ÉCLAIR AND PRESENT DANGER

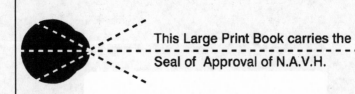

This Large Print Book carries the
Seal of Approval of N.A.V.H.

AN EMERGENCY DESSERT SQUAD
MYSTERY

ÉCLAIR AND PRESENT DANGER

LAURA BRADFORD

WHEELER PUBLISHING
A part of Gale, Cengage Learning

GALE
CENGAGE Learning·

Farmington Hills, Mich • San Francisco • New York • Waterville, Maine
Meriden, Conn • Mason, Ohio • Chicago

GALE
CENGAGE Learning·

Wheeler Publishing Large Print Cozy Mystery.
The text of this Large Print edition is unabridged.
Other aspects of the book may vary from the original edition.
Set in 16 pt. Plantin.

LIBRARY OF CONGRESS CATALOGING-IN-PUBLICATION DATA

Names: Bradford, Laura, author.
Title: Éclair and present danger / by Laura Bradford.
Description: Large print edition. | Waterville, Maine : Wheeler Publishing, 2016. | Series: An emergency dessert squad mystery | Series: Wheeler Publishing large print cozy mystery
Identifiers: LCCN 2016042832| ISBN 9781410495297 (softcover) | ISBN 1410495299 (softcover)
Subjects: LCSH: Large type books. | GSAFD: Mystery fiction.
Classification: LCC PS3602.R34235 E27 2016 | DDC 813/.6—dc23
LC record available at https://lccn.loc.gov/2016042832

Published in 2017 by arrangement with The Berkley Publishing Group, an imprint of Penguin Publishing Group, a division of Penguin Random House LLC

Printed in the United States of America
1 2 3 4 5 6 7 21 20 19 18 17

For Emily.
If Winnie can do it, so can you.

ACKNOWLEDGMENTS

Everything about writing this book was magical — from the moment the concept first came to me (while driving my car), until the very last word (I think I actually squealed when I typed "The End"). As this story (and the stories that will soon follow in the series) unfolded on my computer screen, I found myself becoming quite attached to Winnie, Renee, Mr. Nelson, and the rest of the gang. Getting to live in "their world" for a little while was an absolute joy.

A huge thank you goes out to Lynn Deardorff and Eileen Pearce for helping me brainstorm some of the same dessert names Winnie brainstorms with *her* friends. They had me giggling and saying, "Yes!" just like Winnie does.

I'd also like to thank my editor, Michelle Vega, for her continued belief in me.

And, finally, I'd like to thank you — my readers. Whether you're just now finding me through the Emergency Dessert Squad Mysteries, or you've been reading my work (such as my Amish Mysteries) for a while, the fact that you're here — with this book in your hand — matters to me. Thank you.

Chapter 1

"I'm sorry, could you, um, read that one more time, please?" Winnie Johnson rested her elbows on the edge of Charles Woodward's desk and willed herself to concentrate. "I've been a little scattered these last few weeks, and I think my mind might be playing tricks on me."

For a moment, she wasn't sure he'd heard, but, eventually, he nodded, cleared his throat, and began reading from the semi-tattered paper in his hands.

"I, Gertrude Redenbacher, being of sound mind and body, do bequest my precious angel, Lovey, to my sweet neighbor, Winnie Johnson. I'm sure, given time, Lovey will come to adore Winnie just as much as I have these last two years." Charles glanced up, his tired eyes pinning hers. "Are you still with me, Miss Johnson?"

All she could do was nod, and his focus shifted back down to the paper as she did.

"Additionally, having never been blessed with any children of our own, I also must bequest to Winnie my late husband's beloved vintage ambulance. He may not have finished restoring it to its original grandeur, but it runs, and it will keep Winnie from having to walk to the bakery in the rain."

Nope. Her mind wasn't scattered. She'd heard every last word exactly the same way the first go-round. Only this time, when the attorney's monotone delivery came to an end, it touched off an almost maniacal laugh track in her head.

"Miss Johnson? Are you all right?"

She glanced around the room, her gaze falling on a miniature bonsai tree on the corner of the man's desk. "Oh, I know what's going on here . . ." Without waiting for a reply, she reached over, parted each branch, and then moved on to a complete and thorough inspection of the soil in which the tree was planted.

No camera . . .

"Miss Johnson, I notarized Gertrude's wishes myself not more than six months ago." Charles pulled the pot closer to his chair and brushed the disturbed soil back into place. "Her body was failing her, of course, but her mind was sharp as a tack. This is what she wanted."

"Wait." She fell back against her chair, a new and different laugh making its way past her lips. "Mr. Nelson put you up to this, didn't he?"

"Mr. Nelson?" Charles parroted.

"Yes. Parker Nelson. My downstairs neighbor." Suddenly, it all added up. Mr. Nelson was always playing tricks on her — whoopee cushions on her porch furniture, toy mice on her steps, even hiding her newspaper in a different place each day. Surely this whole cat-and-ambulance-bequeathing thing was just more of the same. "Okay. You got me."

"I *got* you?"

"Yes. But how'd he get you to do it?"

"Excuse me?"

"Mr. Nelson. How'd he get you to read *that* version instead of the real one?"

Charles let her finger guide his attention back to the paper on his desk before he pushed back his chair and stood. Then, leaning across the polished mahogany surface, he pressed the intercom button on the side of his phone. "Susan? Could you please bring in Miss Johnson's items?"

"I'll be right in, Mr. Woodward."

Releasing the button, he spun the paper around and scooted it across the desk to Winnie. "I'll need to keep the original, of course, but I'll see that Susan makes a copy

11

for you before you leave. That way you don't have to worry about taxes on the vehicle in the event the government should ever question —"

A door opened behind her, and she turned to see the same kind yet efficient woman who'd whisked Winnie into the attorney's inner sanctum within moments of her arrival. This time, though, instead of Gertrude's file and a mug of steaming black coffee, the secretary handed her boss a pair of keys and a brown and white tabby cat who promptly turned and hissed at Winnie.

She took a deep breath and yanked open the bakery door, the tower of boxes lined up along the southern wall no different than she'd left it an hour earlier. Likewise, its unassembled counterparts on the opposite wall also remained unchanged.

"What a difference an hour makes," Winnie mumbled to no one in particular as she set the cat carrier beside the counter, exchanged her new set of keys for the folded pink apron she'd left behind the counter, and braced herself for the questions that were no more than five seconds away.

Five . . .

Four . . .

Three . . .

Two . . .

"Welcome to Delectable Delights, how may I help — Winnie! You're back! Oh my gosh, how did it go? Are you rich? Can we stay open?" Renee Ballentine did a little jig halfway across the room, her voice dripping with unbridled excitement. "I didn't bother packing any more boxes because I figured we'd just end up unpacking them the minute you got back, anyway. So? Tell me what happened. And don't leave *anything* out."

Me-owww . . .

Renee shoved a wisp of white blond hair behind her ear and looked around. "Did you hear that?"

Meee-owwwww . . .

"There it is again!" Renee craned her head to the left and then the right as her emerald-colored eyes surveyed the sidewalk outside the bakery. "It almost sounds like it's in here *with* us, doesn't it?"

Winnie stared up at the ceiling and weighed her options. She could pretend she didn't hear anything and let her one and only soon-to-be-let-go employee think psychosis was setting in, she could act shocked to see the cage and the cat, or she could simply share the details of her morning and wallow in any pity that would likely come her way as a result.

She opted for the latter. "It sounds like it's coming from inside because it *is*. And its name is Lovey."

"Lovey?"

"Look, I didn't name it. I just inherited it. From Gertrude." She led Renee over to the cage and pointed at the cat. "See?"

Renee squatted her ample figure atop her three-inch stilettos and peeked inside the cage. "Oh, Winnie, she's really, really cute."

"Cute?"

"You don't think so?"

"It's hard to think much of anything when she so clearly hates me," Winnie said.

"Hates you?"

"She hisses every single time she even looks at me."

"C'mon, Winnie, why would she do that?"

"I don't know. Maybe she knows some-how."

"Knows?" Renee asked. "Knows what?"

"That I killed the family goldfish when I was three."

Renee laughed. "You killed a goldfish?"

"Yup. Two of them — Goldie and Silver."

"And how did you do that?"

"I fed them salt."

"Salt?"

Even now, thirty-one years later, she felt the need to explain the actions that had led to her first and only true dalliance with crime. "I'd watched my mom shake the box of food over the tank countless times. It looked neat and like something I wanted to try, too. A saltshaker fit the bill. Next thing I knew, I was attending my first and last toilet-side memorial — as a murderer." Winnie slumped against the counter and tried not to look at the boxes lining the walls of her dream. Two hours earlier, she'd actually thought there was a chance to keep her doors open. Now, unfortunately, she knew better.

"So the moral of this story, Lovey, is to be wary of your food, okay?" Renee poked a finger inside the cage, stroked as much of Lovey's head as she could access, and then looked up at Winnie. "So what else did Gertie leave —"

The jingle of the door-mounted bell that had alerted them to customers over the past two years brought their collective attention to the front of the store and Renee to her feet.

"Oh my gosh, oh my gosh, oh my gosh! It's *him*," Renee whispered. "Master Sergeant Hottie."

"Good almost afternoon, ladies."

Winnie quickly parted company with the wall on which she'd been leaning, her

15

mental eye taking in each and every detail of the man now standing inside her bakery in a standard paramedic uniform. A quick glance pegged him to be in his thirties, though if she had to venture a more specific guess, she'd put him around thirty-eight. A longer look had her noticing his hair (which was cut close at the sides and well shy of his ears), his shape (quite toned), his dimples (capable of causing momentary heart stoppage), and his eyes (the exact color of chocolate melting in the double boiler) . . .

Renee's elbow found Winnie's ribs and brought her back to the present and the odd look now sported on Master Sergeant Hottie's ruggedly handsome face. "Oh. Yes. Good afternoon. Welcome to Delectable Delights. I'm sorry to say our inventory is a bit low today, but I can promise what we have is still —"

"*Delectable*," Renee interjected. "Get it? *Delectable* Delights?"

He closed the gap between them in three long strides only to stop when he noticed the cat carrier. Bending down, he peered inside the cage and was rewarded with a quiet purr for his efforts. "Cute cat. What's her — or is it *his* — name?"

"Her name is Lovey."

"Pleased to make your acquaintance,

Lovey." Straightening, Master Sergeant Hottie offered his hand to Renee, and then to Winnie. "I'm Greg. Greg Stevens."

She resisted the urge to reach across and wipe the hint of drool from the corner of Renee's mouth and, instead, shook Greg's hand. "I'm Winnie Johnson."

"You're new in town, aren't you?" Renee asked in her usual get-to-the-point way. "A retired army medic, yes?"

A flash of surprise rolled across Greg's features only to disappear behind a nod. "That's right. Moved here about two months ago." He smiled at Winnie and then pointed out the front window to the vintage ambulance parked across the street. "Is that your ride out there?"

Renee tried to cover her snort with a well-placed hand, but she was about a second too late. "Winnie doesn't own a ride. She *walks* to —"

"Yes. That's mine." She could feel Renee's eyes burning into the side of her scalp just as surely as she felt the noticeable cooling that came with the woman's subsequent glance toward the road.

"Wait. You already bought a *car?*"

Ignoring her friend's question, Winnie captured the end of her mousy brown ponytail between her fingers and kept her

17

focus on Greg. "If someone called to complain about the siren, it was a mistake. I tried to find the blinker, and, well, didn't."

"Siren?" Renee echoed. "What siren?"

"That's a 1960 Cadillac Miller-Meteor ambulance. And it appears to be in pretty good shape," Greg said as he gestured toward the window. "How long have you had it?"

She turned around, took note of the clock, and then wandered behind the dessert case with a renewed sense of dread. "An hour. Give or take a few minutes on either side."

The paramedic's surprise was back, this time in the form of a raised eyebrow. "Where'd you buy it?" he asked. "I've been looking for one of those for almost three years."

Renee moved closer to the window, the mental wheels in her head virtually clacking along with the remaining hours Winnie had left as a bakery owner.

"I inherited it from a dear friend who passed away a few weeks ago." Winnie peered through the rear access door of the glass-fronted case and then dropped back against the wall. "Now, instead of owning a bakery, I own an ambulance."

Renee spun around. "Wait. Are you telling me that Gertie left you an *ambulance*?"

"I'm telling you she left me an ambulance *and* a cat. We must not forget the cat."

"And?"

"That's it, Renee. Just an ambulance and a cat."

"No money?"

A lump rose inside her throat, making it difficult to speak. Instead, she shook her head and blinked rapidly against the tears that threatened.

"Oh. Wow." Renee's shoulders dropped a good inch or two. "So today really *is* our last day? *For sure?*"

When Winnie didn't answer, Renee turned to Greg. "Winnie, here, is the most amazing dessert maker on the face of the earth. Every time you think you've eaten the greatest treat you've ever had, she follows it up with something even better. It's been her dream since she was a little girl, isn't that right, Winnie?"

She tried to shake off the conversation, but Renee barreled on. "You should see her when she's baking. It's like this calm comes across her and she slips into her own little world. It's mesmerizing to watch, really."

Greg looked from Winnie to Renee and back again, the lighthearted aura he'd had only moments earlier suddenly gone, as if he sensed he'd walked in on something

19

deep. Renee, of course, prattled on, filling in gaps the man never requested to be filled. "Anyway, the landlord has this crazy notion that Silver Lake is the next up-and-coming town. That people are going to flock here by the hundreds to do God knows what. So, in preparation of such a miracle, he's raised the rent so high on this shop that we can't afford to stay here anymore."

"So reopen somewhere else," Greg suggested.

Winnie liberated an unassembled box from the top of the pile and began to put it together. "There really is nowhere else unless I want to pick up and move."

"Which she doesn't," Renee said emphatically. "There'd be a mutiny of old people if she did."

Greg drew back. "A mutiny of *old* people?"

"That's right. In fact that's why you've probably never seen Winnie around town before. She prefers to hang with folks over seventy. She finds it more fulfilling."

Winnie waved Renee off with a tape roll. "It's not like that. It's just . . ." She let the words fall away as she realized an explanation didn't matter. Very few people understood her, least of all men. So really, why bother? "Anyway, if you'd like something from the case, it's yours for half price. Maybe one day, you can say you had one of the last chocolate soufflés I ever made as a bakery owner."

His gaze lingered on hers far longer than necessary before he stepped up, pulled a twenty from his wallet, and set it on the counter. "I'll take what's left of the tray. I lost a bet the other day at the station, and the guys have been giving me grief ever since. Maybe if I drop this off for them on my way home, they'll finally shut their traps."

She rested the tape roll on the edge of the counter and plucked the last to-go box from the shelf below the register. With quiet efficiency born from experience, Winnie placed each of the soufflés into the box and handed it to the man. "I hope they stop giving you grief now."

"So do I. Though, working with these guys isn't much different than what my sister went through in middle school. Same maturity level, same drama." Greg reached into his front pocket, pulled out a notebook and pen, and wrote his name and phone number on the first page. When he was finished, he ripped it out and handed it to Winnie. "I know you've got a lot going on right now, but if you think you might be interested in selling that ambulance, give me a call. I'll make an offer."

Winnie folded the paper and shoved it into her back pocket. "I'll give it some thought."

"What's an ambulance like that worth?" Renee asked as she came to stand beside Winnie. "Enough to keep a bakery going for a few more years?"

Greg took his box of soufflés and shrugged. "Probably not, I'm afraid." He retraced his steps back to the door and then stopped to look at Winnie one last time, his warm, chocolate-colored eyes narrowing in on her blue ones. "Even if you decide you don't want to sell, I've been told I'm a pretty good listener on occasion. So if you need a friendly ear, the number will work for that, too."

And then he was gone, the odd silence that followed his departure quickly squelched by Renee. "*Oooh . . .* I think Master Sergeant Hottie likes you!"

"Because there's so much to like about a thirty-four-year-old with no job, right?"

Renee's face fell. "I'm sorry, Winnie. I'd really hoped that call from Gertie's attorney would have been the ticket to keeping Delectable Delights open."

"Me, too. But hey, maybe it's time I find a new dream. Something less . . . *messy.*"

Winnie grabbed hold of the box she'd successfully assembled and began loading it with trays and other paraphernalia she'd accumulated over the years, the pain in her heart making it difficult to breathe, let alone think. Still, she trudged on. Stalling the inevitable would change nothing. Her days as a bakery owner were over. "Come on. Let's get this over with. I've got to get Lovey home and fed, and make good on one more order before I hang up my measuring cups and spoons once and for all."

CHAPTER 2

She was halfway up the steps when Parker Nelson, affectionately dubbed Nosy Nelson by all who knew him, poked his head into the hallway below. "Hello? Winnie? Is that you?"

Part of her wanted to keep going, to let the elderly man's eyes provide the answer his ears weren't always capable of catching sans hearing aids, but she couldn't. It wasn't Mr. Nelson's fault her life had just blown up in her face. That honor was hers alone.

Slowly, she turned, bumping Lovey's cage against the edge of the step in the process. "Yes, Mr. Nelson. It's me."

"Home a bit early, aren't you?"

"Maybe a little, I guess."

"Whatcha got there in that cage, Winnie Girl?" Parker held tight to the top of his hand-carved wooden cane with his left hand and pointed to the pet carrier with his right.

"Gertrude Redenbacher's cat, Lovey." She

leaned forward, peered into the cage, and was greeted with an exhausted hiss. "Lovey, I believe you've probably met Mr. Nelson a time or two. Mr. Nelson, you know Lovey."

Lifting his cane off the ground, he gestured for Winnie to follow him into his first-floor apartment. "Well bring her in here and let me have a look at her," he commanded. "Can't give her a proper welcome to our home with bars between us, now can I?"

More than anything she wanted to ignore the invitation and simply go upstairs. If she did, she could rustle through her cabinet for something to sustain a cat until morning, and finally give in to the cry she'd held at bay for most of the afternoon. Then again, if she did as Mr. Nelson asked, she could stave off reality a bit longer . . .

Sighing, Winnie retraced her path down the stairs and into her housemate's quarters — a nearly identical layout to her own space with decidedly far more manly touches. She set the carrier on the living room floor and sunk onto the closest end of the plaid settee from which Mr. Nelson viewed the comings and goings on Serenity Lane. Ever the gentleman, he chose the straight-backed chair held together by duct tape.

Once he was settled with his cane propped against the side of the chair, the elderly man leaned forward, unlatched the pet carrier, and lifted a grateful Lovey to freedom. "I wondered what happened to you after Gertie passed on."

She watched with a mixture of awe and dejection as the cat flopped onto the man's lap and began to purr with reckless abandon. "Charles Woodward's been holding on to her since the funeral, apparently."

"So how'd she end up here? With us?"

Something about the elderly man's pronoun choice broke through her funk and solicited her first true smile of the day. Sure, she might feel lost at that moment, even down on her luck in a way she never had before, but she wasn't alone. That had to count for something, didn't it?

"Gertie bequeathed Lovey to me in her will," Winnie explained. "Lovey *and* the classic ambulance her late husband was restoring until his death a few years ago. I parked it on the street under that elm tree between our house and Bridget's."

"You've got an ambulance parked on the street?"

"For now, yes."

"Then Bridget O'Keefe should be coming through that door any minute, sniffing around for a juicy piece of news she can stick into that gossip column of hers."

26

A gasp from the doorway met his words. "I do not write a *gossip* column, Parker Nelson! I deliver the news the people of Silver Lake really want to read!" Belying her eighty-year-old legs, the stout, white-haired woman glided across the living room with noticeable ease, planting a kiss on the top of Winnie's head as she passed. Without waiting for an official invite, their next-door neighbor dropped onto the couch beside Winnie and stared at Lovey through her bifocals. "Since when did you start stealing cats, Parker?"

"Mr. Nelson didn't steal Lovey. She's *my* cat now."

Bridget turned a raised brow in Winnie's direction. "*Your* cat?"

"That's right. I got the news today." Winnie wiggled her fingers at the semi-comatose cat across the coffee table and, again, was rewarded for her efforts with a hiss. "Lovey is positively thrilled, can't you tell?"

"Gertie always did have a soft spot for you, Winnie," Mr. Nelson said. "Just like the rest of us, I reckon."

A soft grunt off to her right drew Winnie's focus back to their next-door neighbor and the pen that was feverishly gliding across a small spiral-bound notebook. "I really don't think Silver Lake cares that I have a cat, Bridget."

The woman stopped writing long enough to shake off Winnie's words and point to the window overlooking Serenity Lane. "They might not care about a cat, but they will surely care about that ambulance parked out on the street. Any thoughts on why it's here?"

"To cart you away to the looney bin, perhaps?" Mr. Nelson joked, slapping his knee with such glee Winnie couldn't help but laugh.

Bridget turned her infamous stink eye on Parker and then dismissed him entirely to focus, again, on Winnie. "Did you see anything when you came home, dear?"

"*See* anything?"

"You know, an accident, a fall, a seizure?"

"No. The ambulance is mine, Bridget."

Lowering her pen to the notepad, Bridget took hold of Winnie's hand and squeezed it tightly. "Has your stomach been bothering you, too, dear? Because, let me tell you, mine has been positively awful these last few days. Makes me wonder if I should have a scope done."

She rushed to head off Bridget's latest list of ailments and to set the record straight before a far juicier version of reality surfaced in the next edition of the *Silver Lake Herald.* "Gertie left the cat and the ambulance to me. In her will."

Bridget swapped Winnie's hand for the pen and began writing once again. "How wonderful, dear. Now you don't have to walk to work in the rain anymore."

Work . . .

Just like that, any momentary reprieve from her lousiest day ever was gone, the pain she'd managed to shove aside now back with a vengeance. If she wanted pity, if she wanted coddling and hugs, she knew it would be forthcoming from this crew. But as tempting as that was, it was time to take Lovey upstairs and make good, once again, on the promise she'd made to another deceased friend, Ethel Wagner.

"How's Bart doing today?" she asked in a not-so-subtle attempt to change the subject.

Not ones to disappoint whenever the subject of their still-mourning neighbor came up, Bridget opened her mouth to speak but closed it as Mr. Nelson took the floor. "What's happened to that man is exactly why I never got married. Live with a woman long enough and she'll steal your soul."

"Oh shut up, Parker." Bridget's hiss wasn't unlike Lovey's, and Winnie found

29

herself marveling at the similarities while simultaneously trying to process the conversation taking shape between her friends. "Bart and Ethel were married for nearly fifty years, Parker. You don't get over a love like that in six *years,* let alone six *weeks.*"

"Tell that to that nasty little Donovan woman."

Winnie leaned forward. "You mean Sissy Donovan down the street?" At Mr. Nelson's and Bridget's matching nods, she pressed on. "What happened?"

Bridget crossed her ankles and sat up straight, keenly aware of her role as neighborhood informant — a responsibility the elderly woman took quite seriously. "This was yesterday, actually, but we didn't get to tell you because you went to bed early in preparation for your meeting with Gertie's attorney."

Ah yes. Naïveté at its finest . . .

"Anyway," Bridget continued, "Bart had just stepped onto the porch with that new young man from the end of the block — you know, the history teacher at the community college . . ."

"Lance. Lance Reed," Winnie supplied.

"That's right. Lance Reed. For the first time since Ethel's passing, Bart was actually talking, even *smiling,* when . . . all of a sud-

den, on their way back from the bus stop
—"

"Ava ran through Ethel's flower bed!"
Clearly delighted with his information
bomb, Mr. Nelson, too, sat up tall.

"Uh-oh."

"Uh-oh is right." The tall, thin seventy-
five-year-old stroked a trembling hand down
Lovey's back, his voice booming off the
walls as much for his own auditory benefit
as anyone else's. "I was a sailor in the navy
when I was a young man, and even *I* learned
a few new words by the time Bart's tirade
on that child was over."

"I take it Sissy witnessed this tirade?"

Bridget and Mr. Nelson nodded in perfect
unison.

She winced. "Oh. Wow. I don't know what
to say."

"You know how Sissy is with that child.
Ava can do no wrong. And when she saw
me furiously writing in my notebook as
everything unfolded, she wasn't pleased.
Not one little bit." Bridget patted her lap
and was openly delighted to see Lovey leave
Parker's in favor of hers. Smiling triumphantly at Winnie's housemate, the woman
continued, her eyes widening with excitement. "But that was only the beginning of
things going from bad to worse."

31

"Oh?" Winnie looked from Bridget to Mr. Nelson and back again. When it became clear they were holding out for a more worthy reaction, she upped the ante. "So? Don't keep me in suspense. What happened?"

Satisfied, Bridget supplied the rest of the story. "Ava was so surprised that someone was actually yelling at her, she started running. She'd gotten no more than five feet down the sidewalk when she fell and —"

"Popped a tooth clear out of her mouth!" Parker shouted.

Not to be undone at the finish line, Bridget added, "There was blood everywhere. And by everywhere, I mean *everywhere*. Isn't that right, Parker?"

Mr. Nelson nodded, forcing Winnie to raise her instinctual "uh-oh" with a loud, sustained groan. "Oh no . . . Ava's big pageant is this weekend, isn't it?"

Again, her elderly neighbors nodded in perfect unison, prompting Winnie to say what was most surely on all of their minds. "I hate to say this, but maybe Bart's stepson is right. Maybe it's time for Bart to give up the house. The change of scenery might be good for him."

"Can you imagine what would happen to our street if Mark Reilly got his hands on that house?" Having won the ultimate battle for Lovey's affections, Bridget lifted Lovey from her lap and deposited the cat back in Parker's. "If he *does,* I give it two months before Ethel and Bart's home is turned into one of them gambling casinos or, even worse, a — a . . . *brothel!*"

"A pothole?" Mr. Nelson parroted. "How on earth could someone turn a home into a pothole?"

Winnie shook her head in amusement as Bridget rolled her eyes and repeated her original word at full volume. "I said *brothel!* Broth-el. Turn on your hearing aids, old man. That, or go get yourself a muzzle."

"What was that?" At Bridget's exasperated eye roll, Mr. Nelson fiddled with his hearing aids and then stared down at the cat, his voice surprisingly quiet. "We're starting to drop like flies around here, aren't we? First Ethel, then Gertie, and now maybe even Bart."

Winnie stood, walked around the table to Mr. Nelson, and gave him a hug much to Lovey's chagrin. "If Bart goes, Mr. Nelson, it's only to an assisted living facility. Not death," she said, gently.

"Same thing if you ask me," he grumbled.

She hugged him again and then headed toward the hallway and the stairs beyond.

When she reached the doorway, she glanced back at her friend. "Mr. Nelson? Could you hang on to Lovey for just a little while longer? It sounds like Bart could use his peach pie sooner rather than later."

Not a Tuesday night went by that Winnie didn't cross the street to Bart's home without Ethel's final request looping its way through her thoughts.

"Winnie, promise me you'll bring one of your peach pies to Bart every Tuesday night with a reminder that I love him . . . and that we'll be together again one day when the time is right? I'd be eternally grateful."

She'd made that promise as she sat next to one of the half dozen or so machines tasked with monitoring various aspects of Ethel's health as her life drew to a close. And it was a promise she'd held true to in the six weeks that had come and gone since Ethel's final breath.

At first she'd worried the edible reminder would be too hard on a man already paralyzed by grief. But something about the gesture, and the knowledge that it had been requested by Ethel herself, made it the one moment each week Winnie could count on seeing the man smile.

This time, though, Winnie couldn't help

but notice the trepidation in her step as she left the porch she shared with Mr. Nelson and headed across the street. Bart was growing increasingly agitated with each passing day. It was an agitation she knew was born of grief, but still . . . If he could feel needed, if he could get back to being Bart, maybe he could stay in the home he'd shared with his beloved Ethel.

The tricky part was how to make him feel needed when they'd all been living on the same street for years. Bart was an intelligent man. If his help was sought for something bogus, he'd know it in an instant.

Then again, she *had* just gotten a cat. Maybe he could help with Lovey . . .

Or maybe she could use him as a sounding board on what to do with her life in the weeks and months to come . . .

Better yet, maybe she could ask for his help in planting a flower bed outside the Victorian she shared with Mr. Nelson. After all, she had time on her hands now that the bakery was gone . . .

She made her way up Bart's driveway and over to his front porch, the slow, steady breath she needed finally finding its way through her lungs.

Help him feel needed . . .

Let him know we all care about him . . .

35

Encourage him to live for Ethel . . .

The plan made perfect sense. Now, all she had to do was execute it.

She knocked on the navy blue door and waited. When he didn't answer, she knocked a second and third time.

No answer.

Double-checking the driveway for Bart's car, Winnie tried the doorknob and found it unlocked.

"Bart?" she called through the now-open door. "Are you here? It's me — Winnie."

When there was still no response, she raised her voice a bit louder in the event he'd fallen asleep in his favorite chair. "Bart? It's Winnie. I have your special peach pie from Ethel."

She stepped all the way into the foyer and closed the door, the click of the lock echoing eerily in a house that was far too quiet.

"Bart?" Slowly, step-by-step, she made her way down the hallway and into the living room, her gaze skirting the mantel and its plethora of framed photographs artfully arranged around a glass-fronted display case before finally landing on Bart's empty chair.

An odd sense of unease skittered up her spine as she returned to the hallway and continued toward the rear of the house, checking the study and the dining room as

36

she passed.

Maybe he was in the kitchen . . .

Or sitting out back on the patio . . .

"Bart? It's me . . . W—"

Rounding the corner into the kitchen, she froze, her name morphing into a bloodcurdling scream even Mr. Nelson was sure to hear.

CHAPTER 3

Breathe in . . .
  Breathe out . . .
  Breathe in . . .
  Breathe out . . .

Winnie pulled the brown paper bag from her mouth and did her best to muster a reassuring smile for Bridget. "I'm okay. Really."

"You say a *willow* was over his face?" Mr. Nelson shouted from his observation station at the front window. Having secured a prime location to watch the comings and goings of the Silver Lake Police Department and the medical examiner's office, Winnie's friend showed no sign of moving anytime in the next century.

"A *pillow*, Mr. Nelson. A pillow." She dropped the bag onto the coffee table and joined her elderly friend in his quest to be in the know. It took a moment, but Winnie managed to pick out the detective who'd

38

grilled her for information upon his arrival on the scene.

"Why in God's name would Bart hold a pillow over his own face?"

"He wouldn't," Bridget rasped. "Someone else would."

"Bridget?" Winnie glanced over her shoulder toward the couch she'd just vacated. "Are you okay?"

"How can I be okay? How can any of us be okay with a — a *murderer* on the loose?" Bridget looked down at her Lovey-topped lap and closed her eyes. "The elderly make perfect victims because we aren't strong enough to fight back. Particularly those of us with health ailments."

"Still thinking you need a scope done?" Mr. Nelson asked.

Bridget peeked through her lashes then quickly closed them when she saw that she had Winnie's concern. "I'm *convinced* I do, Parker. Here I am, chilled to the bone over Bart's passing, yet my abdomen is strangely warm. My blood must not be flowing properly."

Winnie crossed back to the couch and claimed the cushion closest to Bridget. Lovey popped up from her peaceful slumber (against Bridget's abdomen) and whirled around to glare at Winnie. Her attempts to

39

soothe the feline via a soft pet were met with two short hisses and something that sounded an awful lot like a growl.

Ahhh, that's nice . . .

Giving up, she squeezed Bridget's hand, instead. "I'm sure the police will figure out who did this to Bart and why." Yet even as she said the words, she knew the likelihood of them being true was slim to none. The Silver Lake Police Department was small — as in *really* small, and deduction and logic weren't their forte.

Bridget looked up. "Please tell me that Detective Wyatt at least *pretended* to ask good questions?"

She cast about for some sort of positive spin she could use to deliver her answer, but there was none. Besides, Bridget was sharp; she knew the drill. "Not really, no."

"He asked if he could eat that peach pie, didn't he?" Mr. Nelson released his hold on the curtain and let it drift back across the window, momentarily inhibiting his view of the action. At Winnie's nod, he waved his cane in the air. "I hope you didn't give it to him, Winnie."

"How could I say no?" She fidgeted with the hem of her powder blue top and tried to think back on the conversation she'd had with the detective. He'd confirmed that

40

Bart's door was unlocked . . . he'd asked if she saw anything unusual . . . and he'd asked if Bart could have simply fallen, pulling the pillow with him as he went.

Rising to her feet once again, Winnie made her way back to the now-unmanned window, her gaze searching for (and finding) Detective Wyatt and the handful of officers who'd arrived on the scene with donut powder on their uniforms. Maybe they'd figure out what happened to Bart; maybe they wouldn't. Either way, she refused to let Bridget, Mr. Nelson, and the remaining dozen or so elderly folks on Serenity Lane live in fear.

Besides, it wasn't like she had anything else to do with her time at the moment.

"We're smart," she said without turning around. "We can figure this out."

"Figure what out?" Mr. Nelson hobbled back to his spot next to Winnie.

"Figure out who did this to Bart."

This time, when she looked back at Bridget, she saw hope pushing through the fear — hope that Winnie was right and that she would deliver on her word.

And she would.

One way or the other . . .

It was ten-thirty by the time she and Lovey

finally made it upstairs to their apartment. She was tired, the cat was hissy, and Bridget and Mr. Nelson were safely tucked away behind locked doors in their respective homes.

Now that Winnie was finally alone (save for Lovey, of course), and able to have the cry she'd been fighting off since she locked the bakery's door for the very last time, there were no tears.

Sure, she was still sad — devastated, even. But seeing Bart's lifeless body stretched across his linoleum kitchen floor and hearing Bridget's subsequent fear that she or Mr. Nelson could be next had put things in perspective, at least a little.

Did she still want her bakery back? Without a doubt.

Was she still at a complete loss for what to do with her life? Head-spinningly so.

But wallowing did nothing. *Baking* did.

From the time Winnie's line of vision was able to clear the countertop in her mother's kitchen, she'd loved baking. Her favorite picture books as a pre-reader had been those containing desserts. Once she started reading, she'd shunned the fiction books favored by her peers and devoured every cookbook she could find. In her teens, she'd pushed aside those same cookbooks to experiment with her own flavors and tastes, techniques and presentation.

Soon, blue ribbons for her pies and cakes at the county fair segued into money prizes and inclusion in several dessert-specific cookbooks and magazines. By the time she was done with college, her destiny was all but certain. A few stints in various bakeries elsewhere in the state eventually led her, and the money she'd managed to sock aside in a drawer, to Silver Lake and her very own bakery, Delectable Delights.

She reached for the row of canisters beside the sink, measured out two cups of flour, and sifted it into a large mixing bowl. When the flour was as fine as dust, she added salt, shortening, and cold water. With clean hands, she mixed the dough until it was ready to be rolled out across a lightly floured board and then transferred to a waiting pie dish.

In a different bowl, she mixed sugar, cornstarch, salt, and cinnamon, and sprinkled it over the blueberries Mr. Nelson had picked for her the previous day. Quickly, she scooped the blueberry mixture into the crust, dotted it with butter, and then latticed it with strips of remaining dough.

As she worked, she could feel the day's tension slipping away and the rational side of her brain engaging.

If she had money, she could take a class at the community college. If she had money, she could remain in the two-family house she shared with Mr. Nelson. If she had money, she could —

The ambulance!

Winnie slid the pie onto the top rack of the oven and shut the door. Once the timer was set, she crossed to the opposite side of the kitchen and her purse. A quick search of the unzipped center compartment yielded the phone number of her one and only chance to stay afloat.

Granted she had no idea how much money she could get for a 1960 ambulance, but she had an interested buyer in Master Sergeant Hottie, er — she peered at his handwritten note — *Greg Stevens.* And thanks to the Internet, she could access the approximate value of just about anything under the sun.

Fifty minutes later, she had an asking price for the ambulance in her head and a freshly baked blueberry pie sitting atop her kitchen counter. Buoyed by her accomplishments, she carried the dirty bowls and measuring cups to the sink, turned on the tap, and looked out the window at her next-door neighbor's still-lit home.

As she watched, she could just make out Bridget's stout frame as it paced back and forth behind a too-sheer parlor curtain. A glance at the oven clock confirmed what she already knew to be true. Bridget was scared — scared to go to sleep, and scared to take her eyes off the doors and windows that separated her from a killer who, in the elderly woman's eyes, had already preyed on one comrade in age.

Winnie turned off the water, shooed a not-so-happy Lovey back into the cat carrier, retrieved the still-warm pie from the cooling rack, and made her way out of her apartment, down the stairs, and out into the night. Slowly, carefully, she picked her way across the yard that separated her two-family Victorian from Bridget's single-family home and knocked softly on the parlor window. "Bridget . . . it's me, Winnie."

The back door swept inward just long enough for Bridget to reach onto the top stoop and pull Winnie inside. "Is everything all right? Did the killer come back? Did he get Parker?"

She set the cage down, shifted the pie to her now-empty hand, and released Lovey with the other. "Everything is fine, Bridget. You need to get some sleep. It's one o'clock in the morning."

"I have a horrible case of amnesia," Bridget said, bringing her hand to her head with award-winning theatrics.

"When did that start?"

"An hour ago." Bridget pointed at Winnie's hands as Lovey wound her tail around the woman's legs. "What's that?"

She followed the path forged by Bridget's finger and remembered the pie. "Oh. I made this for you. Here. It's my" — she searched her thoughts for an appropriate name — "Don't-Be-Blue Berry Pie. Because everything *will* be okay. I promise."

Bridget looked from the pie to Winnie and back again, a single tear slipping down her weathered face as she did. "Oh, Winnie. Thank you. I've nearly worn a hole in my carpet thinking about what happened to Bart. Worked myself up so much I can't even think about sleep. But you being here? Checking up on me? It means more than you can ever know, dear."

"I love you Bridget, you know that."

The woman's slow nod gave way to a pointed look. "Don't think I'm not aware of what's going on with your bakery, dear, because I am. And I'm awfully sorry, Winnie. I know how much running that place meant to you. That landlord of yours is a good-for-nothing, and everyone in this town

46

knows it."

Steeling herself against the kind of senti-ment capable of unearthing the tears she'd managed to escape thus far, Winnie forced herself to smile, to keep her mood light. "I'll figure something out, Bridget. Really."

"I know you will, dear. You're a smart cookie." Bridget held the pie to her nose and inhaled. "Even so, with everything on your plate right now, it was mighty thought-ful of you to rescue me with one of your special desserts the way you —"

Rescue?

"Wh-what did you just say?" Winnie stam-mered.

The late hour, coupled with the stress of Bart's murder, weighed on Bridget's tired frame, bringing with it a momentary flash of irritation. "Which part, dear?"

"The last part. About rescuing you."

"Oh. *That.* I just said that it was mighty thoughtful of you to rescue me with one of your special desserts."

Rescue . . .

Desserts . . .

Stepping forward, Winnie planted a hand on each of Bridget's shoulders and pulled the woman in for a hug — pie and all. "That's it! Bridget, you are a veritable *ge-nius!*"

"I am?"

"You sure are." Winnie released the woman and her pie and headed back into the night. Halfway down the porch steps, she stopped as Bridget called her name.

"Winnie, wait. Didn't you forget something?"

She looked down at her empty hands and then back up at Bridget. "No. The pie is for you, remember?"

"I'm talking about Lovey!"

And then it dawned on her . . .

She was a cat owner now. Lovey's care and well-being were her responsibility.

Turning, she started back up the steps only to stop as Lovey peered up at Bridget and began to purr as if her ninth life depended on it. "Actually, on second thought, why don't you hang on to her for the night? Something tells me you'll both sleep a lot better that way."

CHAPTER 4

Winnie was just reaching for her third cup of coffee when she heard a vibration somewhere in her general vicinity. It was faint at first, but thanks to her caller's persistence, she finally located its source beneath six hours' worth of discarded ideas strewn across her kitchen table and most of the living room floor.

"Hello?"

"Let me in. I have coffee."

She looked from the digital oven clock (6:45 A.M.) to her relatively full mug and back again before giving voice to the confusion now clouding her caffeinated thoughts. "Renee, the bakery is closed, remember?"

"I'm not at the bakery. I'm downstairs. On your front stoop." Renee's voice petered off momentarily only to return with a rare sense of hesitancy. "Um, Winnie? Do you know that . . . um . . . there's yellow cop tape around that peach pie guy's house?"

"It's called crime scene tape and, yes, I'm aware. I'm the one who found Bart's body."

She ended the call in the middle of Renee's gasp, took one last look at the effects of her all-night brainstorming session, and made her way over to the door and down the steps.

"Who's there?" Mr. Nelson called from inside his apartment. "If you're preaching, I've already got religion. And if you're selling, I ain't buying — unless you've got binoculars. I could use some new binoculars . . ."

Even in her sleep-deprived state, Winnie managed to stifle her laugh in favor of the reassurance she knew was needed. "It's just me, Mr. Nelson. I'm letting Renee in."

The second she mentioned her friend and former employee's name, she wished she hadn't. After all, nothing had Mr. Nelson off his couch and clipping on a bow tie faster than a chance to flirt with Renee.

Sure enough, by the time she unlocked the series of bolts Mr. Nelson had installed on the front door during a bout of extreme boredom six months earlier, the seventy-five-year-old was standing behind her, straightening his bow tie and puffing out a chest that was decades past the point of puffing.

"Fine morning we're having, isn't it, Miss Ballentine?"

She started to remind him of Renee's age in comparison to his but let it go when it became apparent Renee was all too happy to do a little flirting, too. Eyelashes were batted, cheeks turned crimson, and throats were cleared before Renee put a stop to it by shoving a finger into Winnie's shoulder. "And you! You had to drop that little bomb just as you were hanging up, didn't you?"

"Bomb?" Mr. Nelson's shoulders rose up alongside his ears. "What bomb?"

Instinctively, Winnie rested a calming hand on the man's back while simultaneously stepping aside to afford Renee entrance into the vestibule. "Not that kind of bomb, Mr. Nelson."

His shoulders returned to position in time to look Renee up and down, a sly smile claiming his weathered face. "Aren't you a sight for sore eyes . . ."

Renee pointed at Mr. Nelson. "Can I keep you?" Then, sliding her gaze left, she looked at Winnie. "Can I keep him? He's really good for my ego."

"You can keep me whenever and however you want, Miss Ballentine," Mr. Nelson said, winking. "I'm not picky."

"Okay, you two. Enough is enough. It's

only —" Winnie stopped, looked down at her watch, and then back up at Renee. "Wait just a minute. Why is it that today — when there's no bakery to open — you can be standing at my door, coffees in hand, at seven o'clock, when you were routinely thirty to forty minutes late for a *nine* o'clock start?"

"It's a school day."

"It's a school day five out of seven days," Winnie reminded before putting two and two together and coming up with Renee's ex-husband, Bob, and his mid-week visitation with their son.

Renee leaned toward Mr. Nelson, giving him a bird's-eye view of her ample cleavage in the process. "Did someone give our Winnie cranky pills this morning?"

Mr. Nelson brought a hand to his heart. "I — I —"

"No one gave me cranky pills, Renee," Winnie said as every hue of red known to mankind took a turn on the palette that was Mr. Nelson's face. When he became aware of her scrutiny, he took one last (and lengthy) glance at Renee's chest and then busied himself with a nonexistent speck of dust on the handle of his cane. "I've just been up all night, that's all."

Mr. Nelson's chin shot upward. "You

should've heard Winnie scream when she found Bart the way she did. Why, I heard it over that ditty they play during Final Jeopardy! You know — do, do, do, do, do, do, do, do, do, do, do, DO, do do do do do."

"So you really *did* find a real live dead body?"

"I think that's a contradictory sentence, Renee, but in the spirit of moving things along — yes." Winnie leaned back against the closest stretch of wall she could find and rubbed at the headache she felt building behind her temples. "It appears he was murdered. Which explains the crime scene tape you referenced on the phone."

"It's a dangerous world out there, Miss Ballentine," Mr. Nelson mused. Then, cocking his head toward his open doorway, he offered a ready-made solution to Winnie's internal how-to-get-upstairs-alone-without-hurting-his-feelings dilemma. "I'm sorry, but I have to leave you two gals to your own devices for a little while. That cute little weather anchor on Channel Five is about to smile out at me from my TV, and I don't want to miss that."

In a flash, Mr. Nelson was gone, a stunned and somewhat dejected-looking Renee staring at the spot where he'd once stood. "I can't believe it. I've been cast aside for a female who studies *clouds* all day?"

"There could be far worse fates, I'm sure." Winnie removed her fingertips from her temple and motioned Renee to follow her up the steps and into her apartment. "Besides, you already have a man — one that's six plus decades younger, worships the ground you walk on, and doesn't need batteries in order to hear you."

"Semantics." Renee stopped halfway into the living room and stared. "Whoa. What happened here?"

Plucking one of the semi-warm to-go cups from Renee's hand, Winnie took a sip. "I told you. I've been up all night."

"Most people, in the throes of depression, merely sit on their bed and cry . . . or take up residency in front of the television watching infomercials until the wee hours of the morning. But you? You *trash* the joint."

Slowly, Winnie looked around, her gaze falling on the crumpled balls of paper that fell shy of the wastebasket, as well as the intact sheets covered with lists and doodles that covered just about every available surface in sight. "I was thinking."

"Thinking?" Renee parroted. "Why couldn't you think like this at the bakery when my shift was over and your incessant

neatness made it so I couldn't use cleaning as an excuse to stay?"

"Sorry."

She watched her friend veer into the kitchen, lift a piece of loose leaf off the table, and turn it so Winnie could see the series of rectangular shapes she'd drawn at some point during the night. "What are these?"

"Pillows."

Renee looked back at the paper. "Pillows? Why? Are you thinking about getting into the bedding business now?"

Snapping off the lid of her drink, Winnie stared inside at the liquid that was no longer steaming. If it was, she would have added a touch more milk. And maybe a little sugar . . .

"Winnie?"

She shook herself back into the conversation and the question she was expected to answer. "Bart was suffocated to death with a pillow. I guess it went through my mind at some point during the night."

Renee shot her right index finger into the air in a request for silence. "Wait. Where's the cat?"

"Cat?"

"Yes. *Lovey.* The one you inherited from Gertie yesterday, remember?" Renee's hand drifted back to her side. "Oh God. Please tell me you haven't gone all saltshaker on the poor thing already . . ."

"Of course not! She's next door with my neighbor! I left her there last night after Bridget said . . ." Her sentence fell away as, once again, Winnie found herself transported back to the exact moment inspiration hit.

Now, six sleepless hours later, that same inspiration was mixing it up with equal parts self-doubt.

She, of all people, knew just how hard it was to get a new business off the ground. Did she really want to try and do it again? Especially now that —

" *'It's Okay, Don't Scream Puffs*'?"

The sound of Renee's voice, coupled with its background accompaniment of shifting papers, broke through her pity party and brought her back into the present.

" *'Down in the Dumps Cake*'? What is this, Winnie?"

Setting her coffee cup down on the closest surface she could find, Winnie rescued the paper from Renee's hand and studied the half dozen or so cockamamie thoughts that had come to her at various points throughout the night. "It's . . . it's just an idea I'm working on, that's all."

"Oh?"

To tell or not to tell, that was the question . . .

Fortunately for Winnie and her dilemma, Renee had the attention span of a flea and was already on to a slightly smaller sheet of lined paper and another, far different question. "So? Are you going to call him or what?"

"Him?"

"Master Sergeant Hottie," Renee said, waving the hastily scrawled phone number in the air. "I mean, c'mon, Winnie. The guy is gorgeous. Though, if you *do* call, you have to let me do something with your hair . . . and your makeup . . . and — wait! Isn't that the same shirt you were wearing yesterday?"

She took in the powder blue top she'd donned the previous morning in the hope it would bring good luck at the attorney's office and shrugged. "I told you. I was up all night."

"Okay, get some sleep first and *then* call. I'll take care of the rest."

Again, she returned her focus to the list still clutched in her hand and lowered herself down to the same chair she'd inhabited up until Renee's call. So much of her night had been spent jotting down ideas, yet now that she had some, she couldn't

57

help but wonder if she was grasping at straws.

"Winnie?"

She lowered the paper to her lap and peered up at her friend. "I don't think I'm going to call him. I mean, if I give this" — she gestured toward the various notes — "more thought and it isn't feasible, I can always sell, but if it *is* feasible, it could put me back in the driver's seat. Literally and figuratively."

"You lost me," Renee said. "I mean, don't get me wrong. Being in the driver's seat with a guy is a good idea. Provided, of course, he doesn't *realize* you're steering. Ignorance is bliss, if you get my drift."

Her mouth gaped, closed, and then gaped again as Renee continued to go off on a tangent far different than the one firing away in Winnie's head. "But, either way, I don't get why you're saying you won't call him. It's not like you travel in the same circles and can just assume you'll bump into him. Then again, if one of your neighbors happens to fall and you have to call 911 for ambulatory assistance, maybe you could see him then . . ."

The headache was back, and this time, instead of trying to knead the pain away, she vacated her chair in favor of the cabinet above the sink where she housed her over-the-counter pain medicine. Two pills and a glass of water later, she was ready to set Renee straight.

"I'm not going to call Master Sergeant Hottie — I mean, *Greg* — because I'm not going to sell the ambulance. I'm going to keep it."

"Keep it?" Renee echoed. "What? Why? Are you nuts?"

"No . . . Maybe . . . Okay, yeah. But I think this is worth a shot — for me, and for you. *If* we can make it work, that is."

"Sleep deprivation really messes you up, you know that?"

She laughed. "It does. But if it keeps *me* baking, and *you* from climbing the walls while Ty is otherwise occupied at school, then I think it's worth a shot, don't you?"

"Keeps you baking? And me . . ." Renee fairly ran around the kitchen table to meet Winnie next to the sink. "Did you figure something out about the bakery?"

"Sort of."

"*Sort of?* What does that mean?"

She took a deep breath and slowly released it along with the idea that had made it impossible to sleep. "We're taking the bakery on the road, Renee. With Gertie's ambulance."

If a mirror were nearby, she might have actually checked to see if she had grown the second head Renee's expression indicated, but since there wasn't, she jumped into the deep end of the pool and hoped for the best.

"And we're calling ourselves the Emergency Dessert Squad."

CHAPTER 5

Pinching her fingers together, Winnie tonged the sixth and final piece of bacon from the sizzling grease and transferred it to the serving plate.

"Don't forget women in the throes of menopause! They like dessert!"

She turned off the oven, grabbed hold of the plate, and carried it across the tiny kitchen to the still paper-strewn table. "Okay . . ."

"You know, something to tame the mood or soothe the hot flash — that sorta thing." Renee stopped nibbling on the end of her pen and, instead, helped herself to a slice of sustenance. "Mmmm. Yes! Bacon."

"It's the least I could do after making you listen to my sleep-deprived ramblings for the past hour." Shoving a haphazard pile of papers to the side, Winnie set the plate down between them and reached for the crispiest piece, her mind already at work on

Renee's suggestion. "Moods. We could change the word *mood* to *moon* . . . as in a moon pie of some sort. Or —" She stopped, mid-bite, and shook the remaining half piece of bacon at her friend. "I got it! Hot Flash Fudge Sundae! And we'll top the homemade sauce with a variety of chocolate bits — dark, milk, white. Whatever the customer prefers."

Renee's wide mouth flapped open. "Wow. You're really good at this name thing."

"You wouldn't have said that if you'd heard the things I was coming up with between the hours of four and five A.M.," she joked. "You Deserve Batter Cake was the one that finally convinced me it was time to darken up the coffee."

"Maybe, but You're a Peach Pie is adorable! I love that one. And Down in the Dumps Cake is a pretty creative way to get one of our customers' favorites back on the menu." Renee stood, took another piece of bacon, and wandered over to the window that looked down on Serenity Lane. "So, uhhh . . . how awful was it?"

Winnie looked up from her notes and studied the back of her friend's pixie-style haircut, its wash-and-go ease lost on a woman who believed preening was akin to breathing. "I'm not a huge fan of black coffee, but it was necessary."

"I mean about finding a dead body." Renee leaned her forehead against the glass. "That's like one of my worst nightmares in the event I've never mentioned it before."

Suddenly, the lightness she'd managed to capture over the past few hours was gone, in its place a sense of foreboding she simply wasn't ready to give in to quite yet. "I thought your worst nightmares tended to be about at-home birthday parties with twenty of Ty's closest friends."

"When his friends are ten years old? Yes. When they're twenty-five and all muscled out? Not so much."

"When they're twenty-five, you'll be fifty," Winnie reminded.

"And your point?"

She pushed back her own chair and came to stand beside her friend. Draping her arm around Renee's back, she pulled the woman in for a side hug. "Cut the act, Renee. I hear your jaw flapping, and I see the way you eye everyone from Sergeant Hottie to Mr. Nelson, but it's me, remember? I know you're not ready to move on from Bob yet. Just remember, when the time is right, Bob's loss will be someone else's gain. Of that, I have absolutely no doubt."

Seconds turned to minutes as the silence

63

between them continued. Then, finally, "Did he suffer?"

Oh, how she wanted to protest the obvious subject change, but, in the end, she opted to let it go. After all, the topic of Renee's reticence to date in the aftermath of her divorce had been born on the back of another blatant change in subject.

Hers . . .

"I don't know much about suffocation, but I'm hoping it happened pretty fast," Winnie finally said in lieu of waving a white flag she didn't have. "Bart was always a really nice man."

"I thought you said he had a trigger temper."

Had she really said that? She couldn't remember. But, even if she had, it didn't justify someone waltzing into the man's home and holding a pillow over his face. She said as much to Renee as they watched an officer from the Silver Lake Police Department removing the crime scene tape from around the house on the other side of the street. "Bart had certain things he wanted a certain way. He spent hours on his flower beds and didn't take kindly to those who let their dog or cat undo his work. He took pride in his house and in knowing that he'd paid it off with the blood, sweat, and tears of a forty-year career as a corrections officer. He didn't want anyone telling him it was time to give it up. Especially when he saw it as one of the last remaining connections to Ethel."

"How long were they married again?" Renee asked, her voice surprisingly quiet.

"Almost fifty years. And these past six weeks without her have been awful for him. Just awful. It's no wonder he couldn't control his emotions very well."

Renee pulled her forehead off the window and rested the side of her head on Winnie's shoulder. "Maybe this is better, then. He doesn't have to miss her anymore."

"I'd agree if it happened naturally. But Bart was *murdered,* Renee. Someone has to pay for that."

"Indeed they do!"

As if powered by one body, Winnie and Renee whirled around to find Bridget standing at the top of the stairs with Lovey in one hand and the empty cat carrier in the other.

"Bridget," Winnie scolded as she closed the gap between the window and her next-door neighbor, "let me take those from you. You shouldn't be carrying that kind of weight up those stairs by yourself."

She reached out for the carrier, only to

pull her hand back as Lovey hissed. "Good morning to you, too, Lovey."

Bridget relinquished the carrier to Winnie but held tight to the clearly perturbed feline. Nodding a greeting at Renee, the elderly woman peered down at Lovey and then back up at Winnie. "I can't thank you enough for the pie, your concern, and allowing Lovey to stay with me last night. It made all the difference in the world, dear."

Lovey hissed again, prompting Winnie to retreat in surrender.

"Put the cage away, Winnie," Renee suggested. "Maybe she's protesting *that* rather than *you.*"

"She didn't hiss at *me* when *I* was holding the cage."

"Thank you, Bridget." Still, in the hope that Renee was right, Winnie carried the cage into her bedroom, deposited it in the closet, and then returned to the main room.

Lovey hissed again.

"So much for that theory," Renee mumbled. "Maybe she's hungry."

"Hungry . . . Yeah, maybe that's it." She opened her pantry closet, searched the shelves for tuna or anything else a cat might like, and came up empty-handed. Then, on a hunch, she returned to the table and the last remaining piece of bacon on the plate.

"Do cats like bacon?"

At Renee and Bridget's matching shrugs, she broke off a small piece and held it in Lovey's direction. The cat hissed back at her from the safety of Bridget's arms.

"I guess that would be a no . . ."

Renee stepped around Winnie and helped herself to a piece of bacon. "Here. Let me try." Flipping her freshly manicured (yet still nibbled) hand palm side up, the single mom held the bacon within smelling distance of the cat.

Lovey ate the bacon.

Winnie snorted.

"Maybe it was just your technique," Renee said, following an exchange of raised eyebrows with Bridget. "Like maybe your hand shook or something."

"Maybe Lovey just hates me."

"I'm beginning to suspect you're right, dear." Bridget stroked the top of the cat's head with her wrinkled hand and then set the animal free to roam around her legs. "I noticed, on my way in just now, that the police have concluded their investigation. I stopped and talked to Adelaide's grandson — you do remember Adelaide, don't you, Winnie? She's that nasty little thing I've told you about that gets inside everyone's head at bingo on the second Tuesday of the month . . ."

Renee laughed, earning her — and Winnie (guilt by association, apparently) — an irritated look from Bridget in return. Renee stopped laughing.

"Anyway, her grandson, Roger, is on the police force, and he was outside just now, removing the crime scene tape. I asked him if they've solved Bart's murder, and he said no. I asked him if an arrest would be imminent and, again, he said no. He said there are no leads at this point. Nothing to indicate who or why. All they know is how."

"As in the pillow?" Winnie asked for clarification purposes.

"Of course, the pillow. And *that's* something a mere bakery owner was able to figure out." Bridget's eyes widened the second her mouth stopped moving, and she reached out for Winnie's hand. "Oh dear, I'm sorry. I didn't mean to bring up the loss of your bakery. Forgive me? Please?"

"I under —"

"I'm just so distraught by what happened on the other side of our peaceful little street. It's — it's *frightening.*" Bridget took a deep breath and released it slowly through her nose. "Regardless, it wasn't right to drag up your failure the way I did just now. Especially after you were so kind to me last night."

Failure?

Ouch.

"I wouldn't count her out just yet, Ms. O'Keefe." Renee circled back and stood in solidarity beside Winnie. "In fact, I think she's about to be a million times more successful with her new plan than she ever was or could have been downtown."

Bridget dipped her chin and peered at first Renee and then Winnie atop the rim of her glasses. "Please tell me you're not moving, dear."

"She's not moving," Renee supplied. "The bakery will be."

"You're going to *commute*?"

Again, Renee answered for Winnie. "Nope. The bakery will move . . . literally."

"I don't understand —"

Winnie turned to Renee and gave her what she hoped was the universal nonverbal sign to shut her mouth. It didn't work.

"Winnie is going to start the Emergency Dessert Squad with that ambulance she got from Gertie. And her menu is going to be created around the kind of emergency situations that might prompt a person to need dessert — like menopause, or a broken heart, or a horrible day at work. That sort

69

of thing. We've been working on cute dessert titles all morning. Like Hot Flash Fudge Sundae and —"

Bridget stopped all further explanation from Renee's mouth with a well-placed hand and turned her undivided attention toward Winnie. "Or like when your neighbor is afraid because an old friend has been murdered?"

More than anything, she wanted to smack Renee upside the head for sharing Winnie's plans with Silver Lake's premier (and only) gossip columnist, but news of employer/employee abuse would be bad for business. So, instead, she simply smiled. And nodded.

"Don't-Be-Blue Berry Pie will be on the menu, yes?" Bridget asked.

Winnie nodded again. "It will."

"I love it, dear. Absolutely love it."

The same relief she'd felt in the wake of Renee's reaction to her idea was back, tenfold, and she sunk into the closest kitchen chair with relief (and, yes, exhaustion). "Really? You don't think it's silly?"

"I think it's utterly brilliant, dear. And you can count on me to use my connections to get you coverage in the newspaper when you're ready. Provided, of course, I'm not lying in a hospital bed undergoing some sort of lifesaving procedure."

Winnie nibbled back the smile she felt forming and, instead, gave the elderly woman the concern she was seeking. "Still dealing with those waves of warmth across your abdomen?"

"Yes. It even moved to my lower legs a few times while I was sleeping. And once, I even woke to find the same area vibrating as if I was having some sort of — of muscle attack!"

"Was Lovey at least a comfort?" She felt Renee's eyes on her but refused to meet them for fear any reaction might hurt Bridget's feelings.

"She was, dear. She was always right there — at the source of the warmth or the tremor, doing her best to support me through the moment." Bridget wandered over to the table, perused some of the notes Winnie had made throughout the night and with Renee's help that morning, and then handed a pen to Winnie along with instructions to start writing. "You and Renee will need uniforms. Perhaps with EDT written on the back."

"EDT?" Renee repeated.

"Wait. I know this. Emergency Dessert Technician, right?" At Bridget's nod, Winnie wrote it down and then looked back at her elderly neighbor. "I love it. It's perfect."

"The more authentic you make your mobile bakery, the better." Bridget moved her index finger in a circular motion until Winnie was poised to write again. "Cute dessert names are a good first step. The way they come out of the ambulance is another . . ."

She paused the pen above her list of ideas and looked from Bridget to Renee and back again. "I don't know what you mean."

"It's like I just said, dear. You need to be *authentic*."

Before she could process the woman's words, Renee began to squeal. "Oooh . . . You know what this means, don't you, Winnie? You need to call Master Sergeant Hottie — stat."

"For?" she prompted.

"I'll take this." Bridget folded her arms across her chest in obvious exasperation. "To *assist* you with that authenticity I mentioned, of course."

CHAPTER 6

"Don't you dare fall asleep, Winnie Johnson!"

Winnie tightened her grip on the phone and willed herself to focus on something other than the hint of warmth on her cheek from the waning sun. "I — I'm not falling asleep."

"Liar. I just saw your head loll to the side like a rag doll."

Straightening up on the bench, Winnie darted her gaze left to the empty sidewalk, straight ahead to the front window of Hudson Hardware, and then right to the all-too-familiar Easter egg blue compact car parked no more than a block away. "You *followed* me?"

"You're darn straight I did. If I didn't, you'd be fast asleep on that bench by now, and I'd be wondering why you stopped talking." Renee rolled down the driver's side window and made what Winnie suspected was a not-so-nice face. "Besides, I know you. You're afraid he's going to bite."

"Oh, stop it, Renee. Do I need to remind you I've owned my own bakery for the last two years?"

"And do I need to remind you that you haven't gone on a date in all that time, either?"

"I've dated!"

"Treating Mr. Nelson to a spaghetti dinner at Mario's doesn't qualify as a date, Winnie."

"I'm going to tell him you said that."

"Go ahead. It won't matter. I'm the only one he clips on those bow ties for and you know it."

She had to laugh. It was either that or run into traffic (if there was any) . . . "I'm just here to gather information for the Dessert Squad, Renee. That's all."

"But if he happened to ask you for a date during that process, you would go, right?"

Sinking against the wooden slats at her back, she tried to find the humor in the situation. Her efforts were futile. "Look, Renee, how about we make a deal? I don't try to analyze your feelings about the divorce, and you don't try to set me up on dates, okay?"

"I'm not trying to set you up on a date, Winnie. I'm just helping you with your new business. It's not my fault that in order to fully execute your plan to the best of your ability you need to spend some quality time with Master Sergeant Hottie."

Master Sergeant Hottie . . .

She felt her eyes start to glaze over as, once again, her head dipped to the side.

"Don't you do it! I swear, I'll drag you into that station by the ear, if you do."

She shifted to the shadier end of the bench and stared up at the sky. "You do realize I haven't slept since the night before last, yes?"

"Sleep is overrated, Winnie."

"And in that time, I've inherited an ambulance and a cat that hates me . . . closed up shop on something I poured my heart and soul into for the past two years . . . baked a pie and delivered it to my friend, only to find his dead . . . um . . ."

Focus . . .

Focus . . .

Prying her droopy eyes open with her fingers, she tried to remember where they were. At a loss for an answer, she stepped onto an entirely different train of thought . . .

"Is it just me, or did you happen to notice how my eighty-year-old neighbor knew exactly who you were talking about when you referenced Master Sergeant Hottie this morning?"

"Of course she did, Winnie. Bridget is the one who coined the phrase."

She looked back toward Renee's car. "You're kidding, right?"

"Nope. Used it in the first column she wrote after he moved to town. I'm shocked you didn't see it."

"I've had bigger fish to fry the past few months, I guess." Slowly, she leaned her head against the back of the bench, the memory of carrying the last box out of the bakery — almost exactly twenty-four hours earlier — still fresh in her thoughts. "I can't believe Delectable Delights is really gone."

"The Emergency Dessert Squad is better. Much better."

She watched a plane dart between clouds thousands of miles overhead, her mind shifting gears as she did. "Do you really think so, Renee?"

"Absolutely. It's genius, Winnie. The names, the concept, it's all there. You just need to put the cherry on top."

"The cherry?"

"Go inside, Winnie. Greg will help you if you ask."

Lifting her head from the bench, she turned her attention back to the car and the woman now pointing at the one-story brick building behind Winnie's bench. "You called him *Greg*."

"Because it's the only way you'll go inside."

"Am I really that transparent?"

"Yes." Renee pointed again and then rolled up her window. "I'm hanging up now, but I'm not leaving until I see you get off that bench and walk inside that station."

"I won't bother calling your bluff, but —" She stopped at the click in her ear, removed the device from the side of her face, and returned it to the backpack purse next to her leg. There was no denying the excitement she'd felt coursing through her body as she'd brainstormed ideas throughout the night. No denying the excitement she'd felt when Renee had reacted to those ideas with such enthusiasm. The concept was there. Talking to Greg and getting inside a real ambulance could only help.

Winnie stood, hoisted the purse onto her shoulder, and stepped inside the rather nondescript building. A balding man looked up from behind a half wall separating the lobby area from the inner workings of the Silver Lake Ambulance Corps and smiled. "Good afternoon. Are you here for our EMT class?"

"No. I . . ." She took a deep breath and made herself step closer. "I was wondering if Greg Stevens might be in today?"

"Yeah, Greg's here. Got in about an hour ago. You want to talk to him?"

"If I could. If he's not busy. If he is, I could just come back another time."

"Nah, he's not busy." Bypassing the intercom system on the desk in front of him, the man whose name tag read "Stan" yelled, "Yo, boss. You've got company up here."

She didn't need the framed mirror to her left to know her face was red. That just served as irrefutable proof.

A door behind Stan swung open, and Greg stepped out. "I guess you don't need that megaphone I was planning to buy for you —" He stopped, mid-step, his eyes widening as they came to rest on Winnie. "Oh. Wow. Hey. *Winnie,* right?"

"Yes."

"Well this is a nice surprise."

Stan leaned back in his chair, an amused expression snaking its way across his face. "Should I leave you two kids alone?"

Ignoring his coworker, Greg emerged from behind the half wall to stand in front of Winnie. "You have a price?"

"A price?" she echoed.

"For the ambulance. That's why you're

here, right?" A flash of something that looked a lot like embarrassment changed his eyes from a milk chocolate shade to one more befitting a darker, richer cocoa . . .

Focus . . .

Focus . . .

"You know what?" he said, changing gears. "How about we step outside for a minute? There's a bench out front we could sit on."

She resisted the urge to share her familiarity with the bench and opted, instead, to simply nod.

"If you need me, Stan, I'm outside."

"You got it, boss."

She followed him back out to the sidewalk and over to the bench she'd vacated not more than five minutes earlier. A visual sweep of the street to her right showed no sign of Renee. Surprisingly, that didn't give her the relief she would have anticipated . . .

"By now, Stan is back in the lounge, making up all kinds of stories about the two of us. You do realize this, don't you?"

She made herself laugh despite the dread rising up in her throat. "Guys do that?"

"I'll let you in on a little secret, Winnie. Cops, firefighters, paramedics — they're worse than a group of middle school girls. In every way. Trust me on this."

"You mentioned that yesterday when you came into the bakery." Easing back against the bench, she forced herself to relax. "I'm sorry if my showing up here causes any problems for you. In fact, I even told Renee it was probably a bad idea."

"Renee," he repeated, his head nodding as he did. "That was the woman with the short blond hair in your bakery yesterday morning, right? The one that seemed to know more about me than even I do?"

"Yup. That's her. She's harmless, though. I swear."

"Good to know."

Their laughter died away, leaving them with a semi-awkward silence that had Winnie's face warming despite the sun's rapid descent behind the hardware store. Hiking his thigh onto the bench between them, Greg was the first to speak. "I'm sorry about your bakery. That really stinks."

She felt the pain of her loss tickling at her heart and willed it away. "Mr. Nelson reminds everyone who walks by our house that you just need to find a little sun in your day and you'll be fine. And he's right."

"Who's Mr. Nelson?"

"The man who lives in the apartment below mine. It's a two-family house — only he lives in his place alone, and I live in my

80

place alone." Feeling suddenly foolish about her over-the-top chattiness, she inhaled every ounce of courage she could muster and got to the point of her visit. "I'm not here to sell the ambulance."

The slump to his shoulders was quick but still noticeable.

"I was considering it, I really was," she rushed to explain. "But then I realized it just might be the ticket to getting my business up and running again."

"I think you might be overestimating what you can get for it, Winnie. I mean, it's beautiful, don't get me wrong, but . . . it still needs work to restore it to its original condition."

She, too, swiveled her body so that they were facing each other. "I know. That's why I'm here. I'm hoping you'll help me with the details."

Lifting his hand off the back of the bench, Greg raked it across the top of his head, his minimal amount of hair undaunted by the motion. "I don't understand."

"I'm thinking about taking my bakery on the road via the ambulance. I've got a name — the Emergency Dessert Squad — and I'm working on creating a menu to reflect that theme."

"The Emergency Dessert Squad? Are you

serious?"

She felt her own shoulders slump. "You think it's stupid?"

A smile like she'd never seen on a person's face before suddenly covered his, bringing with it the dimples she remembered from the previous day. "Are you kidding me? It's awesome!" He leaned the side of his body into the bench and propped his head against his hand. "You can't run the siren, though. That would be against the law."

"No siren. Got it."

"So how can I help?" he asked.

"Well, in order to really make this a success, I think I need to work the whole emergency rescue theme into my presentation."

"You mean in more than just the name of your business and the name of your desserts?"

"Exactly." She leaned forward, powered, no doubt, by the notion of getting her dream back on its feet in a new and more creative way. "So I was hoping that maybe you could let me see a real ambulance. And, if it's okay, maybe I could take notes and see how I might tweak my idea in the name of authenticity."

"I think that can be arranged," he said,

letting his foot drop back down to the concrete.

She clapped her hands and then stood, her mind already racing ahead to the kinds of things she might see on her personal tour. "Fantastic. Thank you. Just name the day and time and I'll be here."

"How about today? How about right now?"

"You can do that?" she asked, stunned.

"I'm not doing anything at the moment, are *you?"*

"No."

"Then come on." Touching his hand to the small of her back, he guided her around the bench and toward a different door than the one she'd used to access the station. "As long as we don't get any calls, you can look for as long as you'd like. Just know that if you do, Stan's jaws will be flapping for days to come."

CHAPTER 7

"So this is what we refer to as the bay, but it's really just a super big garage." Greg flicked on a secondary overhead light and then gestured toward the lone ambulance in the center, the vehicle's predominately white exterior sparkling with the effects of a very recent waxing. "Now, *this* ambulance is quite a bit different than *your* ambulance, but you'll still get a good sense of what we bring along on a call."

Winnie trailed him over to the back of the ambulance and then stepped to the side as he opened the back. "One big difference between the ambulance of today and the ambulance of the 1960s is that we can stand up inside this one. Or at least anyone smaller than I am can."

Pulling her purse around to her side, she reached inside for a notebook and pen and flipped to a clean page. "How many people can fit inside the back of this thing?"

"Three. The person we're transporting, the paramedic or EMT, and, if necessary, a family member of the sick or injured party."

She stopped writing long enough to point at the silver pole to the left of the empty gurney. "What's that?"

"A drip pole. In case we have to administer an IV en route to the hospital." He hopped into the back of the ambulance and pulled out a bag with a clear liquid inside. "See this loop? It fits right here on the top of the pole. It hangs there while the fluid is administered into the patient's arm."

"I couldn't have one of those in my ambulance, right? The patient transport area is way too short."

Greg put the fluid bag back in the drawer and pulled the pole closer. "No, you could have one. You'd just have to collapse it down like you would with the gurney. Like this . . ." He wrapped his hands around the pole and twisted. Sure enough, the pole shrunk down in much the way a microphone stand could. "See?"

"Hmmm . . ."

He extended the pole once again, returned it to its original spot inside the ambulance, and then eyed her with obvious amusement. "I see your wheels turning."

Flipping the page over, she sketched the

pole and a tube running from a bag straight to the top of a piece of cinnamon cake. When she was done, she shifted the notebook over so Greg could see. "I'm thinking I could have a drip pole in the Dessert Squad, too. I wouldn't need it for all desserts, of course, but for those that should have a drizzle of icing — like maybe a cinnamon cake or a pastry puff of some sort — an IV pole could be a really fun way to add it when I'm making the delivery to the customer's door, don't you think?"

At his silence, she looked up, a hint of a smile tugging at the corners of his mouth. "No good, huh?" she asked, dropping her gaze back to the primitive drawing in her hand.

"Actually, I think it's a pretty clever idea." His smile opened wide, bringing with it such an intense dimple sighting she actually had to hang on to the ambulance's bumper for support. "Not something I would have thought of, but then again no one has ever accused me of being creative —"

"Oh, c'mon, boss, don't sell yourself short. You got Stan to shut his mouth last week by making up some disease he was in danger of contracting if he didn't."

Greg's face reddened slightly, and Winnie turned to see who was speaking.

"Hey, I remember you!"

She racked her brain for a name to go with the five foot six red-haired man, but she came up empty. "I'm sorry, you look familiar but . . ."

"I'm Chuck. Chuck Rogers. I was one of the EMTs on the scene yesterday. How are you holding up today? I know that had to be quite a shock to your system."

And then it clicked. Chuck had been the one who'd sat her down on Bart's front porch the previous evening and checked her vitals. She'd been so consumed by sadness and shock and fear over finding the elderly man's body that many of the peripheral details of what came next were fuzzy at best.

"Wait a minute." Greg jumped down from the back of the ambulance and looked from Winnie to Chuck and back again. "You were the one who found that body last night, Winnie?"

She closed her eyes against the memory of Bart's sock-clad feet . . . Bart's spindly legs . . . Bart's navy blue shirt . . . and, finally, the navy blue throw pillow atop Bart's face — a memory that had risen to the surface of her thoughts many times over the past twenty-four hours only to be shoved to the side in favor of her sanity.

"Winnie?" She felt Greg's hand on her

arm and willed herself to focus on that, instead. "Are you okay?"

Breathe in . . .

Breathe out . . .

Breathe in . . .

She looked down at the drawing of her IV icing bag and waited for the excitement over her new business idea to return and help deflect the horror of finding Bart's body. But it didn't. "I thought I was," she finally said. "But I think maybe I've just been fooling myself."

He slid his hand behind her and gripped the back of her arm. "Why don't you come into the lounge with me and sit for a while. You're looking a little pale."

Chuck closed the back of the ambulance and then flanked her on the other side for the walk across the bay. Thanks to the interior wall that provided a visual of the ambulance at all times, Winnie could see that the lounge held a large metal table, a few comfortable recliners across from a wall-mounted television set, a refrigerator, a sink, and a stove.

"Welcome to our home away from home," Chuck said at the door before excusing himself to speak with Stan up front.

When he was gone, Greg ushered her over to the most intact-looking recliner and stayed at her side as she sat. "I'm sorry I wasn't on duty last night when all of this happened."

Desperate to stop the trembling in her hands, Winnie tucked them underneath her thighs. "I don't know how you do what you do," she whispered. "I — I wouldn't want to see someone like that ever again."

"We all have our job to do, Winnie. But most of the time, we get to people before it's too late. *That's* why I do what I do."

"I just don't understand why someone would hurt *anyone,* let alone an elderly man. I mean, what kind of threat could he have possibly been?"

Greg lowered himself onto the recliner closest to Winnie's and propped his elbows atop his thighs. "I wish I could answer that, Winnie. I really do. But sometimes the world just doesn't make any sense. All we can do now is let the police department do its job and hope their efforts lead to justice."

"I hope so." She pulled her right hand out and used it to stop the sudden bounce in her legs. Why now? Why was Bart's death just now starting to bubble to the surface?

"Was this man a relative of yours?" Greg asked.

"No. He lives — I mean, *lived* — across the street from me, and he was my friend.

He and his late wife, Ethel, were my friends." Closing her eyes, she tried to block out her final memory of Ethel and the promise she'd made to the woman. Little did either of them know at the time that Winnie would only have to make six peach pies for Bart . . .

"Ahhh, I get it now," Greg said. "You live on Serenity Lane."

"Meaning?"

"What Renee said at your bakery yesterday morning makes sense now. You know, the part about the mutiny of old people. Serenity Lane is where the elderly in this town seem to live."

"Which is why I *chose* to live on Serenity Lane in the first place. I've always been more comfortable with people in their seventies, eighties, and nineties." She peered at him through parted lashes and then looked away, the intensity with which he studied her more than she could take at that moment. "Most people find that weird."

"It's different, I'll give you that, but it's also kind of telling," Greg mused.

Her gaze ricocheted off the blackened TV screen and back to Master Sergeant Hottie. "Telling? Of what?"

"Of the kind of person you must be."

She felt the lump making its way up her

throat and did her best to swallow it back down. "I don't understand."

"So many people our age and younger seem to write older generations off. The fact that you don't speaks to a sort of patience and tolerance that isn't necessarily the norm, you know?"

"Patience and tolerance?" she echoed.

"Those are the best words I can think of right now."

Unsure of what to make of his word choices, she hurried to set the record straight. "My life is richer because of people like Ethel and Bart."

"And obviously they feel the same. That *is* how you got your ambulance in the first place, yes?"

Her ambulance . . .

The reason she was there with Greg in the first place . . .

"Yes, the ambulance *and* the cat were left to me by another former neighbor, Gertrude Redenbacher. Only Gertrude died the way we're meant to die — of old age."

He nodded and then brought his chin into his waiting hands. "So how's the cat? Lovey, right?"

"She hates me."

"Oh, c'mon, she doesn't hate you. She's probably just trying to adjust to a new environment and a new face."

"She has no problem with Mr. Nelson's face. Or Bridget's face. Or Renee's face. Or even your face yesterday," she said. "Just mine."

"Can't imagine why."

There was something about his words, combined with the slight rasp to his voice, that sent a tingle up her spine and made her eternally grateful she hadn't brought Renee. If she had, those three words would have had Renee shopping for bridesmaid attire.

Unsure of what to say in response, Winnie stood and wandered around the lounge, her thoughts vacillating between her surroundings and the man still seated on the recliner watching her every move. She took in the pair of soda cans on opposite ends of the table with a stack of playing cards between them, the upside down paperback novel (a thriller) wedged into a corner of the tattered couch, the mug of coffee grounds (sans water) seemingly forgotten atop the single laminate counter along the far wall . . . "Don't mind the mess," he said from over her shoulder. "I work with slobs."

"You should see *my* place right now. It looks like a bomb went —" She stopped, mid-step, and pointed at a corkboard on the other side of the room. "Why do you have a picture of Bart's house in here? Is that because of yesterday?"

"Bart's house?" he repeated as he, too, rose to his feet and joined her beside the tan-colored board with its brightly colored tacks and various flyers and business cards.

She removed the tack that held the picture in place and began to read the detailed description of the home she saw from her front porch every morning as she left for work and again every evening as she shared dessert and tales of her day with Mr. Nelson. Two lines into the flyer, she heard herself gasp. "Wait a minute. This says Bart's home is for sale! I — I don't understand. I just found him *yesterday*."

"I don't know who put this here, but I can sure find out." Greg opened the lounge door, poked his head into the bay, and whistled. "Chuck? Stan? Can you guys come in here for a minute? I want to ask you a quick question." Within seconds, Chuck (the redhead) and Stan (the balding middle school girl) were standing beside the corkboard. Chuck gave a passing glance to the flyer Winnie handed him and then passed it to Stan. "Yeah, I know about this. Pinned it to the board myself yesterday

93

afternoon. Still trying to decide if I want to
—"

"Yesterday afternoon? As in *before* I saw
you?" She heard the shrillness in her voice
and worked to soften it as she saw Chuck
nod and then exchange a confused glance
with Stan. "Where did you get this?"
Stan handed the flyer back to Winnie. "A
friend of mine stopped by as I was finishing
up lunch and asked if he could run off a
few flyers on our copier. He only ran off ten
so it wasn't a big deal. When he was done, I
offered to hang on to two here at the station to help get the word out. I pinned one
to the bulletin board in the lobby for the
public to see, and asked Chuck to put the
other one in here in case any of the crew is
looking to buy a new place."

"But that house wasn't for sale!"

"According to Mark it was." The jingle of
a bell somewhere outside the lounge had
Stan gesturing toward the door from which
he'd just come. "Oh, sorry, but I gotta get
back to my desk. Duty calls."

At Greg's reluctant nod, Stan headed back
out of the lounge.

"Mark?" she said, whirling around to face
Greg. "*Mark?* Who's Mark —"

And then she knew.

"Winnie?"

Mark Reilly. Ethel's son.

"Winnie?"

Had Bart conceded to the sale? Or was Mark proceeding ahead on his own despite the wishes of his stepfather?

A click off to her right snapped her back into the moment, and she realized Chuck was no longer in the room.

"Do you want to sit down again?"

She looked up from the flyer as a different, far more disturbing scenario began to play out in her thoughts. "Is there a way to know how long Bart had been dead before I found him?"

"Sure. The autopsy will be able to tell us that. But, even before that report comes in, rigor mortis can get us pretty darn close to time of death."

"Would Chuck know if that had started to set in?"

"Sure."

"Could you call him back in one last time?" she asked. "So I could ask him?"

Greg shifted from foot to foot, his gaze never leaving her face. "You sure you want to hear this?"

"I don't want to," she whispered. "I *have* to."

CHAPTER 8

It was a beautiful evening.

The kind of evening capable of relaxing even the most tightly wound nerves.

Unless, of course, those nerves had been wound to the breaking point by the kind of details no one should have to hear about a friend or loved one.

"What's got you so distracted this evening?"

Winnie traced her finger around the top of her glass and weighed her options.

If she told Mr. Nelson and Bridget what she'd learned from Chuck, she risked getting them upset over Bart's murder all over again. Then again, if she could use them as a sounding board, maybe they could hand the man's murderer to the police with a great big bow tied neatly on top.

"Probably that iced tea of yours, Parker." Bridget pulled her hand from the top of Lovey's head and repositioned herself against the back of her favorite wicker chair. "Did you even put iced tea mix in the water?"

"What's that, Bridget?" Mr. Nelson shouted. "You want more iced tea?"

Bridget raised her gaze to the porch ceiling, rolled her eyes, and muttered something under her breath about men and stubbornness. While Winnie couldn't make out each and every word, she got the general gist.

Winnie guided Mr. Nelson's confused eyes to her ear. "Turn up your hearing aids, Mr. Nelson."

He stuck his finger into first his left, and then his right ear. When he was done, he turned back to Bridget. "Do you want more tea?"

"No!"

Waving their neighbor off with a flick of his hand, Mr. Nelson focused his attention back on Winnie. "What's on your mind, Winnie Girl?"

"Mark put Bart and Ethel's place up for sale." There. She said it.

Bridget snapped forward in her chair so fast, Lovey aborted the liftoff attempt that would have landed her safely in the elderly woman's lap and, instead, scurried in the opposite direction. "Bart's body isn't even in the ground yet!"

Pushing her glass into the center of the tiny table between herself and Mr. Nelson, Winnie patted her lap in the hope that Lovey would come over.

Lovey simply looked at her and hissed.

"True. But he *was* dead . . ."

Bypassing her offer, Lovey jumped onto Mr. Nelson's lap as the man leaned forward, eyes wide. "What makes you say that?"

"I — I just know, that's all." She knew she was being evasive, but she wasn't sure filling in details was advisable, either.

"*How* do you know this, Winnie?" Bridget persisted.

"I saw the flyer. I spoke with the person Mark gave it to before I'd even found Bart . . . but *after* he was dead."

Lovey turned herself around in Mr. Nelson's lap and then settled herself against his stomach. "But if you hadn't found him yet, Winnie Girl, no one could have known he was dead."

"No one except the killer," Bridget said, her voice dripping with irritation. Then, to Winnie, she said, "What do you know?"

"This is off the record, Bridget. I'm not law enforcement." When she got the nod of agreement she was seeking, she continued, the nature of her words bringing a hesitancy to her voice she wouldn't otherwise have.

"According to Greg Stevens and one of the EMTs —"

"Greg Stevens?" Mr. Nelson parroted. "Who's that?"

"Master Sergeant Hottie."

She smiled at Bridget and then continued, all momentary amusement disappearing rapidly. "Rigor mortis tends to set in after about three to four hours. A body will reach full stiffness, if you will, at about twelve hours. Bart was nearing full stiffness when I found him yesterday evening."

It was Mr. Nelson's turn to look at the ceiling while Bridget closed her eyes and wrapped her hand around the tiny gold cross that dangled from a chain around her stubby neck.

"I'm sorry," Winnie said, pushing back her chair and making her way over to first Bridget, and then Mr. Nelson. "I shouldn't be sharing this with you. It's too much. Too soon."

Bridget held fast to her cross but opened her eyes to look at Winnie. "No. Bart was our friend. We want answers."

At Mr. Nelson's slow nod, Winnie returned to her chair and continued. "Even without the results of Bart's autopsy, we know that it's likely Bart was killed sometime between eight and nine o'clock yesterday morning."

"I was eating breakfast," Bridget mumbled. "I've been having this thing where it feels as if my throat is closing in on itself, and I was focused on making sure not to choke . . ."

Mr. Nelson's brow furrowed in thought only to release as he returned to petting the cat. "I think I was out back, readying the garbage to go out. Or maybe here, playing chess."

"Did you see a car parked outside Bart's?" Winnie asked, sitting up tall. "Any sign of someone going in or out of his house? Any unusual people? Sounds?"

"Can't say that I did."

Bridget snorted. "Not that Parker would hear anything, anyway, when he's staring at that chessboard of his . . ."

Anxious to avoid a fight, Winnie took up where she left off, her suspicions and fears finding their way into their most articulate form yet. "I guess I'm wondering why — if Bart was killed between eight and nine and I didn't find him until ten hours later — Mark was running off house flyers at lunchtime for a house *he* didn't own . . . but Bart did."

Lovey's head popped up over the edge of the table at the sound of Bridget's gasp. "He knew his stepfather was dead because *he* killed him! I knew it! Why, I've been saying that man was up to no good for years, haven't I, Parker?"

Mr. Nelson tried to keep Lovey from jumping down, but the cat, having been disturbed from her lap-induced slumber, was having none of it.

Without waiting for Parker's nod, Bridget continued, her excitement tempered by a resigned sadness. "From what Ethel told me, Mark was just shy of two when she met Bart, and Bart accepted and loved that baby as if he was his own. What a kick in the head it is to know that none of that mattered in the end."

"Bridget, I can't say for certain that's —"

"He couldn't wait another year or two until nature ran its course? He had to help it along by suffocating the only father he'd ever known?"

"Bridget. Please. This is just a theory. It will be up to the police to see if it has any merit."

"Did you take it to them?" Mr. Nelson asked as he struggled to his feet and followed Lovey around the porch, stopping every few steps to look across the street at Bart's home.

"No. Not yet."

When he reached the end of the porch, he leaned his cane against the railing and shuffled himself in a half circle until he was facing Winnie and Bridget. "Now that you mention this rigor mortis thing, I saw something strange yesterday afternoon. Before you came home from work, Winnie."

"Oh, Parker, please," Bridget moaned, dropping her head into her hand. "This is not time for one of your silly little stories or jokes."

A flash of something resembling hurt zipped across Parker's face just before he locked glances with Winnie. "What is it, Mr. Nelson?" she asked, over a second, louder moan from Bridget.

"I was here on the porch, sitting in that seat you're sitting in right now."

"Okay . . ." she prompted, waiting.

Bridget looked from Winnie to Mr. Nelson and back again, her exasperation at an all-time high. "Why are you humoring him, dear? You know this is going to end up in one of his ridiculous little jokes that aren't the slightest bit funny."

Winnie stood and joined her housemate next to the railing. "Go on, Mr. Nelson."

"The school bus stopped at the end of the road just like always. And just like always, I watched Sissy meet Ava outside the bus and

102

walk with her down the street."

Lovey wound her way around Mr. Nelson's legs . . . the cane . . . the legs of just about every chair on the porch . . . and then looked up at Winnie and hissed. This time, though, Winnie gave the exchange only a passing notice as she waited for her friend to continue.

"When they got to right there" — Mr. Nelson pointed to the street between their home and Bart's — "Sissy whispered something in Ava's ear, and Ava ran right through Bart's flower bed, trampling everything in sight. See?"

Winnie's gaze traveled beyond the road to the flower bed that encircled Bart's mailbox. Sure enough, all signs of spring that had been starting to form had been crushed into the mulched earth.

"I guess I missed that when I brought the pie over after dinner," she mused.

Bridget's hands moved to her mouth but not before she released yet another gasp. Eventually, she spoke, her disgust rivaled only by disbelief. "How could she tell her child to do that especially after what happened the first time?"

The answer was on the tip of Winnie's tongue, but she let Mr. Nelson spell it out for their next-door neighbor. "Based on what Winnie just said, Bart was already dead by as much as six or seven hours when school let out."

"I realize that," Bridget said. "But Sissy couldn't have known that."

Mr. Nelson's hand tightened on the handle of his cane. "She could if she was the one who held the pillow . . ."

CHAPTER 9

Winnie pulled the sponge from the bucket, squeezed out the excess soapy water, and moved around to the driver's side of the ambulance. "Don't look now, Renee, but your number one fan is headed this way."

Renee's head popped up from the other side of the car as she, too, took note of Mr. Nelson and his cane headed in their direction. Lovey followed at a safe distance and with a slightly lazier pace. "Maybe he wants to help dry."

"Maybe he wants to gawk at you in that formfitting T-shirt." She finished the door panel and moved down the length of the ambulance, stopping to dip her sponge into the bucket as she went. "In fact, if I'm right on the time, Mr. Nelson is giving up his noon sighting of Channel Five's meteorologist to get a closer look at you."

"He *is* good for the ego," Renee said in a half whisper before she made her way around the hood of the ambulance to meet Mr. Nelson at the end of the driveway. "Mr. Nelson, hello. Don't you look dapper today?"

Winnie stopped washing and turned in time to see Renee straighten the man's clip-on bow tie, a gesture that earned her former and soon-to-be-again employee a sweet smile in return. She shook her head in amusement and returned to the task at hand.

Mr. Nelson cleared his throat and hobbled a few steps closer to Winnie. "Lovey seemed anxious to come outside and see what you were up to, so I let her out. I hope that's okay."

"It's fine, Mr. Nelson." She waved a soapy finger in the direction of the gold-colored eyes staring out at her from the oak tree on the opposite side of the driveway.

Lovey, in turn, blinked twice and then hissed.

Progress . . .

"Once you get to rinsing, make sure you rinse and dry one section at a time. Looks better that way."

"Will do, Mr. Nelson. Thanks for the tip." She got to the end of the driver's side and stood, the ache in her legs after three sides of bending and washing making her more than a little grateful for Renee's help. "Phew. Time to rinse. Renee, you want to spray it down?"

"I'll do that!" Mr. Nelson stepped forward, took the garden hose from Renee's hands, and hit her with the first shot.

"Oooh!" Renee squealed. "Oooh, that's cold."

He released his hold on the trigger, his eyes wide. "Oh. Miss Ballentine. I'm so sorry. Can I help dry you off?"

Winnie snorted, then laughed, then snorted again. "You're as bad as a teenage boy, Mr. Nelson!"

"What?" he countered, his non-cane-holding hand splayed. "My hand slipped. It happens sometimes."

She stepped over to the folding chair tasked with holding their car-washing supplies and liberated the first towel from the pile. "Here, Renee."

Renee took the towel, dried off, and then wrapped it around her body. "Th-that's b-better."

"You gonna keep that towel there?" Mr. Nelson asked.

"F-for a lit-tle while," Renee managed between teeth clatters. "Th-that wa-ter is c-cold."

"Oh." Mr. Nelson dropped the hose, lifted

his left forearm into view, and consulted his watch. "Well, I better head inside. The noonday weather report will be coming on in four and a half minutes, and I need to see what the day will bring."

Winnie retrieved the hose and pointed at the sky with the nozzle. "I'm pretty sure it's going to be sunny today, Mr. Nelson. There's not so much as a cloud in the sky."

"You never know, Winnie. You never know." And then he was gone, hobbling down the driveway and up the front steps to their porch with a speed he rarely possessed — unless Renee or a weekday forecast was at the other end.

"Was it something I said?" Renee asked.

"Nope. It was something you did."

"What did I do?"

"You covered up the T-shirt he intentionally soaked." Slowly, Winnie moved around the car, spraying off soap as she went. When she reached the end, she waited for Renee to catch up and then handed the woman a can of soda from the cooler. "Thanks, Renee. For everything. I'm not sure I could pull this thing off without you."

Renee tossed the car-drying towel onto the chair, took a sip of soda, and then added her body towel to the mix. "Think that'll get him back out here?"

"Not until the weather report is over." She leaned against the pin oak tree at the edge of the property and took a sip of her own soda. "You haven't asked about my time at the ambulance district with Master Sergeant Hottie. You feeling okay?"

"I'm fine," Renee said, shrugging. "Just missing Ty, I guess."

"He's only with Bob for two more days." She looked at her friend closely and noticed some unfamiliar circles under the woman's eyes. "Are you sleeping?"

"Some." Then, with a flick of her hand, bubbly Renee was back. "So tell me . . . how'd it go?"

She considered pressing Renee on the subject of her recently finalized divorce and the resulting split custody schedule, but she let it go. Her friend needed a distraction from life, not a rehashing. When Renee was ready to talk, she'd talk. "It went well. Greg is really nice. He thinks my —"

"Nice?" Renee shouted. "Nice? I don't want to hear that he's nice!"

"Well he is. And as I was starting to say, he thinks my idea for the Emergency Dessert Squad is great."

Renee finished off her soda with two long pulls, set the can down on the chair next to the towels they hadn't used, and reached for Lovey. Instantly, the cat settled into Renee's arms and began to purr. Loudly. "Anyone with a brain in their head would think it's a great idea, because it is. Did he let you look at one of the ambulances?"

"Yup. And I came up with an idea for those desserts that call for a drizzle of icing or glaze." It was hard not to feel a little hurt by the affection her new cat seemed to show everyone except her, but she shook it off. Besides, she had bigger fish to fry. "When we deliver them up to the door on the gurney, I'll drizzle on the topping via an IV bag."

"An IV bag?"

"That's right. And it will hang from an extendable pole just like a real IV bag would."

"Cute." Renee stroked her hand down the top of Lovey's neck and then returned her fingers to the same general starting place to administer a well-received scratch. "We'll have to figure out a way to keep the chocolate warm so it stays at the right consistency, won't we?"

"Yes, but I don't think that will be too difficult. We won't have to hang the bag until we're unloading the ambulance for delivery." She set her half-empty can down on the ground at her feet and slowly walked toward Renee and Lovey. The closer she got, the narrower the cat's eyes became. Two feet from her intended destination, she stopped. "Do you think this cat is *ever* going to like me? I mean, she was left to *me,* you know . . ."

"It's probably just a reaction to your stress. Cats can sense stuff like that, I think." Renee clicked her tongue against the back of her teeth and smiled down at Lovey. "The day you got her, you closed down the bakery *and* found a dead body. That's not the kind of stress a person can hide real well."

"You're stressed about Bob and not seeing Ty this week . . ."

"Okay, but —"

She held up her hand and continued. "And Mr. Nelson and Bridget are both stressed beyond belief about Bart's death . . ."

"Yeah, but —"

"So your stress theory doesn't hold up, Renee."

"Then I've got nothing." Shrugging, Renee lowered herself to the ground and repositioned the cat against her legs instead of her arms. Once she was sure Lovey was going to stay, she pointed to the house across the street. "So what's going on over there, anyway?"

Winnie retraced her steps back to the tree and leaned against its trunk. "We have no idea. Since the crime scene tape came down yesterday morning, we haven't seen any more police."

"No suspects?"

"I can't speak for the Silver Lake PD, but Mr. Nelson and Bridget and I have come up with two."

A flash of movement at Mr. Nelson's front window let her know that the weather report was over and that her neighbor was trying to determine whether it was worth venturing outside again. The fact that Renee's chosen patch of ground was outside of the man's visual path had Winnie guessing Mr. Nelson would remain inside.

"Did one of you see something?" Renee asked.

She smiled and waved at the elderly man. "I saw something *after* the fact that gave us the first suspect, and Mr. Nelson saw something that gave us the second."

"Care to share?"

"Yesterday, while I was at the station talking to Greg, I saw a flyer on a bulletin board listing Bart's house for sale. When I asked how it got there, one of Greg's coworkers said it came from Bart's stepson, Mark Reilly."

Renee made a face first at Winnie and then at Lovey as the cat abandoned her cuddle spot in favor of smelling her way around the ambulance and the assorted car-washing paraphernalia scattered across the ground. "I admit the timing is pathetic, but maybe the guy can't afford the mortgage on the house now that his stepfather is dead."

She watched Lovey lick a bead of water off the outside of the garden hose and then continue on, stopping only to stalk a butterfly and a falling leaf before contemplating a dash across the street. "Lovey, stay over here," she cautioned. Surprisingly, the cat lowered herself to the grass, swished her tail from side to side, and remained on their side of the road.

Looking back at Renee, she continued. "But here's the thing. Mark was copying these flyers hours before I found his stepfather's body."

"Maybe Bart agreed to the sale."

It was a wrinkle she hadn't considered.

Now that she did, though, she couldn't help but wonder if Renee was right. Bart had grown increasingly more depressed since the death of his beloved Ethel. Even Winnie's peach pie deliveries couldn't keep a smile on his face for more than a few minutes. Maybe the memories of a life shared in that house had become too painful . . .

"I guess I hadn't thought of that possibility," she finally admitted. "I suppose you could be right."

"Maybe. Maybe not — oh, there she goes!"

Winnie pushed off the tree and whirled around in time to see Lovey dash across the street and right through the middle of Bart's trampled flower bed. "Lovey! Come back! Come back here right now!"

Renee stood, readjusted her still-wet T-shirt against her body, and joined Winnie in her own dash across Serenity Lane. "Cat Lesson Number One: Cats only listen if they want to listen. So that whole 'come back, come back' thing you just yelled? Completely ineffective."

"*Now* you tell me," she mumbled as Lovey scampered around the side of the Wagners' house. Darting left, Winnie half ran, half jogged around the back of the house and stopped. "Lovey?"

When there was no response, she threw her hands in the air. "Great. Two days into my role as cat owner and I've already lost the cat."

Renee called for silence with her index finger and then cocked her head toward the house. Seconds later, she lowered the same finger to point at a partially askew screen next to Bart's patio. "Cat Lesson Number Two: Cats are curious. Period."

She looked from Renee to the basement window and back again. "Huh?"

"Lovey is in there."

Again she followed the path of Renee's finger, and again she took note of the gap between the screen and the windowsill. "In *there*?"

"Uh-huh."

"But how am I supposed to get her out?" she asked.

"You're the creative one. You'll figure it out." Renee waved, pivoted on the toes of her bare feet, and headed back around the side of the house.

Winnie ran to catch up. "Aren't you going to help me?"

"Nope."

"Why not?"

"Because I'm not about to blow your chance to play damsel in distress."

"Damsel in distress?" she repeated.

Renee's answering grin was decidedly wicked. "That's right. Lovey just did you a huge favor."

"A — a favor?" she stammered. "How the heck do you figure that?"

"Damsel in distress, Winnie. Damsel. In. Distress."

CHAPTER 10

A cup of chocolate chips — check.

A half teaspoon of baking powder — check.

Three-quarters of a cup of brown sugar — check.

Winnie looked up from her list of ingredients and shook her mixing spoon at the four-legged creature eyeing her with boredom from the windowsill. "You have no idea how lucky you are that you came out of Bart's house all on your own."

Lovey yawned, her mouth opening wide enough to display her long pink tongue. When she was done, she stood up, walked around in a circle, and then dropped into a ball, clearly undaunted by Winnie's reprimand.

She kept talking. "I get that you're not happy about this situation. I'm not, either. But Gertie was my friend, and she left you in my care. One way or the other, we're going to have to make this work. I'm doing my part by providing you a litter box, food, and a window bed. How about meeting me in the middle and at least *pretending* you like me?"

"Knock, knock . . . It's me, dear." Bridget peeked around Winnie's always-open door, gave a quick scan of the kitchen and living room, and then cocked her head ever so slightly. "Winnie, dear? Who were you speaking to just now?"

"Myself, apparently." She loosened her grip on the spoon and used it to wave her neighbor into the apartment. "If you stick around for a while and you're game, I have a new dessert I'd like to try out on you."

Bridget crossed the entryway and stopped at the edge of the counter. "Will this one have a cute little rescue name, too?"

"I'm working on that." Winnie returned to her drawer of measuring tools and selected the sizes she needed for the next two ingredients on her self-made list. She pointed the four-ounce cup at Bridget's left hand. "Are you heading off to work?"

"I'm *here* to work, dear."

"I don't understand."

"I'd like to talk to you — on the record, of course — about the Emergency Dessert Squad."

She lowered the cup back down to the counter, bouncing her attention between her latest recipe and Bridget. "While I think I can be up and running on a limited scale as early as Monday, I'm not sure anyone will be calling. Maybe we should wait until I have customers."

"A piece in the paper will *get* you customers, dear."

"That makes sense, I guess. So? What do you need from me? To let you" — she let go of the cup and used her fingers to make air quotes — "*overhear* something about my new business venture?"

Bridget's stare was so intense, Winnie recovered the measuring cup and took a half step back. "What? Your column is called 'Overheard.' "

"My column is, yes. But I'm going to interview you for a full article that will run in this weekend's paper . . ."

"Oh. Wow. Thanks, Bridget. That would be fantastic." She looked at the mess in front of her and then back at her neighbor. "Um, do you want me to put this on hold while you ask me questions?"

"First, I want to know why you were talking to yourself when I arrived. Is everything all right, dear?"

Winnie used the one-cup measuring tool

to scoop sugar, and the three-quarter-cup tool to scoop white chocolate chips. One by one, she added each ingredient to the first of two bowls and then gave them a quick mix. "Mostly. But, honestly, how do I get Lovey to like me?"

At the mention of the feline, Bridget inventoried the floor around the counter and the various seating options in the living room before finally locating Lovey in her spot in front of the window. Within moments, the cat was awake and purring as Bridget lovingly scratched around her ears and under her chin. "Just do what I do, Winnie."

"I would if she'd let me get close. But she doesn't. Every time I try, she hisses at me."

"Have you tried bribing her, dear?"

"Bribing her?" Winnie set the dry ingredients to the side and moved on to the next bowl and the eggs, milk, and oil waiting to be mixed together. "With what?"

"Kitties love tuna. And the leftover soupy part of vanilla ice cream."

With expert hands, she cracked each of the trio of eggs against the side of the bowl and watched as the yolk slid down the inner edge. "I suppose I could give that a try — later. Doing it now might seem like she's being rewarded for her misbehavior earlier."

Bridget stopped rubbing Lovey's neck. "Misbehavior?"

Winnie wrapped her fingers around the mixing spoon once again and pointed it at Lovey. "Do you want to tell Aunty Bridget what you did today? Or should I?" The cat turned her head and her attention toward the bird's eye view of Serenity Lane she favored. "Okay, fine. I'll tell her."

With her free hand, Winnie poured in the oil and the milk and began to mix. "Lovey, here, decided to cross the street, run around the back of Bart's house, and wiggle her way through a gap in the basement screen."

"And?"

"Mr. Nelson came over and managed to coax her back outside."

Bridget folded her thinning arms against her chest and cast a knowing smile at first Lovey, and then Winnie. "You should have called Master Sergeant Hottie."

She stopped mixing and stared at the woman. "You are as bad as Renee, do you know that?"

"We just want to see you happy, dear."

"I *am* happy, Bridget. It's just been a stressful few weeks with the pending demise of the bakery and then thinking I might be getting a reprieve by way of Gertie's will." She returned to the liquid mixture and the next handful of ingredients still to be added. When everything was in, she mixed again. "But things are looking up now."

"It *does* certainly seem as if this new business idea has given you a lift. And I'm glad about that. I truly am. But you're young. You should be out dating instead of spending your evenings sitting on the front porch with old fogies like Parker and me."

"I love my time with you. I always have." She added the dry ingredients to the second bowl and swapped her spoon for the electric hand mixer. Slowly, she moved the bowl in a circle with one hand while holding the beaters steady with the other. "Why should I waste my time on something that's probably not going to go anywhere?"

"Because it could."

Winnie looked down at the creamy mixture taking shape in the bowl and tried to think of something clever to say in response. But there was nothing. Bridget was right. She had the drive for a career down pat. It was just the rest of her life that seemed rather rudderless.

"Can we talk about something else for a little while?" Winnie powered off the mixer and set it to the side. A peek over her shoulder confirmed that the oven had, indeed, reached the proper baking temperature.

"Such as?"

"Whether Bart had decided to sell the house prior to his death." She poured the mixture into the prepared pan and then popped it into the oven. When the timer was set, she turned back to face her neighbor. "Maybe being there, without Ethel, had simply become too much for him."

Bridget returned to the window, pushed the simple sheer curtain to the side, and looked across the street, her back to Winnie. "There is no way Bart would have sold that house. Just think about all those pictures he had around his living room — pictures highlighting nearly fifty years spent loving Ethel. Think about the case on the fireplace mantel that held his beloved coin. Think about all of the parties they had in that house along the way, all the milestones that were celebrated there."

"Pictures and coins are portable, Bridget. They could have just as easily been displayed around a condominium or an apartment in an assisted living facility. And as for the memories, they were in his heart and his head." She carried the empty bowls, measuring tools, and mixing spoons over to the sink. Normally, she'd wash them right away if for no other reason than to ensure they were at the ready for her next baking whim. But today, she left them and wandered over to the window and Bridget. "Ethel's death really took its toll on him, Bridget. You know that. Maybe he'd realized it, too, and decided it was time to make a change."

The curtain fell back into place as Bridget turned to face Winnie. "Bart wouldn't have sold. I'm as sure of that as I am that Parker is a certifiable pain in the neck."

She ignored the woman's slap at Mr. Nelson and stayed on point. "Why? He was painfully lonely in that house without Ethel. Maybe he just didn't want to be there all by himself anymore. Ethel was quite a lively personality. Having her there one minute and gone the next would be tough. Especially for someone who'd doted on her the way Bart did."

Bridget gestured toward the living room and, at Winnie's nod, walked over to a chair and sat. "Late last week, I was on the way home from a meeting at the paper when I saw Bart sitting on his front porch. I waved and mentioned the vitamin C I'd stopped to buy at the pharmacy — I'd woken with a horrible cold that morning, dear — but he didn't respond."

"Okay . . ." Winnie perched on the front edge of the couch opposite from Bridget and waited for the woman to continue, the anguish in her friend's eyes impossible to miss.

"Well, you know how I am, Winnie. I couldn't leave well enough alone. I couldn't just assume he was sleeping or simply preoccupied with his thoughts. I had to get to the bottom of why he hadn't waved back at me." Bridget picked at a nonexistent piece of lint on her flowered skirt and then leaned her head back against the chair. "What I ended up doing, though, was interrupting a rather pleasant memory of a trip he and Ethel had taken after Mark had moved out on his own. There Bart was, sitting on his rocker, smiling and laughing in a way I hadn't seen him do since it became apparent Ethel wasn't going to pull through."

"That sounds lovely," Winnie said. "But I don't understand what that has to do with your absolute conviction Bart hadn't decided to sell . . ."

"When I stepped onto his porch and he still seemed completely unaware of my presence, I clapped my hands." The woman closed her eyes as if the image accompanying her words had become too painful. "Bart's smile disappeared, his laughter stopped, and the utter sadness that crept over his face left me wishing for a sweater to combat the chill I felt to my very core. I apologized, of course, but it was too late. My need to be noticed and acknowledged had snapped Bart back into reality."

"You couldn't have known, Bridget."

Slowly, Bridget's lashes parted to reveal a regret that seemed far bigger than the situation deserved. "Bart said something that made me realize what I'd done, and so I asked him to tell me about the trip, hoping desperately that revisiting the moment again would bring his happiness back. But it didn't work. He was *sharing* the memory rather than *experiencing* the memory the way he had been when I clapped.

"It was like . . . it was like I'd taken Ethel from him all over again."

Something about the way Bridget's voice cracked made Winnie stand, bypass the coffee table between them, and crouch down beside the woman. Reaching up, she took Bridget's wrinkled hand in hers and caressed it gently with her thumb. "Bridget, don't."

"That's when Bart told me that Ethel was still with him — in the living room where they watched television each night, in the kitchen where they sat across the table from each other, and in their bed where he'd held her as she fell asleep for virtually all of their nearly fifty years together. He told me that when his grief became so great, he would go into one of those spaces and simply feel her." Bridget flipped her hand inside Winnie's gentle grasp and squeezed. "That's why I'm absolutely certain that those flyers you saw yesterday had nothing to do with Bart. And why I'm absolutely certain that he knew nothing about them, either."

Once again, Mark Reilly was back in the forefront of Winnie's thoughts . . .

"Okay," she said as her thoughts moved ahead into the processing stage. "Then how could Mark have honestly thought he could put the place up for sale without Bart's say-so? I mean, what was he going to do when the place sold? Say, 'Oh, by the way, Dad, a moving truck is coming to deliver the next family, so you gotta go'?"

But even as she lost the male-sounding mimic to her voice, she knew it was a silly thing to say. After all, if Bart were dead when the sale happened, there would be nothing to say, no cajoling to be done. Mark could simply put the place up for sale, sign on the dotted line, and pocket the money.

Then again, anyone with a brain in their head knew Bart was old. His health had been declining even before Ethel's death. So why not just wait? Why jump the gun?

Winnie stood but remained beside Bridget's chair, one question after the other firing from between her lips. "Do we know for certain that the house was to go to Mark upon Bart's death? And if it was, is the printing of a few flyers really enough proof? Do we take this to the police?"

Bridget's head parted company with the back of the chair as she, too, struggled to her feet. "Part of me thinks yes, and part of me thinks no."

"Why the no?" Winnie asked. "I mean, it seems pretty likely to me on account of what we know about the flyers and Bart's disinterest in leaving his home anytime soon."

"I don't know. Call it a nagging feeling."

Winnie meandered her way back to the couch but didn't sit, her thoughts far too jumbled not to keep walking, keep processing. On one hand, it seemed to make perfect sense to go to the Silver Lake Police Department and at least share their suspicion, but, on the other hand, what did she know? She baked desserts for a living — or did . . .

And will again!

She rounded the back of the couch and headed toward the kitchen, the timer on her oven beginning its final second-by-second countdown.

Concentrate on the Dessert Squad, dummy . . .

Leave the police work to the police . . .

"Besides, we can't forget what Parker said about Sissy and Ava," Bridget reminded.

Winnie stilled her mitted hand on the oven door and waited for the official beep. "You mean about Sissy telling Ava to trample Bart's flower bed on the day I found his body?"

"It seems to me that woman had to be mighty confident Bart wasn't going to come tearing out of the house screaming at her precious angel again."

When the cake pan was safely in the center of the cooling rack, Winnie removed the oven mitt from her hand and hung it on the magnetized hook on the side of the refrigerator. "The kid lost a tooth, Bridget. Do you really think that's worthy of murdering someone? I mean at least with Mark you can see how his actions might have been propelled by greed. A house like Bart's, on a street like Serenity Lane, could potentially go for some nice money. A lost tooth can't compete with that. Not even close."

Bridget wandered back into the kitchen, stopped in front of the cooling cake, and sniffed. "I could take offense over the way you seem oblivious to my career, dear, but I won't. Simply see that I get a piece of this marvelous creation when it's ready, and I'll overlook it."

"What are you talking about? I — I read your column."

The woman's left eyebrow shot upward.

"What?" Winnie protested. "I *do.*"

The right eyebrow rose in solidarity with the left.

"M-most of the time," she whispered.

Bridget crossed her arms, only to uncross them in favor of drumming the fingers of her right hand atop the counter. "What's the last column of mine you remember reading?"

She searched her memory bank but came up empty. Unless —

"You wrote about Greg Stevens. You called him Master Sergeant Hottie!"

Thank you, Renee . . .

Bridget's eyes narrowed on her face.

Uh-oh.

"Did I call him that in the *body* of my column, dear?"

She swallowed. Could she claim a sudden urge to use the restroom and call Renee for help?

"That's what I thought." Bridget shuffled

130

over to the top of the staircase that would take her past Mr. Nelson's door and out into the late afternoon sunshine. But when she reached the exit, she turned and made a beeline back to the window and the cat licking herself on its sill. Lovey retracted her tongue from her hind leg, looked up at Bridget, and began to purr. "This pageant Ava was supposed to be in this weekend wasn't just about winning a sash and wearing a cute little crown for photographers, Winnie. It was about much more than that."

"Oh?"

"There were rumors that a talent scout was to be in attendance as a favor to a judge he'd known since college."

She made a mental note to read Bridget's column on a weekly basis and then forced herself to focus on what the woman was saying.

"Sissy was absolutely convinced this talent scout was going to take one look at Ava and sign her for commercials, soap operas, prime-time television, movies, you name it."

"I would imagine *most* of the moms associated with this pageant probably believed the same thing, Bridget."

"True. But how many of those moms had the foresight to contact the man ahead of time to tell him about their daughter?"

131

Bridget's hand moved around to Lovey's chin. "And how many of them were actually contacted by that same scout two weeks ago for additional pictures and a résumé?"

She started to lean against the refrigerator but stopped as the woman's words took hold. "Seriously? He really contacted Sissy for pictures and a résumé?"

Bridget stopped petting Lovey to nod. "He did. From what Sissy told me when it first happened, this guy thought Ava would be perfect for a commercial he was helping to cast for this coming week. In New York. He was to meet Sissy and Ava after the pageant to sign the papers and, potentially, take them back to New York with him that very night."

"So why couldn't that still happen?"

"It was a toothpaste commercial, dear. Teeth are rather essential, don't you think?"

CHAPTER 11

"What about a dessert for someone who's fit to be tied and needs a treat to calm them down?"

Winnie looked up from the notepad in front of her and smiled at Mr. Nelson across the porch table. "I'm listening . . ."

"You could call it Fit To Be Tied." Mr. Nelson dug his knife into the margarine container, slathered the butter substitute onto his second of three croissants, and then pointed at Winnie's list. "Or maybe Hopping Mad."

"Those are good, Mr. Nelson, but I'm trying to incorporate the problem my dessert will solve with the actual name of the dessert. Like, Don't-Be-Blue Berry Pie for someone who is feeling sad." She set down her pen long enough to take a sip of coffee and then returned to her notes and the slowly growing list of items for the Dessert Squad's menu.

The man took a bite of his croissant and then popped a blueberry into his mouth from the bowl Winnie had placed in the center of the table. "People get mad, too, Winnie."

"I know that, Mr. Nelson. And it's certainly a problem worthy of a dessert rescue, but I need to equate it with a specific —"

"Heck, we saw plenty of examples of that with Bart these last few weeks," he said, helping himself to an entire handful of blueberries.

He tried to sound removed, as if it was just another morning on the porch, but Winnie knew her friend was still shaken by what had happened across the street. "The police will figure out what happened to him, Mr. Nelson."

"If Bart were twenty-five, instead of eighty-five, I could believe that. But I don't think getting to the bottom of a crime against us old folks carries the same urgency as, say, that bad stretch of road on the north side of town where all those accidents keep happening."

"Bart was *suffocated*," she reminded him. "They can't ignore that."

"Maybe they can't. But they can control where it falls on the priority list." Mr. Nelson returned to his butter knife and the last of his croissants. "I suspect the person who did this is right under our noses."

"Then we'll figure this out, Mr. Nelson. With or without the police."

His hand trembled ever so slightly as he placed the knife back on the table and brought the croissant to his mouth. "And if we do," he said, winking, "that lazy, good-for-nothing Chief Rankin will be seeing red."

Seeing red . . .

Seeing red —

"That's it!" She tightened her grip on her pen and added another dessert to her menu. "Mr. Nelson, you did it!"

He stopped chewing and tapped his hearing aids. "I didn't hide anything."

The momentary confusion born on his words quickly gave way to understanding. "You did it, Mr. Nelson. *Did* it."

"Oh." The man leaned across his now-empty plate. "Did what?"

"You just came up with my next dessert — Seeing Red Velvet Cake."

Mr. Nelson smiled triumphantly. "My parents always used to tell me I was one smart cookie."

Smart cookie . . .

One smart cookie . . .

"One Smart Cookie!" She returned to her

list again as her mind raced ahead to the various choices that could be placed in parentheses on the menu — chocolate chip, double chocolate fudge, butterscotch, et cetera. "A perfect choice for a really good report card or some other school-related milestone . . . Mr. Nelson, these are awesome. Thank you!"

With the help of her index finger, Winnie ticked off the boxes she'd opened in relation to the shipping order in her opposite hand.

Yup. She'd unpacked them all.

Then again, if she had, why was one of them moving?

Painfully aware of the lack of sleep she'd been getting, Winnie rubbed her eyes. When the box continued to move, she rubbed them again.

She was about to rub them a third time when her backside began to vibrate. Sliding her hand into her pocket, she pulled out her phone, checked the caller ID screen, and held the device to her ear. "Hey, Renee."

"Whatcha doing?"

"Right now? I'm staring at a box I could swear I unpacked, yet it's — it's —" She stopped, swallowed. "Moving."

"Where's Lovey?"

"Lovey?"

She didn't need to see Renee's face to pick up the hint of condescension in the woman's laugh. "You've forgotten Cat Lesson Number Two, haven't you?"

"No," she protested. "I remember. Cats are curious. Period."

"Well, that leads to Cat Lesson Number Three."

The movement inside the box stopped, and she felt her shoulders relax. "You never told me there was a third lesson . . ."

"Cats like boxes."

"Cats like —" She took a deep breath, walked over to the now-quiet box, and folded back the lid. Inside was Lovey, her ears lowering in preparation for (you guessed it) the hiss that invariably followed.

"Yup. It's Lovey . . ."

"I heard," Renee said between sighs. "We've really got to find a way to make her like you, Winnie."

"Tell me about it."

"Have you tried tuna?"

"I gave her some for breakfast this morning."

"And?"

"She hissed when I put it in her bowl, and she hissed when I asked her if it was good."

"Have you tried petting her?"

Wedging the phone between her ear and her shoulder, Winnie looked down at the angry red line (about two inches in length, mind you) on her wrist and nodded.

"Winnie?"

"Oh. Sorry. Yes. I've tried petting her."

"And she hissed?"

"Actually, no." She reclaimed the phone, stuck her tongue out at the cat, and then returned to the last box she'd unpacked. "She just scratched me."

"Oh." Renee's yawn made her yawn, too. "I'm not sure if that's progress."

"Yeah, me, neither." She crouched down beside the box, glanced at the order sheet, and mentally compared it to the items scattered across her living room floor. "The delivery guy came about an hour ago. I've got everything we need to get this Dessert Squad on the road come Monday morning."

Renee squealed in her ear. "Really? Already? What about the menu?"

"It's coming along. I've got about a dozen desserts right now — not enough to sustain a business, but enough to get us moving. I suspect more and more will come to us as we go." She stood, crossed to the table and the dessert list, and smiled at the last two entries. "Mr. Nelson helped me add two just this morning."

"Okay, let me hear them."

"Seeing Red Velvet Cake for someone who is feeling angry about something, and You Are One Smart — chocolate chip, double chocolate fudge, et cetera — Cookie for someone who just accomplished something really cool."

"Winnie, I love them." Renee's enthusiasm started strong but waned as she continued. "But, how are we going to get the word out? I mean, we can open for business on Monday, but if no one knows we exist, we'll spend the entire day staring at each other. Not that that's a problem, because it's not, but . . . well, I want this to work for you."

"For *us,*" she corrected. "And it will. Bridget interviewed me yesterday for an article that is going to run in the *Silver Lake Herald* this weekend. I shared a few dessert titles with her, talked about the concept of wanting to turn someone's day around with a tasty dessert, and how the rescue theme will play out in both areas."

"Oooh. Good . . ."

"So maybe we'll get a customer or two from that article. Then, people will see me out and about in the ambulance, and they'll call to order something, too."

"Can I come up with a clever way to take

the calls?" Renee asked. "Maybe answering them like an actual dispatcher?"

"Sure. Why not? I think that sounds like a great idea." Movement from Lovey's box claimed her attention momentarily. Seconds later, two ears poked through the top of the box followed by two large golden eyes and a little pink tongue that unfurled along with a yawn. "I think our chat is interrupting Lovey's sleep."

There was no sound in her ear except a very faint sniff. "Renee? You still there?"

A second sniff was followed by a third and a fourth.

"Renee? Are you okay?" she asked.

"Winnie?"

"Yes?"

"I know the concept behind the Emergency Dessert Squad is to rescue people with dessert, but it's kind of rescued me, too."

Lovey jumped out of the box and into the next one with such force, the whole thing toppled over — Lovey and all.

Winnie laughed, brought her friend up to speed on what had just transpired, and then got back to the conversation at hand. "What do you mean the Dessert Squad has rescued you?"

"I always loved working with you at the

bakery, as you know. But . . . this . . . it's different. No one has done this before. And I get to be there from the start — watching it go from an idea on paper to a reality. It's really . . ." Renee's voice petered off only to return wrapped in the kind of enthusiasm no phone line could damper. "It's really exciting."

"For you and me, both, Renee. For you and me both."

CHAPTER 12

More times than she probably should have, Winnie found herself stealing glances in Mark Reilly's direction as he flitted around the private room, sharing memories of his stepfather with a tear in his eye.

With Mr. Nelson, he'd looked back fondly on his mom and Bart's annual flower beds, sharing a behind-the-scenes account that included tales of drawings and spreadsheets in the weeks leading up to planting season.

With Bridget, Mark lamented his good fortune in being raised by a man like Bart.

With Peggy Landon, one of Serenity Lane's earliest settlers, he recounted the patience his stepfather had shown him when he'd resisted riding his first bike as a young boy.

Observing (and, yes, eavesdropping) from a distance, it was easy to view each and every encounter as insincere — a show put forth by a very viable suspect in Bart's murder. Yet, the moment Mark got around to Winnie and started talking about how much her peach pie promise to his mother had truly meant to Bart, she couldn't help but want to scratch his name off her mental suspect list.

Up close, Mark's grief over Bart's death seemed sincere.

Up close, his outrage over the manner in which Bart died seemed true.

But was it?

"Nice article in this morning's paper."

She looked up from her half-eaten lunch to find Greg Stevens's dimples on full display. "Oh. Greg. Hi." Pushing her plate forward, she wiggled out of her chair and extended her hand to the uniformed man. "I didn't know you knew Bart."

Greg's broad shoulders shrugged beneath the dark blue fabric of his shirt. "I didn't, really. But Chuck" — she followed the line of his finger to the redhead talking to Mark at the far end of the table — "over there wanted to stop by."

"Do you always go to the funerals of people you aren't able to save?"

"Sometimes. Depends on the circumstances." He took inventory of Winnie's dress and then gestured to her hair. "I like your hair down like that. It's really pretty."

"Thank you."

"We wanted to come by the service, but a call on the other side of town prevented us from being able to do that. So here we are at the repast — although we're not staying to eat."

Mr. Nelson pushed his chair into the gap between them and pointed up at Greg. "That's right, young fella, there's meat . . . but it's a bit rubbery if you ask me."

The dimples disappeared as Greg drew back, confused. "I'm sorry, I —"

She reached out, placed one hand on Greg's forearm and one hand on Mr. Nelson's shoulder. "Mr. Nelson, he said *eat* . . . not *meat*. And he's not staying to do that."

"Smart man," Mr. Nelson muttered as he scooted his chair back to the table and resumed his conversation with the thirty-something brunette on his other side.

A flicker of amusement brought the paramedic's dimples back in play. "You know this guy?" Greg asked, lowering his voice to a near whisper.

Unsure of how to take the question, she merely nodded.

"A bit hard of hearing, I take it?"

"He does okay." She heard the defensive note to her tone and, instead, let her gaze return to the far end of the table and the two men now in full-blown conversation. "So you came to accompany Chuck?"

"We're riding together today."

"I see." But she really didn't. She was still trying to decide whether his comment about Mr. Nelson had been a simple case of making conversation or the first sign of a person she didn't care to continue knowing.

"Turns out, Chuck has known the victim for a while."

"Oh?"

"From what I gather, Mr. Wagner used to run some sort of collectors club in town and Chuck started attending meetings with his dad when he was a kid." Greg widened his stance and rocked back on his heels. "I think his dad was into old Lionel trains and Chuck did something with baseball cards. When Chuck's parents moved to Florida a few years ago, Chuck stayed on with the club.

"Anyway, enough of that. I saw the article in the weekend section of the *Herald* this morning. You must be really excited."

"I am. Bridget did a great job."

"Have you slept at all in the last day or so?" he asked.

She hated that her hands moved to her face as she revisited her brief look in the bathroom mirror at the church, but she couldn't help it. "It's that obvious, huh?"

Again his dimples disappeared as reality dawned across his handsome face. "No. That's not what I meant. You — you look fine — great, actually. I just saw the pictures of the inside of the ambulance and know it must have taken some time to doctor it up like that."

"Oh." She brought her hands back down to her sides and resisted the urge to hug Chuck for the distraction that came from his sudden appearance at her elbow. "It's — it's nice to see you again, Chuck."

"You, too, Winnie." Chuck looked from Greg to Winnie and back again before clearing his throat awkwardly. "So, uh . . . nice piece in the paper this morning. Are you excited to get going on Monday?"

"Excited, and a little bit scared, too."

"Scared?" Greg echoed.

She reached across the top edge of her chair and rescued her water glass from the table. "Sure. This whole business idea could be the cleverest thing in the world. But it won't matter if no one calls and places an order."

"They'll call." Bridget sidled up alongside Greg, locked gazes with Winnie, and hooked her thumb in the paramedic's direction.

The gesture alone was embarrassing all

on its own, but it was the not-so-subtle cluck of appreciation that accompanied the gesture that had Winnie trading her next sip for a gulp.

"I agree."

She knew she should acknowledge Greg's faith in her idea with something more than a quick glare in Bridget's direction, but she couldn't. Not at that moment, anyway. No, what she truly needed (and desperately wanted) at that exact moment was a trapdoor beneath her feet.

She leaned back against the lip of the porch and watched as Lovey jumped off her housemate's lap and wandered toward the staircase on which Winnie sat. "So what did you think about the service and the repast today, Mr. Nelson?"

Mr. Nelson moved his white knight, smiled triumphantly, and then glanced up from his chessboard. "I think the showing from Serenity Lane was nice to see . . ."

"Minus the Donovans, of course."

"That's just as well. Not sure I'd have been able to hold my tongue about that intentional flowerbed trampling the other day." Mr. Nelson leaned back in his chair and lifted his chin to the gentle late afternoon breeze. "The service was nice. Father

Deagen did a fine job, although he needs to secure a different organist."

"I thought the organist was fine."

"That's because I was sitting *between* you and Bridget."

Lovey lowered her body to the floor, flapped her tail from side to side, and then darted past Winnie in an attempt to kill a lone dandelion swaying in the breeze. "What does your placement between Bridget and me have to do with the organist?" she asked.

"His playing encouraged her to sing."

"We were at a funeral, Mr. Nelson. That's what we were supposed to do."

Mr. Nelson crinkled his nose and then dropped his gaze back to the dark brown pieces on the table in front of him. "I will say, I found myself wondering, from time to time, if a reevaluation of Mark Reilly was in order. Especially at the repast."

She sat up tall. "You, too?"

He paused his hand on the rook, mumbled something unintelligible, and then switched to the bishop. "Seems as if Bart meant a good deal to that young man."

Seems . . .

There was that word again. Only this time, it wasn't just taking up space inside her head.

"Do you believe it?" she asked.

Mr. Nelson moved the rook four spots, held it between his fingertips a few beats, and then backed it up one spot. "I know he gave his parents a hard time for a lot of years. He was one who always wanted things handed to him — second chances, money, accolades, you name it. But Mark wouldn't be the first person to look back on his youth and realize he could have been more appreciative."

She processed her friend's words while simultaneously watching Lovey stalk her way around the yard — a leaf, another dandelion, a butterfly . . . "I wish I'd had the courage to ask him outright about the house, but it just didn't seem to be the appropriate time or place, you know?"

"*I* asked him."

She turned in time to watch Mr. Nelson remove his hand from the rook and gesture toward his nonexistent opponent. "You *asked* him?"

"I sure did."

"What did he say?"

"He didn't. Someone came over and tapped him on the shoulder the second I finished the question."

"Okay, but did you see any sort of reaction before he turned away?"

Mr. Nelson caressed his stubbled chin and

contemplated the white side's next move. "You mean other than the way his eyes darted around his head and the color drained from his face?"

"Interesting . . ."

"That's one word for it." Mr. Nelson moved his white knight around his forwardmost pawn and sat back. "The one that came to mind at the time, though, was *guilty*."

"But he seemed so sincere, so genuinely distraught over losing them both so quickly."

"I take it Bart or Ethel never told you what Mark pursued in college?"

She searched her memory bank for an answer to the question but came up empty. "I thought Mark dropped out of college . . ."

"He did. But he went for a few months."

"Okay . . ."

"He wanted to be an actor. And, from what I saw when he was in high school, he was quite good at it. One minute he could be a swashbuckling pirate in *Treasure Island*, and the next he could be down on his luck in *Death of a Salesman*."

"So you think he was faking today?"

"I can't say for sure." Mr. Nelson reached for his cane and used it to steady himself as he stood. "But I've got my eye on that young man, Winnie Girl. If Mark had something to do with Bart's death, I will do everything I can to see that he pays for his crime."

"I know you will, Mr. Nelson. And I'll help."

Mr. Nelson caned his way over to the stairs, winked at Winnie, and then looked out over their shared front yard. "You're a good girl, Winnie Johnson. A real blessing to all of us, you know that?"

"The feeling is mutual, Mr. Nelson." And it was. She'd be lost without her friends. They kept her grounded as to what mattered most in life.

"Now, if we can just get Lovey to realize how lucky she is to have you as her new owner, we'll be all set."

She didn't mean to snort when she laughed, but she couldn't help it. Some things just seemed impossible to imagine. Lovey warming up to her was one of those things.

"I don't know what Gertie was thinking when she left Lovey to me. It's not like I've ever really had a pet before."

"That's not what I heard."

She opened her mouth to protest but closed it as a certain pixie-haired female flitted her way through Winnie's thoughts.

"You've been talking to Renee, haven't you?"

"Don't worry, Winnie, your secret is safe with me."

"It *shook*!" she insisted. "I was *three*! How was I supposed to know?"

Holding tight to his cane with his right hand, Mr. Nelson started to lean down to pat her shoulder but stopped and pointed across the yard instead. "There she goes again, that little rascal."

"Little ras—" Winnie turned in time to see a flash of brown and white hightail it across the street and around the back corner of Bart and Ethel's house — a gap in the late couple's basement window Lovey's likely destination.

Chapter 13

"Good heavens, Parker, you bring new meaning to the word *slow*," Bridget said mid-moan.

Mr. Nelson inserted the key in the top lock and turned it to the right, the answering click exactly the same as it had been the first five times he'd tried. "Hush, woman, this is tricky business!"

"Top lock to the right, bottom lock to the left is tricky business?" Bridget rolled her eyes up to the porch ceiling and released an audible breath of air through her nose. "Do you hear this, Winnie? This is why the youth of America write us off once we hit seventy. Because we lose our common sense."

Winnie stepped forward, reached around Mr. Nelson, and laid her hand atop his. "How about I give it a try?"

For a moment, she thought the man was going to protest, his trembling grip on the key as determined as ever. Eventually, though, he let go and took a step backward, mumbling under his breath. "I tell you, Winnie Girl, if I'd have wanted to be nagged all the time, I'd have gotten married."

At any other time, she probably would have laughed, but this wasn't any other time. In fact, when it came right down to it, what they were doing was probably illegal. That is, if she could actually unlock the door — which she couldn't. "And you're sure it's okay for us to be letting ourselves into Bart's house like this?"

"That's why I have a key," Mr. Nelson said for what had to be the fifth time. "Got it from Bart, myself."

"But Bart's dead now. Shouldn't we be checking with his son, first —"

"Excuse me. Can I help you with something?"

Winnie, Bridget, and Mr. Nelson turned in unison toward the road and the thirty-something bearded man staring back at them across the front seat of a now-familiar silver two-door sedan that had seen better days.

"Oh, Mr. Nelson . . . Ms. O'Keefe . . . Winnie . . . I didn't realize it was you." Lance Reed's face rescinded from view through the open window only to reappear across the roof of the car via his now-open driver's side door. "Sorry about that. I just knew Mr. Wagner had passed and was afraid someone was trying to break in."

Bridget crossed to the railing. "That would imply that Parker had actually managed to open the door."

Winnie could feel the defeat that weighed Mr. Nelson's shoulders down and rushed to make things right. "My new cat went and got herself into Bart's house via a bad screen out back. Last time she did this, she came back out on her own. This time, she's being a bit of a pill."

"And that, right there, is why I've always been a dog owner." Lance raked a hand through his coarse auburn-colored hair and then let it thump back down on the top of his car. "A lot less stress."

"And this, right here, Lance," Mr. Nelson said, pointing the end of his cane at Bridget, "is why I've always been single."

She was grateful for the instinct that had her biting back the laugh Lance didn't. After all, Bridget's glares were legendary around Silver Lake. Still, Winnie didn't want Serenity Lane's latest newcomer to bear the brunt of Bridget's wrath (a wrath that could mean exclusion from the annual summer block party invite list if he wasn't careful), so she, too, stepped over to the rail. "Thank you for paying such close attention, though. Awareness is what will keep another tragedy from happening on this street."

Bingo.

Sure enough, any irritation Bridget harbored on the heels of Lance's ill-advised laugh gave way to an energetic and heartfelt nod from Winnie's left and right.

"Yes. Winnie is right, Mr. Reed. Thank you."

"My pleasure, Ms. O'Keefe." Lance tapped his hands on the roof of his car and then stepped back. "Well, I better get home. I spent way too much time at the car lot this morning, and I've got to start preparing for Monday's class."

"Finally getting a new car, eh, young man?" Mr. Nelson asked.

Despite the expanse of front yard between them, there was no mistaking the smile that accompanied Lance back into his car. Then, shifting the car into drive, he leaned across the seat one last time. "Wait until you see it, Mr. Nelson. It's a real beauty."

They watched as the man drove away, the small white ranch home on the end of the quiet street his final destination.

"Well, that's one less body at the block party this summer," Bridget groused as she returned to the door and the key still poised in the lock.

Slowly, Mr. Nelson turned his back on the now-empty street. "Decided not to come this year, eh, Bridget?"

Bridget's wrist turned to the right.

Click.

Bridget's wrist turned to the left.

Click.

"Ha-ha, you old goat." Pulling the key from the second lock, Bridget pushed the door open with her free hand. "I'll be there, Parker. Will you?"

With a rare burst of speed, Mr. Nelson hobbled past Bridget and into Bart's house. "I will be. Winnie will be. Lance will be. It's a block party, Bridget. You don't get to call the shots."

Bridget stamped her foot against the porch floor. "*I* send out the invites."

"I'll send 'em," Mr. Nelson snapped.

"I bring the tablecloths!"

"We'll go without!"

"I —"

Winnie took hold of Bridget's upper arm and propelled the woman through the door and into Bart's foyer, the closed-up feel of the once-welcoming entry point making it difficult to remember why they were there in the first place. "Please, you two. Now is not the time. We need to concentrate on

157

finding Lovey. The sooner we do that, the sooner we can be on our way."

She braced herself for residual protest from one or both camps, but there was nothing. Instead, Mr. Nelson caned his way toward the living room while Bridget went straight. Moments later, Winnie realized she was the only one actually calling for Lovey.

In fact, with the exception of her own voice and the irritation she was unable to keep out of it, she heard little more than the tapping of Bridget's sensible shoes toward the back of the house, and an occasional grunt from the living room.

She stopped at the base of the stairs that led to the second floor and strained to hear a third set of sounds — a meow, a scratching, a purr . . .

"Lovey?" she called again. "Show yourself, cat!"

A loud gasp from the kitchen pulled her feet in that direction. "Did you find her, Bridget?"

"Winnie, come quick!"

She picked up the pace only to whack her stomach against a kitchen counter. Resisting the instinct to double over in salute of the pain, she bit her bottom lip and powered through. "What's wrong, Bridget? Are you okay?"

158

Bridget held a piece of paper in Winnie's direction and then pulled it back so she could read it aloud. "Mr. Wagner, I realize you have been mourning the death of your wife these last six weeks, but that doesn't give you the right to treat people the way you treated my daughter, Ava, this afternoon. She's eight. She stepped on your flowers. Who the hell do you think you are yelling at her the way you did? She's not your child. You had no right to speak to her the way that you did. It is because of you that she fell and lost her tooth. It is because of you that she will no doubt have nightmares for months to come. And it is because of you that her ability to go to college is now in jeopardy. If you think this behavior of yours will go unchecked, you're wrong."

Releasing her hold on her stomach (and her lip), Winnie walked toward Bridget only to stop as the woman looked up, her face ashen. "*D-Dead* wrong." Then, holding the paper out to Winnie once again, she added, "It-it s-says that, Winnie. It says, *dead wrong.*"

Winnie accepted the paper from the elderly woman, the words in front of her exactly as Bridget had read them.

"She did it, Winnie," Bridget said between labored breaths. "Sissy Donovan actually killed Bart. I didn't want to believe a mother could do that . . . but she did!"

"Whoa. Slow down a minute." She reread the letter a second and third time and then let her gaze drop back down to the table and the pile of unopened mail that had obviously been accumulating for some time. A peek at a few of the postmarks confirmed that Bart had simply stopped opening anything for a good two weeks prior to his death. However, there on the top of the pile was a plain white envelope with no evidence of having been delivered by the post office. "And this letter? It was sitting on top of this envelope?"

Bridget's eyes cast downward.

"Bridget?" she asked again. "This letter was sitting open on top of the envelope, yes?"

After what seemed like an eternity of silence, Winnie's next-door neighbor finally answered by way of a quick head shake.

"Where was the letter, then?"

"In the envelope."

Winnie looked from the tri-folded letter in her hand to the envelope and its broken seal atop the table and waited for Bridget to speak. When the woman finally did, it was in a voice barely above a whisper. "I recognized Sissy's handwriting from those ridiculous little updates she sticks in everyone's mailboxes every time Ava wins another pageant."

"Okay . . ." She saw where this was going and didn't like it. Not one little bit.

"I knew I didn't have one in my mailbox and so I wanted to see what I'd been left out of and why." Bridget propped her elbows on the table and rested her chin on her hands. "But it's a good thing I did. Now we have motive."

"Motive that's been compromised by your hands and mine." She looked again at the letter, the words branding themselves in her head. "Oh, Bridget, you shouldn't have opened this."

"Why not? Now we have proof!"

"Proof of what, exactly?" she challenged.

Bridget's hands dropped to the table with a thump, and Winnie found herself on the receiving end of the kind of exasperated eye rolls usually reserved for Mr. Nelson. "Proof Sissy killed Bart, of course. She threatened him right there in that letter!"

"What's going on in here?"

"I found proof!" Bridget shouted.

"A hoof?" Mr. Nelson said, making his way into the kitchen and over to the table. "What kind of hoof?"

Bridget reached up, stuck her finger in the

man's left ear, and pressed. "Proof! I found proof!"

"Proof of what?" Mr. Nelson asked.

"Proof that Sissy Donovan killed Bart!" Bridget gestured toward Winnie and the letter. "Sissy wrote a letter to Bart the day before he was murdered and threatened him!"

Mr. Nelson tightened his hold on his cane as he shifted his weight more evenly across his lower half. "Is that true, Winnie?"

She nodded. "Looks that way."

Lifting his free hand to his head, Mr. Nelson scratched at a dry patch near his part line and then leaned forward, his nose mere inches from the paper in Winnie's hands. "You . . . will . . . be . . . hearing . . . from . . . my . . . lawyer."

Winnie stared at her friend as he straightened up and released an irritated breath. "That's the problem with people today. Always calling lawyers and muddying the waters. That didn't go on back in the day. No, people settled things in two ways. With fists or by walking away."

Confused, she flipped the letter over.

You will be hearing from my lawyer.
— Sissy Donovan

162

She shook the paper at Bridget and did her best to keep her own irritation in check. "She wasn't threatening Bart *harm* . . . she was threatening *legal action.*"

A hint of red reared itself in Bridget's cheeks just before the woman stood and brushed a hand down the front of her floral blouse. "I suppose we should move on. We are here, after all, to find Lovey, are we not?"

Snatching the letter from Winnie's hands, Bridget folded the page and thrust it back into the envelope. Then, shooting her finger upward, the elderly woman commanded silence as she cocked her ear toward the hallway.

Meow . . .

"Lovey?" Winnie called out.

Meow . . .

Bridget retracted her finger and held her hand up in front of Winnie. "Don't move. If she sees you, she'll take off again."

She started to protest but stopped when Mr. Nelson nodded.

"Great," she muttered. "Just great."

Relegated to kitchen stander, she watched as Mr. Nelson and Bridget crept around the corner of the room and into the hallway, each trying to outdo the other with soothing sounds designed to lure the tabby cat out into the open. While she waited, Winnie looked around, her gaze skirting and then narrowing in on a lone dish and cup in the sink.

It was hard not to feel sorry for Bart — for the emptiness he felt without his beloved Ethel, and for the overwhelming grief that had tainted the man's otherwise blemish-free existence. Grief and loneliness had been the man's constant companions in the days leading up to his death. Neither had needed a plate or a glass, of course, but they'd been there, sitting beside Bart that last morning just as surely as Winnie was standing in his kitchen at that very moment.

She loved her elderly friends. Loved them with all her heart. But she hated the sadness that seeped into their respective worlds as the end drew closer.

"Look who I found?" Bridget reappeared in the kitchen doorway with a wide-eyed brown and white cat in her arms. "Lovey, look, it's your new mama."

Without really thinking, Winnie stepped forward, arms outstretched.

Hiss . . .

She dropped her arms to her side in defeat. "Well, I see some things haven't changed . . ."

"Give her time, dear. She'll come around."

"You sound like Mr. Nelson right now."

164

She stuck out her tongue at Lovey and then headed into the hallway with Bridget in tow. "Mr. Nelson?"

"In here, Winnie."

"It's time to go," she called, stopping to look in each room as she passed — Bart's study, the dining room, and, finally, the living room. Mr. Nelson stood beside a table near the window, deep in thought. "What are you doing?"

"Trying to figure out how to get Bart out of the predicament he got himself into."

"Don't you think you're a little late for that, Parker?" Bridget asked, her voice tinged with boredom. "As in four days too late?"

"Shhh . . . I'm — wait. I got it." Mr. Nelson bent forward across the table, his hand moving forward rapidly. "Checkmate!"

Confused, Winnie peeked around his shoulder only to smile as she saw the chessboard in the center. "Well done, Mr. Nelson."

He puffed out his chest, smiling triumphantly as he did. "Thank you. Thank you."

"Can we please go?" Bridget prodded.

Winnie waved Bridget and Mr. Nelson toward the door and then fell into step behind them as they crossed the room. Four steps from the foyer, the middle body in the

165

parade stopped, necessitating quick braking action from Winnie to avoid a body-to-body collision. "Mr. Nelson? You okay?"

When the man didn't answer, she followed his gaze to the mantel and the series of framed photographs lined up along both the left and right side. In all but one of the pictures, Bart was depicted with either Ethel or Ethel and Mark. In the one to the far left, she recognized a younger Mr. Nelson sitting next to Bart, fishing.

"You miss him, don't you, Mr. Nelson?"

"I do."

"When was that fishing trip?" she asked.

"Fifteen years ago, maybe." Mr. Nelson's Adam's apple bobbed with a swallow. "It was a good trip. We had a lot of laughs that day. But what I miss most about him is the way he told everyone he could about his coin."

This time, she followed the man's finger to the glass case in the center of the mantel — a glass case that sat empty now. "It came to him from his father, right?"

"From President Franklin D. Roosevelt . . . to a member of his Secret Service detail . . . to Bart's father . . . and finally to Bart, yes," Mr. Nelson corrected. "A story that could make Bart smile no matter what."

She slipped an arm around her friend and

rested her head on his shoulder. "Remember him that way, Mr. Nelson. Remember him that way always."

"I will. You can count on that."

CHAPTER 14

Gliding her hand across the logo emblazoned on the side of the ambulance, Winnie couldn't help but marvel at everything she'd accomplished in such a short period of time. Granted, the Emergency Dessert Squad was really just a mobile version of Delectable Delights, but it was different, too.

Her desserts had been tweaked and, in some cases, changed completely.

Her creativity was being tested on a continuous basis.

Sleep, which used to be hers the second her head hit the pillow, was suddenly elusive thanks to the aforementioned creativity that had her reaching for a pen again and again throughout the night.

And suddenly she was very concerned with knowing how many Silver Lake residents actually read the *Herald*'s weekend edition. If readership was good, maybe the phone would actually ring in twenty hours.

If readership was bad —

"Wow. You really go all out, don't you?"

Winnie popped her head over the roof of the ambulance and made a valiant effort to curb the surprise she suspected was written all over her face. "Oh. Greg. Hi . . . What are you doing here?" She cringed at the question and then stepped around the hood of the car. "I mean, I didn't expect to see you. Here. In my driveway."

He ran his hand along the side of the ambulance. "I grew up on the whole don't-show-up-unannounced thing, you know? Even heard my mother's voice in my head the whole way here."

"And here you are, anyway . . ." she said, laughing.

"And here I am, anyway."

Focusing again on the vehicle between them, Greg made his way down the driver's side, around the back end, and up the passenger side, deliberately leaving enough space to take in every detail, every nuance. As he walked, she made a few notes of her own.

No paramedic uniform . . .

A button-down collared shirt (chocolate-colored flannel — a perfect match for his eyes — with the top two buttons undone) looked oh so good on his toned upper body . . .

"I love the logo. It's smart. It's sleek. It's classy." He stopped when he reached the hood, smiled at Winnie, and then retraced his steps toward the back end. "Can you open it up so I can see what you did inside?"

"Sure." She came around the vehicle, unlatched the back panel, and stepped back as Greg swung it open.

"Whoa! Nice!"

"I obviously don't have the room you do in *your* ambulances, but that's okay. I'm really just using it to deliver desserts."

"Nice stretcher," he said, gesturing inside. "The white covering looks good and — whoa . . . you got the collapsible drip pole already?"

"Overnight shipping is a wondrous thing." She reached into the back of the rig, grabbed hold of the pole, and rolled it toward them. When it was at the edge, she pulled it down, set it on the ground, and expanded it to full size. "I also found some heavy-duty clear bags that will be perfect for whatever icing or drizzle I may need on-site. They work well because they can be kept warm en route and then hung on the pole for application when I bring the dessert up to the door. Right now, the desserts that will require the drip pole will be my

Seeing Red Velvet Cake and my Hot Flash Fudge Sundae."

"Hot Flash Fudge Sundae?" he repeated.

"Uh-huh."

"Let me guess . . . For those suffering through menopause?"

She grinned. "Right again."

"And Seeing Red Velvet Cake? What's that for? Anger management?"

"Sort of. I'm envisioning it for those times things just don't go your way. Or your loved one's way, if you're ordering it for someone else."

"You're really good at this," he marveled as he turned his attention to the back of the rig once again. "Is your friend from the bakery going to go out on the calls with you?"

She collapsed the pole back to its compact size and returned it to its original spot inside the rig. "Renee? No. At this point I see her staying back, taking calls from customers and scheduling delivery times. She's also adept at gathering everything I need to make a particular dessert — something that will prove invaluable, no doubt, in a business that will hinge on my ability to respond within a set time frame."

He took one last look inside and then swung the door shut. With a double pat on

171

the latch, he turned, the smile she'd been glimpsing on his face for the past ten minutes or so now fully trained on her. "Excited?"

"About this?" she asked, sweeping her hand toward the ambulance. At his nod, she backed herself against the closest tree for support and looked up at the puffy white clouds dotting the early afternoon sky. "I'm excited, hopeful, anxious, scared, you name it. I just want this to work. To be every bit as successful as Renee and Bridget seem to think it will be."

"And me. Don't forget me."

Slowly, she brought her gaze back down to his, an odd and unfamiliar feeling skittering up her spine. "And you." She tugged the end of her ponytail across her shoulder and fiddled with the ends. "Thanks for that, by the way."

He ventured across the gap she'd created, but stopped short of the standard personal space bubble. "For what? Knowing this business of yours is going to be a smashing success?"

"Something like that."

"I'd be a fool not to." Swooping down to a squat, he picked up a rock and played with it between his hands — turning it over again and again. "So how long have you lived

172

here? In Silver Lake?"

Something about the innocuous question helped lighten an atmosphere that had become suddenly charged. Grateful for the change, she slid down the tree until she, too, was sitting on the grass.

"A little over two years."

"What brought you here?" he asked, looking up from his rock.

"I wanted to give my own bakery a go. And when I was looking around for a place to open one, everything about Silver Lake seemed perfect." She ran her fingers across the recently awakened grass and tried not to think about yet another season of fighting with a lawn mower that had seen its share of better days long before Winnie was even born. "And it was. *Is*."

He dropped the rock and glanced in her direction. "I imagine closing down your first place had to be tough. But honestly, I think what you're poised to do with this Dessert Squad is so much cooler."

"Thanks. It *is* cooler, I'll give you that, but whether that will translate to success remains to be seen." She leaned her head against the tree and lifted her face to the sun.

"And what brought you here? To this house? This street?"

"Luck." At his answering laugh, she lowered her chin and met his eyes once again. "No, really. Mr. Nelson, Bridget, Gertie, Ethel, and Bart made me feel at home the second I moved in. Within a few short weeks, I not only had neighbors, I had friends — *true friends.* A person can't get any luckier than that, in my opinion."

He let himself fall backward out of his squat, plucking a blade of grass from the ground as he did. "That's awfully sweet of you to take all these folks under your wing the way you do."

"I'm not sure I know what you mean . . ."

He pointed the blade of grass over her shoulder at her house and then over his own at Bart's. "The elderly on this street. It's good they have someone looking out for them."

"We look out for one another," she corrected.

There was no mistaking the way his left brow lifted at her response and no ignoring the hint of disbelief in the way his head shook ever so slightly. There was also no mistaking the anger she felt rising up inside her chest.

Bracing the ground with her hands, she stood. "When I came home after my very first day at the bakery, Mr. Nelson met me at the door with a bottle of champagne. Inside his place was Bridget — my next-door neighbor — with a teddy bear dressed in a baker's apron she'd had personalized with the name of my bakery. Ethel and Bart were there, too. And so was Gertie. They were all so happy for me that they took what had been a great day and made it a million times better. That wasn't an isolated incident, either. Those five have cheered me on from the sidelines, offered hugs and encouragement when I needed it, and loved me like family every step of the way. So trust me, Greg, when I say that the people on this street have looked after me every bit as much as I've looked after them."

Depositing the blade of grass back onto the ground, he, too, stood, his hands splayed — waist high — in front of him. "I wasn't trying to offend, Winnie. I was just trying to understand. I'm not used to seeing someone who looks like you spending the majority of her time with old people."

Old people . . .

A familiar creak over her left shoulder let her know Mr. Nelson was on his way outside even before the man ever said a word. "Winnie Girl? Can I let Lovey out? She's been scratching at the door trying to get to you for quite some time now."

175

"Sure thing, Mr. Nelson." Then, swinging her focus back to Greg she said, "There it is again."

"What?"

"Lovey *hates* me, Greg. Despises the very ground on which I walk, quite frankly. But Mr. Nelson just said she's trying to get out here to me."

"I don't understand."

"True friends, regardless of their age, lift you up and make you a better person than you were before. They help make things right."

Lovey beat Mr. Nelson to the tree and then waited by Greg's foot for the elderly man to catch up. Once he did, the animal moved on to the ambulance.

"I was just thinking you need a light, too. A great big honkin' flashlight that you can use to get those desserts of yours up to people's front doors."

It took her a moment to find the man's veer-off point, but she did. "I didn't say *light,* Mr. Nelson. I said *right.*"

Mr. Nelson's shoulders rose in level with his ears as he turned and acknowledged Greg. "I remember you, young fella. Met you yesterday at Bart's repast, didn't I?"

"Yes. I'm Greg Stevens." Greg reached out, took Mr. Nelson's offered hand, and

176

then nodded at Winnie. "Well, I better be heading out, Winnie. Good luck tomorrow. Give me a shout if you need anything."

And then Greg was gone, his long jean-clad legs transporting him up the driveway and over to a dark blue Mustang parked on Bart's side of the street.

"I didn't mean to make him run off, Winnie Girl."

She heard the car start up, heard the wheels start to grip the road as Greg went by, but she kept her focus on the man standing by her side. "You didn't, Mr. Nelson. That was all him."

CHAPTER 15

She was in the middle of a mental debate on the pluses and minuses of smacking Renee's hands with a flyswatter, when the seemingly ceaseless finger drumming finally ceased.

"So?" Renee said, pulling her focus from the clock above the sink and planting it squarely on Winnie. "Are you going to tell me, or are you going to make me drag it out of you?"

"Tell you what?"

"About Master Sergeant Hottie."

Pushing her chair back from the table and the telephone they'd been hovering over for nearly an hour, Winnie stood and wandered over to the open window that provided a fairly uninhibited view of Serenity Lane. To her right, she was able to identify Cornelia Wright and her sheltie, Con-Man, embarking on the first of what had to be a dozen daily walks. To her left, Harold Jenkins was

178

sitting on his motorized scooter trying not to get caught watching Cornelia. "There's nothing to tell."

"That's not what I heard."

She whirled around to find Renee now tapping her finger against her chin. "Excuse me?"

Renee moved her finger around to the wispy pieces of hair that fell against her ear and smiled broadly. "Mr. Nelson told me about yesterday."

"And what did he tell you?"

"That Master Sergeant Hottie was here. To see you."

Moving away from the window, Winnie crossed into the tiny living room and dropped onto the overstuffed armchair that had become another bone of contention between her and Lovey over the past few days. Fortunately for Winnie, Lovey was in the bathroom (drinking from the toilet, no doubt) at the moment rather than napping. "He stopped by to see the ambulance. That's all."

"Mr. Nelson said he was here for close to an hour."

"Apparently Mr. Nelson's vision is far more accurate than his hearing," she droned. Then, in the interest of putting the whole conversation to bed once and for all, she filled in the gaps Renee apparently wanted filled. "I showed him the back of the ambulance, we talked about a few of the items on the menu, and that was it."

"I hear you sat on the grass together."

Groaning, she lolled her head against the back of the chair. "Okay, here's the breakdown. I admit, I was a little — a *little* — jazzed to see him here. But then he messed it up."

Renee left the table to join her in the living room. With a not-so-gentle push, she removed Winnie's feet from the ottoman and sat. "How?"

"He's clearly uncomfortable with my crowd."

"Your crowd?"

She plucked a piece of cat fur off the cushion and stuck it on Renee's pants. "That's right. My crowd. He doesn't get them. Or me."

She waited for Renee to say something, to offer some sort of excuse for Greg or some cheerleader-like encouragement to Winnie about sticking it out, but there was none of that. Instead, Renee merely sighed.

"I just want to focus on the Dessert Squad right now, Renee. If we have a chance at all with this thing, it needs to come first in my life."

"You mean like Delectable Delights always did?"

"Exactly."

"And you think that was a good thing?" Renee pressed.

"I take it you don't?"

"I just don't want to see you end up alone, Winnie. You're far too special for that."

She added a second and third piece of cat hair to the pant leg collection and then gently leaned her forehead against Renee's. "But I'm not alone. I have you . . . I have Mr. Nelson . . . I have Bridget . . . I have this new business —"

Hisssss . . .

Parting company with Renee, Winnie peeked over the armrest of her chair to find Lovey looking not so pleased about the loss of her napping spot. "And, yes, for better or worse, I have Lovey now, too," she added.

Renee invited Lovey onto her lap with a series of quick pats. Lovey, of course, jumped up, turned her back to Winnie, and began to purr. "Is that really enough for you?"

"For now? Yes." And she meant it. Her life was full.

Still, she couldn't help but rejoice inwardly at the staccato ring of the kitchen phone. Whoever was calling had certainly put a much-needed stop to a conversation that had already gone on far too long for Winnie's taste. Rising, she strode into the kitchen with Renee on her heels.

"Do you think it's a customer?" Renee asked, staring down at the phone.

"There's only one way to find out . . ."

With an audible inhale, Renee lifted the receiver with her right hand and reached for the pen-topped order pad with her left. "Emergency Dessert Squad. What's your emergency?"

She hadn't realized she was holding her breath until Renee began writing. Moving closer, Winnie tried to decipher the woman's self-proclaimed chicken scratch, but it was no use. All she could make out was *cookie* and *college.* The rest may as well have been Greek.

"Well, we got it!" Renee declared as she returned the phone to the counter and pumped her fist into the air. "Our first order!"

"Tell me," she said, her voice breathless.

"It's for a sixteen-year-old girl named Caroline. She just passed her driving test, and her dad" — Renee looked down at her notes for confirmation — "Jay Morgan, wants a giant cookie with either white chocolate chips or butterscotch chips deliv-

182

ered to his office at the college. Room 405 in the Cully Business Building. He said it's most easily accessed by the Murphy Street entrance."

"The Murphy Street entrance — got it!" Winnie met Renee's waiting hand with her own and then headed straight for the kitchen and the cabinet of baking ingredients. "Okay, Renee, let's get to work. There's a new driver in need of some special treatment."

Winnie pulled into the closest visitor spot she could find to the Cully Business Building and cut the engine. Two years earlier, when she'd opened the bakery, she'd been nervous, but the realization of a nearly lifelong dream had helped her power through.

Today, the squad of butterflies flapping their wings inside her stomach felt different — like they knew, somehow, that this delivery could very well be a do-or-die moment. And they'd be right. If the Dessert Squad didn't take hold, she'd be forced to hang up her apron and find a new profession.

Removing the key from the ignition, she peeked into the rearview mirror for one last look at her hair (in its trademark ponytail), her eyes (Renee's insistence she wear mascara might actually have been a good idea), and the unexpected reddish tint to her cheeks that was a result, no doubt, of the way her heart was beating double-time inside her chest.

I can do this . . .

I can do this . . .

"I. Can. Do. This." Her mind made up, Winnie pushed open the door, stepped onto the pavement, and made her way around to the back of the ambulance and the giant cookie-topped stretcher visible through the vehicle's narrow rectangular window. Once the cookie and its mode of transportation were safely on the ground, she guided them in the direction of the white-columned brick structure most heavily utilized in Silver Lake College's recruitment brochures. Along the way, she earned a few odd looks, starred in a handful of hastily snapped photographs, and even handed out menus in response to three separate requests.

For her business-owning self, the attention was thrilling. For her quiet, demure self, the attention was downright overwhelming. Somehow, she had to find a way to make the two coexist.

Humming softly to herself, Winnie maneuvered the stretcher around a handful of construction projects and entered the Cully

Business Building on the south side, not far from the bank of elevators tasked with moving students and teachers from floor to floor. The first floor, according to a sign in the elevator, housed a small cafeteria, several large lecture halls, and an atrium. The second floor boasted classrooms, group study rooms, and a business library. The third and fourth floors were dedicated to faculty offices like Jay Morgan's.

She glanced down at the index card in her hand and noted the limited information on her first customer. He was a teacher at the college, with a driving-age daughter, but, beyond that, there wasn't anything of any real consequence.

The elevator lurched to a stop, and she exited onto the fourth floor. A receptionist stationed behind a desk looked up from her book long enough to point to an office at the end of one of four hallways. "Should I let Mr. Morgan know you're coming?"

She started to nod but caught herself just in the nick of time. "Actually, in the event his *daughter* doesn't know I'm coming, would it be okay if I just knocked myself?"

The woman shrugged and returned to her book.

Placing her hands on the side of the stretcher once again, Winnie wheeled the

185

cookie down the hallway indicated by the receptionist and stopped just shy of the one and only open door on the whole wing. A black and gold nameplate affixed to the wall confirmed she'd found the right office.

Anxious to burn the image of her first Emergency Dessert Squad customer into her thoughts, Winnie peeked around the corner and felt her mouth go slack.

Jay Morgan was, in a word, classically handsome. (Okay, maybe that was two words, but who's counting?) In his late thirties — maybe his very early forties — the business professor had light brown hair with a sprinkling of gray near his temples, a strong chin, and a thoughtfulness about his seated demeanor that made her want to know what he was reading . . . what he was thinking . . . what he was —

Suddenly, the eyes that had been engrossed in the pages of a book were now on her, their blue green color, combined with the hint of a sparkle in their depths, bringing a swift end to the pounding in her chest.

Now, if she could only breathe . . .

"You must be with the Emergency Dessert Squad," he said, rising. "Welcome. I'm Jay. Jay Morgan."

"I — I'm Winnie. Winnie Johnson."

He walked around his desk and extended

his hand. "I recognize you from the picture in the weekend paper."

Reluctantly, she pulled her hand from his and ran it nervously down the sides of the simple blue hospital scrubs Renee had worn as a Halloween costume one year. "Um, we're, uh, still working on our uniforms."

"This works." She swallowed hard as his gaze traveled from her head to her feet and then returned along the same path. "Maybe you could add an emblem of some sort in this area" — he pointed at the left side of his chest — "or on the upper arm."

With his eyes back on hers and her feet on comfortable ground, she allowed herself to focus on the moment in a much broader sense. "You know how real paramedic uniforms often say PARAMEDIC across the back in big, bold letters? Well I was thinking about doing the same with the word RESCUER."

He rubbed his chin between his thumb and forefinger and nodded. "That could work." And then, after a beat of silence, "Yeah, I like that. A lot."

She gave in to the smile that tugged at the corners of her mouth, any and all apprehension over her first rescue dissipating in the process. "You're my first call."

"I'm honored."

For a brief second she wondered if the slight husk she heard in his voice had truly happened or was a figment of her imagination, but she let the question go. This was her first call. The one that could serve as a springboard to others if she didn't mess it up . . .

Focus, Winnie. Focus.

"I understand you have a new driver in the family," she finally said.

"I do. Her name is Caroline."

A quick inventory of Jay's office netted no places in which a sixteen-year-old could be holed up. "You know, I'd be happy to deliver to wherever Caroline is. That way she could enjoy the whole effect."

"Now this is probably going to sound awful, but my daughter passed her driving test four months ago."

"Oh." She resisted her shoulders' natural impulse to sag at the disappointment and, instead, shrugged. "It's still a sweet gesture."

"And I'm sure she'll enjoy the cookie when I give it to her. But I really called and placed the order for me."

"F-for y-you?" she stammered.

"That's right. I wasn't blue, so the pie was out — although, truth be told, I love blueberry pie. I'm not angry about anything at the moment, so the red velvet cake wouldn't have worked. I'm not having any hot flashes, so that nixed any notion of a sundae. And, well, the cookie seemed the best fit."

"I still don't understand."

He navigated his head around her and into the hall where the stretcher and the cookie waited. "I'm a business professor, Winnie. I spend my days talking to students about business — what works, what doesn't. But mostly it's the same old stuff all the time. But this" — he gestured from her to the hall and back again — "and you . . . It's incredibly creative. I guess I just wanted to see it up close and personal. Your delivery, your presentation, your . . . all of it."

There was no denying the way his eyes lit from within as he looked at her, waiting. There was no denying the enthusiasm that made it so the man could barely stand still. And there was no denying the way her hands began to shake in response. "Oh. Wow. All of a sudden I'm really nervous."

"Don't be. Please." He spun around and headed back toward his desk and the chair he'd inhabited less than five minutes earlier. Once he was settled, he reached for the reading glasses he hadn't been using when she arrived. "Now pretend you just arrived."

"Pretend I just arrived?" she echoed, confused. "But I —"

"Practice on me. Let me see what you're thinking —" He stopped, smacked a hand to his forehead, and groaned. "And there I go again — doing exactly what Caroline is always calling me on the carpet for doing." He stood, once again, but remained behind his desk, clearly embarrassed. "Look, I'm sorry. I have no right acting like this. You're not a student looking for my opinion on everything."

She liked this man.

She liked his earnestness.

She liked his genuineness.

And, as a result, she didn't like seeing him be so hard on himself. "What's that?" she asked, pointing at a freshly polished plaque in the center of the professor's desk.

For a moment she didn't think he was going to answer, but eventually he followed the path forged by her finger. "That's an award I just got from the president — the president of Silver Lake College, that is."

She opened her mouth to ask for details but, instead, walked closer and read them for herself.

PROFESSOR JAY MORGAN, TOP TEACHER AT
SILVER LAKE COLLEGE

"That's quite an endorsement."

190

"It is," he said, nodding. "Especially when it's voted on by the students." He swiped a hand down his face and then leaned forward, the plaque and its honor all but forgotten. "Winnie. I'm really sorry. I —"

She silenced the rest of his apology with her finger and then returned to the hallway for the stretcher. Squaring her shoulders, she put her hands on the side of the thin mattress and pushed it into the office. "I understand there's a smart cookie in here?"

Jay blinked once, twice, and then slowly lowered himself back down to his desk chair.

Slipping her hand underneath the stretcher, she pulled out the collapsible IV pole and extended it to its full height. Then, reaching back under the stretcher one more time, she pulled out her emergency bag, reached into its still warm interior for the bag of white chocolate icing, and hung it on the pole.

Jay laughed.

Next, she attached a long tube pre-fitted with a decorating tip at the end and drizzled the warm chocolate across the cookie still strapped to the stretcher. When she was done, she unhooked the strap and transferred the dessert to Jay's desk.

"Wow. That was awesome." He looked from the IV tube, to Winnie, and then down at his cookie. "*This* is awesome." He pointed at the pole. "That icing thing in the IV bag — that's genius."

She stepped back behind the stretcher and took a moment to breathe it all in — her first Dessert Squad delivery, her first satisfied customer, her first mental pat on the back in far too long . . .

"So, Professor . . ." she teased with a rare burst of flirtatious confidence, "how did I do?"

He started to laugh off the moment but stopped himself (and her heart, for several beats) with a mischievous smile, instead. "In terms of concept, you get an A-plus. For execution, also an A-plus. For product, well, I'm not sure yet."

She felt her answering smile begin to falter but forced herself to hold it steady. "Oh?"

He broke off a large chunk of the drizzled cookie and took a bite, his blue green eyes disappearing from view behind his unusually long, thick lashes. "Mmmm. Wow. Yeah. Okay. Product gets an A-plus, too."

She bounced up on the balls of her feet and hijacked one of Renee's jigs. "You have no idea how much I needed to hear that. *Thank* you."

Jay took a second bite, groaned, and then shook his head. "Actually, I take that last grade back."

This time, she couldn't stave off the slump. "You do?"

"A-plus doesn't even come close to doing it justice." He looked down at the cookie and then back up at Winnie. "What's *in* this thing?"

"White chocolate chips. Just like you told Renee — I mean, *my dispatcher.*"

He grinned. "Nice."

"Your daughter does like white chocolate chips, yes?"

He shifted in his seat.

"Jay?"

"Well, technically *I* like white chocolate chips."

It felt good to laugh. Great, even. "Even if I hadn't switched the recipient to you just now, your daughter was never going to see this cookie, was she?"

"Tasting *this* good? No. No way. I mean, I love my kid, but . . ." He left his sentence hanging in lieu of their combined laughter. "Seriously, Winnie, this is incredible."

"Thank you. That really means a lot to me." She didn't know why, exactly, but even though the cookie had been delivered and it was time to go, she found herself wanting to stay. There. With Jay.

But she couldn't.

Plucking the icing bag from the pole, she returned it and the tube to the bag, collapsed the pole down to travel size, and placed both under the stretcher. "Well, congratulations again . . . to your daughter, the now-avid driver . . . and to you, for being the kind of teacher clearly appreciated by his students."

Jay stopped eating and pushed back his chair, his smile gone. "Oh. Yeah. I guess you probably have to go, don't you?"

"I should."

Standing, he popped one more bite of cookie into his mouth. "Can I walk you out?"

"You just want to see the ambulance, don't you?" she teased. Then, hooking her thumb in the direction of the hallway, she smiled. "C'mon. I'm not too far from the front door."

"Can I push the stretcher for you?"

"It's my job, sir."

Where on earth did that come from?

Before she could think of a clever way to erase her bizarre teasing, he laughed, instantly easing all unnecessary worry from her thoughts.

Slowly, with her hands on the stretcher, they made their way down the hall, into and out of the elevator, and finally out to the parking lot. Along the way, they talked about desserts, the weather, his favorite building on campus, and finally the ambulance now parked beside them (and the dozen or so students who'd gathered to gawk in her absence).

"It's just a matter of time, Winnie, it really is. Even people who don't necessarily want a dessert are going to be calling just to have you show up in this thing."

"From your mouth to God's ears." She lowered the stretcher, opened the back door, and placed it inside. "I really want this to last."

"It will." He reached around her, plucked a few menus from a holder just inside the back door, and handed them out to the students. "There's a dessert for just about every ailment known to mankind. Broken hearts, bothersome roommates, bad test grades, flat tires, you name it . . ."

"I don't have a dessert for a flat tire," she whispered as he returned to her side. "Or for bothersome roommates."

"Add them," he whispered back. "And add them, stat."

CHAPTER 16

She'd just exited the campus onto Murphy Street when her cell phone rang. Hitting the speaker button, Winnie let out a celebratory shriek.

"I take it our first call was a success?"

"Renee, it couldn't have gone any better." She didn't need the rearview mirror to confirm the near-face-splitting smile she wore as she turned left on Nathan Drive. She felt its presence just as surely as she felt the steering wheel against her hands. "In fact, if this first run had been a school project for Jay's class, we'd have gotten A-pluses across the board."

"Who's Jay?"

Just the mere mention of the man's name ratcheted up her body heat so quickly she couldn't help but wish Gertie's ambulance had come equipped with air-conditioning. "Sorry. I meant Professor Morgan."

"As in our customer?"

She was vaguely aware of Renee's voice in her ear, but all she could really focus on at that moment was the image of the handsome business professor as he'd looked behind his desk . . . smiling up at her . . . eating his cookie . . . walking beside her to the ambulance —

"The customer who placed an order for his teenage daughter?"

His teenage daughter . . .

Crap.

Shaking the euphoric highlight reel from her thoughts, she forced herself to concentrate on the stretch of Main Street that had her slowing for pedestrians and stoplights every few feet. As for when she turned onto Main Street, exactly, it must have happened while Jay was smiling. Or maybe eating . . .

He was awfully cute eating that cookie . . .

"Winnie?"

Focus, Winnie. Focus.

"Oh. Sorry. Someone just . . . uh . . . cut me off and I got distracted." Tightening her hands on the steering wheel, she released her breath along with a well-earned sigh. "Sooo, we did it!"

"Yes, and we're poised to do it again."

"Seriously?"

"Seriously. But as of right now we don't have anything on the menu that fits the

197

request."

"You didn't turn the caller away, did you?"

"No. I told her I'd get back to her in ten minutes. We've got . . ." Silence blanketed the car for a few seconds before Renee's voice returned. "Two minutes left."

"Okay, so what's the request?"

"You mean the *emergency*?" Renee's laugh tickled Winnie's ear and had her smiling all over again. "See how I did that?"

"Very cute."

She heard what sounded like a shuffling of papers and then, "This woman is down in the dumps because her diet isn't working."

"Her *diet*?" Winnie repeated.

"Yup."

"She does realize we deliver desserts, yes?"

"Roger that."

Roger that?

"That's dispatcher talk, by the way . . ."

"Yes, Renee, I got that." She turned east on Fiddler Road, the lack of streetlights and pedestrian crossings making it much easier to drive the speed limit. Surprisingly, the ambulance moved well. "So I'm trying to get how a dessert is a good thing for someone on a diet."

"We can't save everyone," Renee quipped.

"Wait!" She slowed as the approach to

198

Roger's Drive came into view. "I got it. How about Can't Lose a Pound Cake? And I'll make it a low-calorie version for rescue purposes."

When she heard no response, she peeked at the phone to make sure they were still connected. "Renee? You still there?"

"How do you do this?"

"Do what?"

"Come up with this stuff?"

She shrugged then made the final turn onto Serenity Lane. "I don't know. I just do."

"Can you *find* a low-calorie pound cake recipe?"

"I tweak everything I find anyway, so why not?" She slowed to a stop in front of her house and slid the gear shift into park. "Well, I'm here now. Call this woman back and tell her we're on. I can deliver it later this afternoon."

"Roger that."

When she was sure the line had been disconnected, Winnie shut off the speaker function on her phone, retrieved her purse from the floor, and stepped out of the ambulance. An hour earlier, she'd felt equal parts excitement and apprehension as she loaded Jay's cookie and her rescue bag into the ambulance. Now, thanks to the success of her first delivery, excitement ruled.

His teenage daughter . . .

Maybe there really was something to Renee's attempts (unsolicited, by the way) at analyzing Winnie's lack of interest in dating. Maybe she really was afraid. Maybe the reason she found Jay Morgan so appealing was the fact that he was unavailable and, therefore, safe.

Shaking off the frustration threatening to cloud her day, Winnie stole a peek at Mr. Nelson's living room window and then at their shared front door. But short of the front porch light she'd failed to shut off that morning, there was no sign of life on the first floor.

Unless . . .

Smiling, she let herself in to their shared vestibule and waited by his door, the mug of hours-old coffee she could almost imagine him carrying toward her at that moment as clear as if it were already in her right hand. But the door remained closed, and her hand remained empty.

She shook off the feeling of unease slowly creeping up her spine and headed toward the stairs. Mr. Nelson was probably just out, playing bingo or scoping out women from his favorite bench outside the Silver Lake Community Center.

Her worries somewhat placated, she let herself into her apartment to find Renee poring over a pile of opened cookbooks.

"Find anything?" she asked, dropping her purse beside the door. "Remember, we're looking for low-calorie versions."

"I'm looking."

Winnie stopped at the sink, turned on the water, pumped two drops of soap into her hands, and then washed them thoroughly before joining her friend at the table. On instinct, she grabbed one of her favorite books and flipped to the index. Sure enough, she found three different pound cake recipes listed and turned to the first.

"Oh, I saw that one already," Renee said. "But it isn't low calorie."

She turned to the second recipe, read the listed ingredients, and then tapped the page with her finger. "This is it."

"Winnie, that's definitely not low calorie."

"It's not low sugar, either. But it will be both by the time I'm done." She looked at the picture in the book and mentally swapped it with the one taking shape in her thoughts. "Oh, and it will have fresh berries on top. With just a hint of whipped cream. That way our customer gets her treat without hurting her dieting efforts all that much."

"You make my head hurt, you know that?" Renee said, closing the book in front of her.

"Why's that?"

"You're too smart. It's intimidating. And annoying."

She laughed. "Only when it comes to baking. I'm a total dunce when it comes to everything else."

"A *dunce*? Seriously?" Renee scrunched her face and then followed Winnie over to the cabinet. "You really need to hang out with people your own age once in a while. You know, learn some more modern expressions."

"I like Mr. Nelson's expressions better." Winnie pointed Renee toward the flour and sugar containers and then turned her attention toward gathering up the rest of the necessary ingredients — vanilla extract, baking soda, eggs, butter, salt, yogurt, lemon juice . . .

"What's the grater for?" Renee asked, as she deposited the containers on the counter and pulled the electric mixer from its drawer.

"The lemon rind."

Once Winnie had everything she needed assembled around her, she got to work creaming and mixing. "Renee? Have you seen any sign of Mr. Nelson this morning?"

202

"I sure did."

"Okay, good. I was kind of surprised he wasn't home, especially since the twelve o'clock news has only been over for about twenty minutes." She set aside her mixing bowl long enough to spray the tube pan Renee placed on the counter. "I guess the weekday weather girl must be on vacation this week . . ."

"He's home, Winnie."

She stopped spraying and looked at her friend. "He's home?" At Renee's nod, she put down the can. "Then where was my hug . . . and my mug?"

Renee's left eyebrow shot upward. "Huh?"

"Never mind."

"He probably didn't come out because he's not exactly a happy camper at the moment."

"Mr. Nelson?"

Renee pouted her lower lip in time with her nod.

"But *why?*" Winnie asked. "What happened? Was Bridget sniping at him again?"

"No. She was in here with me." Renee paused her hand on the oven's control panel. "What's the temperature?"

"Three-seventy-five." She moved on to the second bowl and the sifter. Slowly, she sifted the flour, baking soda, and salt into the clean bowl and then added all to the first mixture, alternating between the dry ingredients and the yogurt. "Did Bridget need something?"

"Nope. Just wanted to stop by and see Lovey. That cat really loves her."

"I'm aware." Winnie craned her head around Renee and studied the white and brown cat fastidiously preening herself atop the windowsill. "Anything else?"

"She sang your praises for a while."

"That's nice." Winnie added the lemon juice to the bowl, gave it one final mix, and poured the batter into the prepared pan. "Is that all?"

"We plotted a little."

"Plotted?"

Renee leaned across the oven and hit the timer button. "How long?"

"Let's go with thirty-five minutes and then I'll check." She looked at the strawberries and waffled between simply slicing them and making a berry glaze. After careful deliberation, she chose to go with the simple fruit topping as a nod to the customer's dieting issue. She could always switch to the glaze in the future.

Satisfied with her decision, Winnie wiped her hands on the dishcloth and sank onto a kitchen chair. "So what were you two plotting? Or don't I want to know?"

"You don't want to know. But I'll tell you anyway."

Winnie waved the dishcloth in the air. "Actually, let's talk about something else. Like the weather . . . Or your favorite color . . ."

"We were trying to figure out how to get you to give Master Sergeant Hottie a real chance."

She tossed the dishcloth onto the table, grabbed the closest pen, and pointed it at Renee. "Look, you two need to give it a rest. *Greg* is a nice enough guy, yes. And he was helpful when I was trying to figure out how to play out the Dessert Squad theme. But he's really not my type."

Renee snorted as she, too, took a seat. "No one is ever your type, Winnie. That's the problem."

Au contraire, dear friend. Jay Morgan is exactly my type . . .

Dropping the pen onto the table, she cleared her throat and forced Renee and herself into different waters. Safer waters.

"We need to broaden the menu. Cover more problems."

"Such as?" Renee asked, picking up the pen and reaching for their idea pad.

"I don't know, maybe for a college kid

dealing with roommate issues . . ."

"Roommate issues?"

She nodded. "Or a flat tire."

Renee considered that and then wagged the pen at Winnie. "How about a bad date or being flat broke?"

"You mean like Another Bad Date and Nut Bars?" She stared up at the ceiling and then lowered her gaze back to Renee. "And . . . and . . . I got it — All Out of Dough-Nuts!"

Renee repeated the names, laughing as she did. "You do realize you have savant-like tendencies, don't you?"

"Add them." She watched the woman add the desserts to the running list and then refocused their attention on the previous conversation (no, not the one about her nonexistent love life). "So about Bridget being here and Mr. Nelson —"

"She heard a car door shut outside and had to know what was going on."

"And?" she prompted.

"It was the Wagners' son with a prospective buyer."

Suddenly, the notion of an always happy Mr. Nelson being . . . well, *not* happy, made all the sense in the world. Sure, on some level he knew Bart was never coming back. But even so, his friend's body had barely been in the ground for forty-eight hours . . .

"I'll talk to him tonight," she said, standing. "This has to be hard for him. Bridget, too."

She felt Renee's eyes following her as she approached the windowsill and Lovey. "I got the impression Bridget was okay with the person."

Reversing her steps before Lovey even had the chance to hiss, Winnie stared at her friend. "Bridget was okay with *what* person?"

"The guy looking at the house."

"She knew him?"

Renee looked down at the idea pad and then back up at Winnie. "She said you all did."

"Who was it?"

"Some guy from the ambulance district," Renee said, shrugging.

"Greg?"

"Who?"

She rolled her eyes. "Master Sergeant Hottie . . ."

"Wouldn't *that* be convenient?" Renee laughed, pushed the idea pad back into the center of the table, and then crossed to the refrigerator and the sandwich she'd stuck inside earlier that morning. "No. This guy was a redhead — average height, kinda lanky."

"You mean Chuck Rogers?"

Tucking the sandwich under her arm, Renee grabbed a can of soda and returned to the table. "Chuck. Chuck . . . You know, I think that's it." Then, grinning at Winnie across the top of her soda can, Renee added, "He's not Master Sergeant Hottie, but he didn't look too shabby from up here."

This time when she rolled her eyes, she kept them fixed on the ceiling out of disgust and amusement. "Renee, please . . ."

"What? What did I say?"

CHAPTER 17

She backed down the long, winding driveway on the western side of Silver Lake and then stopped, her demeanor bouncing between accomplished and aggravated like a perfectly played game of Ping-Pong.

Narrowing her eyes on the passenger seat, Winnie decided on aggravation only to stifle it back down as her phone began to ring.

"Yes, Renee, what is it?"

"I take it Miss Conklin didn't like the dessert?" Renee asked. "Was it the low-calorie part? Or the name?"

"Neither. She loved it." And she had. In fact, Diane Conklin was so tickled by the delivery of her Can't Lose a Pound Cake, she placed an order for the same thing for a fellow dieter. Winnie passed that part on to Renee, her glare steady.

"Al-right-y then . . . So what's with the 'tude? Two calls on our first day is pretty darn good in my —"

Hissss . . .

"Uh, Winnie? What was that?"

"What was what?" She leaned closer and ratcheted up her glare a few notches.

Hissss . . .

"That!"

Winnie gave up, thumped her head against the seat back, and released her pent-up frustration via a semi-controlled groan.

"What's going on over there? Do I need to call the cops?"

"Does the Silver Lake PD have an animal control officer?" She lifted her gaze to the ceiling of the ambulance as her thoughts drifted to her kitchen pantry and its various contents. "You still at my place?"

"Yes, but I was getting ready to head out if that's okay. Ty's after-school baseball practice should be wrapping up, and I thought maybe I could watch for a few minutes before it's time to actually drive him home."

She knew she should probably be paying attention to whatever her friend had just said, but she couldn't. Her mind was busy inventorying the pantry's second shelf. "Do I have salt?"

"Let me check." She heard Renee set down the phone and head across the linoleum floor in her stilettos. Seconds later,

210

the woman was back. "Yes. Why? Are you planning on knocking off a few more gold-fish?"

She considered a variety of responses worthy of such a barb, but opted to stay mum. Instead, she turned her gaze back to the passenger seat. "I was thinking more along the lines of a very specific cat."

Renee's laughter started out strong, but disappeared against a backdrop that included Winnie moaning.

"Renee?"

"No, I'm here. I just can't seem to find Lovey. I thought she was in the window, sleeping."

It was her turn to laugh, only *her* laugh was laced with a healthy dose of sarcasm. "Nope. She's not in the window . . ."

This time she got the sense Renee was hanging on to the phone as she moved around Winnie's apartment. "She's not in your living room chair, either."

"Nope. She's not in my chair . . ."

"Let me check your bedroom."

"Okay." She checked the rearview mirror to make sure no one was trying to turn into the Conklins' driveway and then rested her head against the seat back once again.

"She's not in the bedroom, either, Winnie."

"Nope. Not in my bedroom . . ." Then, turning her head toward the passenger seat, she held out the phone. "Say hi to Renee, Lovey."

Meow . . .

Renee's initial inhale was so loud, so hard, Winnie half expected to get sucked through the phone. "Nooo!"

"Oh yes."

"But — but how?"

It was the same question she'd asked Lovey again and again from the Conklins' front door all the way back to the ambulance. Unfortunately, in light of the fact Gertie failed to leave a decoder for Lovey's various hisses, she had no answer beyond the obvious. "She stowed herself away in the back of the rig somehow. A major health code violation if I ever saw one . . ."

"Where is she now?"

"Sitting right here next to me. At least now, if we happen to pass a health inspector on the way back to the house, the partition Gertie's husband installed between the cab and the rig will keep us from losing our job."

Silence ensued during which Winnie could almost see Renee sucking on her lower lip in thought. "The customer didn't see her, did she?"

Stretching her front paws over the side of

the seat, Lovey circled once, twice, three times and then flopped onto her side, blinking up at Winnie. Without thinking, Winnie leaned over just enough to scratch the cat's left ear. Lovey, equally confused by the moment, purred for a brief second before putting two and two together and coming up with Winnie.

Hissss . . .

Sighing, she placed her hand back on the steering wheel and glanced down the driveway at the modest ranch-style home. "No, she saw her. In fact, Lovey turned on the charm and wound herself around Miss Conklin's legs. And, wouldn't you know, the woman's cat passed about six months ago and that's when she fell off her diet. Seeing Lovey, she said, has convinced her to get back on her plan, get herself in shape, and rescue another cat from the shelter."

"Sounds like a successful run to me," Renee said around a yawn. "Maybe you should add Lovey to the payroll."

"Fat chance of that." She made a mental note of the time via the dashboard clock and then peeked into the rearview mirror to gage the traffic flow on the street. "I better head back. Enjoy whatever is left of Ty's practice, and I'll see you first thing in the morning, okay? We need to get the new dessert names up onto the website and —"

"Done."

"Seriously?"

"Just call me Dispatcher Extraordinaire."

"Come up with some sort of customer-themed rain dance that will flood the phone line with business tomorrow and we'll talk."

"We're already off to a good start," Renee said.

"We are?"

"Uh-huh. Some kid at Silver Lake College saw you and the ambulance on the way to one of her classes today. She said her roommate is going out with a real loser and needs a little shove to make the break. So, she wants something delivered to their dorm room tomorrow at noon."

It was really happening. Her idea was starting to take off . . .

"I even came up with the perfect dessert!"

Winnie smiled and pulled the phone a bit more tightly against her face. "Oh? What's that?"

"Dump (Him) Cake. For print purposes, we'll put a parenthesis around the 'Him' part, which can, of course, be substituted with 'Her' depending on the recipient's gender —"

"Renee?"

"The dump cake base makes it so people

can choose the one that appeals to them most — cherry, pineapple, peach, chocolate, whatever."

"Renee . . ."

"Your dump cakes were always such a big hit at the bakery, and I figured —"

"Renee," she shouted, successfully (and finally) quieting the ongoing sales job playing out in her ear. "You don't have to keep selling it. I love it! It's . . . perfect!"

"You do?"

"I do. Now get going. Put a forward on the phone directly to my cell for now, and I'll see you first thing in the morning." She dropped her phone into her purse and shifted the car back into reverse. Once she was on the cross street, she headed toward home, her eyes on the road but her thoughts churning over various ways to make the Emergency Dessert Squad's dump cake better than any she'd ever made at Delectable Delights.

Maybe some sort of butterscotch . . .

Or toffee bits and caramel . . .

Street by street she made her way through downtown Silver Lake and out the other side, the excitement of the day starting to eat away at her energy level. For months leading up to the demise of Delectable Delights, she hadn't slept, her mind sifting

215

through various pie-in-the-sky options that simply couldn't or didn't pan out when it mattered most. Then, once she faced the inevitable and its closing became a matter of when, rather than if, she'd lain awake at night trying to imagine a different path for her life, a different career. Word of Gertie's will had given her hope that had faded as quickly as it appeared. Toss in finding a dead body and opening a new business in warp speed time, and, well, nothing sounded better at that moment than sitting in front of her television in the comfiest pair of pajamas she owned.

Yet as she pulled into the driveway at 15 Serenity Lane, she knew the pajamas would have to wait. Mr. Nelson was struggling with Bart's death. He needed her to be a friend, to listen and talk him through the sadness just as he'd done for her when Ethel died. Losing a friend was always hard. Just because that friend was old and had lived a lot of years didn't make the pain go away. If anything, it made it harder. More time to get attached and all that . . .

She hiked the shoulder strap of her purse up her arm, tucked the keys inside the bag's large center compartment, and threw open the driver's side door, glancing at the passenger seat even as she swiveled her feet out and onto the pavement. "C'mon, Lovey. We're home. Time to go inside."

Lovey lifted her head, blinked sleepily back at Winnie, and then followed her out of the car. Running ahead to the door, the cat waited while Winnie retrieved the warming bag from the back of the ambulance and then closed and locked everything for the night.

Once inside the vestibule, Lovey remained in Winnie's vicinity as she knocked on Mr. Nelson's door. When there was no answer, she knocked again. "Mr. Nelson? It's me — Winnie."

Again, there was no answer, no footsteps, no television sounds seeping out from the gap beneath the door. She felt a knot of tension forming at the base of her neck and dug around in her bag for her phone.

Less than a minute later, she was back on the line with a breathless Renee. "Hey, Winnie. What'd I forget?"

"Nothing." She felt Lovey's curious eyes studying her and met them with an anxious shrug. "I was just wondering if you saw Mr. Nelson at all during my last run? He didn't come outside earlier, and now he's not answering my knock. I'm starting to get a little worried."

"He's fine, Winnie." Renee's voice muffled

for a moment as if she was talking to someone in the background, but returned to full power in a matter of seconds. "Well, maybe not completely *fine,* but he's not hurt or anything if that's what you're worried about."

"And you know this how?"

"I ran into Bridget in the front hall as I was leaving a little while ago."

"Okay . . ."

"She told me she was having Mr. Nelson over for dinner tonight and that she was making her famous pot roast just to help cheer him up."

"And he went?"

"I'm not sure he had a choice," Renee said between laughs. "You know how Bridget can be when she makes up her mind about something."

"Yes — she gets just like you." It was true. In fact, if it wasn't for the fact that Renee was tall (even without her stilettos), thirty-five, and voluptuous (as Mr. Nelson liked to mention to anyone who would listen), to Bridget's short, eighty, and boxy, Winnie might actually think they were twins. They were drawn to the same things (Master Sergeant Hottie, anyone?), pontificated on like-minded themes (Winnie needs a man!), and had similar steamroller tendencies when it came to something they wanted.

"I don't make pot roast," Renee argued.

"You obviously haven't tasted Bridget's."

"Bad?"

"That's one word for it." She felt her throat constricting at the memory and forced her thoughts in a different direction. "Well, at least he's with someone — someone who gets what he's feeling about Bart at the moment. That's good."

"I'll see you tomorrow, Winnie."

"See you tomorrow, Renee." She broke the connection and gestured toward the stairs. "Okay, Lovey, let's go. It's an everyone-fend-for-themselves kind of night."

Once inside the apartment, Lovey led her straight to the empty food bowl next to the shoe closet and then looked up, wide-eyed.

"What? You can't feed yourself?" Reaching into the closet, Winnie plucked the two-pound bag of cat food from the top shelf and poured some into the bowl. She was just placing the bag back on the shelf when her cell phone rang.

For a split second she considered letting the unfamiliar number go to voice mail, but then she remembered her instructions to a departing Renee about forwarding customer calls and held the phone to her ear.

"Emergency Dessert Squad, please state your emergency . . ."

"Uhhhh, I need some . . . companionship?" said a decidedly male voice. "And . . . some coffee?"

"I'm sorry. I think you have the wrong number."

"This is Winnie, right?"

She swallowed and looked to Lovey for support. Lovey, of course, continued eating. "It is . . . Who is this?"

She heard the faintest hint of a sigh before the voice (which was actually kind of sexy) returned. "It's Jay. Jay Morgan. From the college. You delivered a cookie to my office this —"

Her free hand flew to her hair, her face, her scrubs only to drop back down as she remembered he wasn't there. "Jay. Hi. Please tell me there wasn't something wrong with the cookie . . ."

"You mean other than the fact that it's all gone?" She imagined the smile that went with his voice and the twinkle it had surely ignited in his gorgeous blue green eyes. "Hey. I was wondering if you might want to go out for coffee with me sometime."

"C-c-coffee?" she stammered. *"Coffee?"*

"We could do a soda if you'd prefer . . ."

She knew she should say something,

anything besides repeating coffee over and over again, but she couldn't exactly focus.

"C-coffee works," she finally managed to eke out. "W-when?"

"We could do tomorrow. We could do the day after. We could even do tonight if that works for you."

"T-tonight?"

"Caroline has a dance class from seven to nine at the studio right next to that new coffee place that just opened up in town."

Caroline?

Ah yes, his teenage daughter . . .

She opened her mouth to decline, yet when her brain finally engaged with her mouth, a very different word came out.

CHAPTER 18

She spotted him the second she walked into Beans. And, judging by the smile and wave he flashed in her direction, he'd seen her, too. (That or he knew the statuesque blond just over her left shoulder.)

Wiping her palms along the sides of her jeans, Winnie crossed to the two-person table in the back corner of the café and slid into the seat across from Jay. "Hey."

"Hey, yourself." His eyes crackled to life as he dropped his elbows onto the table and leaned forward. "It's good to see you again."

She knew she should say something, but like the college version of herself when suddenly in the vicinity of someone she was actually attracted to, she froze. If he noticed, though, he didn't let on, and she was grateful. Instead, he directed her gaze to the counter and the chalkboard menu that hung on the wall behind it. "What can I get you?"

Her gaze slid down the day's liquid offerings and then over to the second chalkboard panel and its list of accompanying treats. "I'm kind of feeling the white chocolate hot chocolate, myself."

"I was eyeing the same thing." He tapped the table with his hand and then rose to his feet, his smile as wide as ever. "Don't go anywhere. I'll be right back."

Two seconds later, he was back. "Can I get you something to eat, too? Or is that like asking a race car driver if they want to drive an off-the-lot economy car?"

Something about the way he asked the question, combined with the earnestness on his face, made it so she didn't have to wipe her palms on her thighs any longer. In fact, oddly enough, she felt . . . comfortable. Happy, even.

"A piece of cinnamon crumb cake might be nice."

"Cinnamon crumb cake it is." She gave in to the need for a really big exhale and then followed Jay back to the counter with her eyes. For a moment or two, she simply studied him — his quiet confidence, his sunny disposition, his genuineness — and then moved on to their surroundings.

Unlike its longtime predecessor, Silver Lake Coffee Shop, Beans certainly had the hip feeling her former landlord, Nick Batkas, was convinced the two-square-block downtown needed. It was present in everything from the expansive (and colorful) chalkboard menu to the high-top tables with the barlike stools. The walls were decorated with photographs of foreign cities and various travel memorabilia. Behind a glass partition bumped out from the back wall, customers could watch coffee beans being roasted. Overhead, music with a steady, almost headache-inducing beat wafted through the dull roar of background conversation.

She'd just set her sights on the customers themselves when Jay returned to the table with a to-go cup in each hand and two plates balanced on his forearms. Plucking the desserts from his arm, she placed them in front of their seats and took her hot chocolate from the man's waiting hand. "Thank you."

"You're most welcome." He reclaimed his seat across from her and lifted his to-go cup into the space between them. "Shall we toast? To a successful first day with the Emergency Dessert Squad?"

Equal parts surprised and flattered, she nodded and lifted her cup. "To a successful first day. Stowaway and all."

His eyebrow cocked upward. "Stowaway?"

At her nod, he leaned in for details, his smile morphing into laughter as she shared details of Lovey and Lovey's first ride with the Dessert Squad. When she was done, he pointed at her still-untouched cake with his fork. "Any chance I could try a bite of that? My lemon square is rather lacking."

"Of course." She nudged the plate forward a few inches. "I think I forgot it was in front of me."

He popped the forkful of cake into his mouth and followed it up with a noncommittal shrug of his shoulders.

"Not good?" she asked.

"It's like the lemon square — nothing special." He guided his plate next to hers. "You try. Tell me if I'm nuts."

Intrigued, she forked a piece for herself, inspected it closely, and then slipped it into her mouth, the suspected issue confirmed inside the first chew. "Too chintzy on the cinnamon."

"Maybe they decided to focus more on the *crumb* part of cinnamon crumb cake?"

She moved on to his lemon square. "Ummm, I think this one needs some confectioners' sugar and maybe a bit more lemon."

Shaking his head in amusement, he gestured her attention back to the menu. "I'd be happy to get you something else. Maybe a piece of chocolate cake or a cookie?"

"I'm fine."

He leaned back in his seat and took a slow, visual inventory of the room before bringing his focus back to Winnie. "I know you'll probably think I'm nuts saying this, but I liked it better the old way."

"Liked what better?" she asked on the heels of her second and last bite of crumb cake.

"This place." The sudden disappearance of his smile was quickly followed by a superfast wave of his hands. "Don't get me wrong, Winnie . . . being here with you is great — awesome, actually. But I guess I preferred the Silver Lake Coffee House better. Less froufrou, more taste."

She was nodding before he'd even finished his sentence.

"You agree?" he asked, relief making its way into his eyes, his returning smile, and his overall body language. "I mean, I guess this place is more — I don't know — *hip* now, but that didn't *grow* the crowd. It just *changed* it, you know?"

"The man that owns most of the buildings on this street is convinced Silver Lake is the next big thing — or can be with the right tenants. So he raised the rent on this place and my place and a few other places and essentially forced us out."

Jay sat back, this time taking a bit longer to survey their surroundings. "Problem is, most of the kids I see in here are from the college. They'll spend money, sure, but their tastes are fickle. Better to build a solid business that has something for everyone. The music alone certainly doesn't help that . . ." His voice trailed off as his gaze returned to hers and then dropped to the table and their half-eaten treats. "Oh. Wow. I think I just showed my inner fuddy-duddy, didn't I?"

"Your inner *fuddy-duddy*?"

"That's what my daughter calls it when I say something she deems completely uncool."

The teenage daughter . . .

She'd forgotten all about that . . .

Winnie's gaze dropped to Jay's to-go cup and the hand that encircled it. No wedding band. No I'm-a-lying-cheat tan line, either.

Dropping her head into her hands, she gave in to the smile she was powerless to hold at bay.

He's not married . . .

"Winnie?"

He's. Not. Married.

"You okay?"

Parting her hands, she peeked out at him

227

and smiled. "I'm fine. Crazy day is all." She brought her forearms back down to the table and willed herself to get back on track like a semi-intelligent human being. Besides, Jay was a business teacher, and she just opened a business. The likelihood he'd suggested this meeting to gather facts for his class was quite high. "So your daughter is sixteen and driving . . . Is that hard?"

"She doesn't have a car of her own, so that makes it a lot easier." He took a long sip of his hot chocolate then set it back on the table. "I remember thinking, when she was little, how much easier it would be when she could get herself places. And now that we're at that age, I wish I could go back to knowing where she was and what she was doing at all times."

"Renee, my friend — the one who worked with me at the bakery and does now again with the Dessert Squad — she says the same thing when her son is off with his father. I mean, she knows Bob is taking care of Ty, but she has to trust that to be the case. She can't see it with her own two eyes."

He nudged the bottom of his cup with his index finger and then pulled his hand back as if suddenly aware he was fidgeting. "I lucked out in that regard. Caroline's mother was an actress, or longed to be one, anyway.

She kept herself busy with community theater as best she could, but she grew bored with that over time. Shortly after Caroline turned five and started kindergarten, she decided it was time to spread her wings."

"Caroline's wings?" she asked, confused.

"Nope. Her mother's wings."

"Meaning . . ."

"Meaning she packed her stuff, kissed a sleeping Caroline, left divorce papers on the kitchen table for me, and headed to California."

Winnie was vaguely aware of heads turning in their direction at her gasp, but she kept her focus on Jay. "She left?"

"Yup."

"Does she at least *see* Caroline from time to time?"

"Nope. She thought a clean break was best."

"Wow." It was all she could think to say under the circumstances. Still, she couldn't help but study his face for any indication his heart was still mixed up in the past.

"I knew I should have been bitter, but I wasn't. I guess I knew it was for the best. But Caroline was five. Her mother walked out of her life with no warning. It was tough on her — still is, on occasion. Especially when we stumble across some press junket from one of her mother's movies and she denies having any children."

"Wow. I'm — I'm sorry. I can't imagine *anything* coming before loved ones," she said, honestly.

"Neither can I." He took another sip of his drink and then smiled, the sparkle returning to his eyes in short order. "Your turn. Tell me something about you."

"There's not much to tell." She wrapped her hands around her own cup and stared down at the hint of steam still rising up through the mouth hole. "You already know about my new business."

"And Lovey," he added.

Winnie rolled her eyes. "Ahhh, yes, my new cat . . ."

"What do you do for fun?"

"I bake."

"And . . ."

Releasing her hold on the cup, she forked another bite of her cake and used the chewing time to think of an answer. All she could come up with though was the truth. "I hang out with my neighbors."

"Cool. What do you do?"

She looked from Jay to the remaining cake and back again and laid the fork down on the table. "You know what? I'm not into pretending to be something I'm not."

"Good. Neither am I."

"You learned about the Dessert Squad from that article in the paper, right?"

He nodded, his eyes never leaving her face.

"So you know *how* I got the ambulance, right?"

"You inherited it. From an elderly friend . . ."

"*One* of my elderly friends," she corrected.

"I don't understand."

She looked around the restaurant for something that would be a nice diversion, but, in the end, she kept on point. "To hear Renee describe it, I collect old people. But the truth is I've always been drawn to the elderly. Have been since I was in fourth grade and my parents and I moved to a new town." Her hands returned to her cup but only for the warmth it provided. "All the kids in my new school had known one another since they were fresh out of the womb. They weren't interested in making friends with me."

Understanding tugged at his features, and she found her voice becoming shaky. "Every day, I couldn't wait for school to be over so I could get out of there . . . but it wasn't any better when the bell rang. I still had to walk home alone. I still had no one to play with when my homework was done. Then, one day, I decided to take a different way home, and I passed an older man named Mr. McCormick. He waved at me and asked me what subject I liked best in school. The next day, I decided to walk that same way . . . and there he was again. Only this time, he waved me over to see a table he was making with his own hands. Soon, I was walking home that way every day, and Mr. McCormick and his wife and their neighbors became my friends. They asked about my day, shared stories about when they were my age, and made me feel special."

"Sounds nice."

"I've gravitated toward the seventy-five-and-older set ever since. It's where I feel most at home and where I can truly be . . . *me.*"

When he said nothing, she prepared herself for the excuse she was sure would come next — I've gotta go, it's getting late, or, if she was really lucky . . . wow, would you look at the time?

But it didn't come. Instead, he leaned closer and helped himself to another piece of her cake. "Tell me about your friends now."

She searched his face for any sign he was humoring her, but there was none. In fact, the only thing she saw in his eyes was interest — genuine interest.

"Gertrude Redenbacher lived down the street. She had the ambulance and Lovey. She taught me how to crochet, and I taught her how to bake the soufflé she'd always wanted to bake. Ethel Wagner lived across the street with her husband, Bart, until she passed six weeks ago. She was like a grandmother to me, and I miss her every day."

She stopped, swallowed, and tried to hold her voice steady as she continued. "As hard as it is to accept she's gone, I'm glad she wasn't alive to see what happened to Bart —"

"Bart?" he repeated, sitting up. "What was the last name again?"

"Yes. I'm talking about the man who was murdered on Serenity Lane last Tuesday. He lived across the street from me." She closed her eyes in an attempt to block out the image that came next, but it was no use. Bart's lifeless body, sprawled across his kitchen floor, was something she suspected she'd never forget. "I — I'm the one who found him."

He reached across the table, tugged her right hand from the cup, and held it tight.

"Wow. I'm sorry. That must have been awful."

"It was." There was no mistaking the electrical charge shooting up her arm at the feel of his hand on hers, and, for a moment, she could think of nothing else. Then, shaking her head, she made herself reengage. "Bridget O'Keefe — the woman who wrote the article about me — lives next door. She's a nosy little thing who lives to talk about her ailments, but I love her."

He smiled, although it stopped short of his eyes.

"And then there's Mr. Nelson. He lives on the first floor of our two-family home. He can't hear a thing without his hearing aids — or, rather, he can't hear an *accurate* thing without his hearing aids. But he's a hoot when he gets going. He's even nosier than Bridget which is why he's earned the nickname Nosy Nelson with a few of our neighbors. He's harmless, though Bridget would disagree with that assessment. Oh, you should see the way he yanks Bridget's chain at every turn. Your face actually hurts from laughing after even half a day with him."

He looked down at their hands and then back up at Winnie, his eyes sparkling once again. "He sounds great. I'd love to meet him sometime."

He'd love to meet him . . .

Reaching down, she secured a piece of skin near her thighs and squeezed. Hard.

Yep, still real . . .

"And, of course, I'd love to see *you* again, too, Winnie."

She pinched even harder.

Real again . . .

CHAPTER 19

Winnie shifted the ambulance into park and peeked at herself in the rearview mirror. She couldn't see much thanks to the tree that stood between the driveway and the dimmer-than-normal porch light, but that was okay. She could feel the smile on her face and knew it was a perfect match for the way she felt at that moment.

Jay was great. He really was.

He was kind, funny, open, and super cute. And he wanted to see her again . . .

She permitted herself the opportunity to squeal within the confines of the vehicle and then cut the engine. In the grand scheme of things, it wasn't that late — only nine fifteen — but she had a dump cake to create before calling it a night.

Shaking her head free of the lingering euphoria that was Jay Morgan, Winnie gathered her purse and stepped from the car. Just as she hit the walkway, a flash of lights over her left shoulder made her turn toward the road and the dark-colored sports car slowing to a crawl at the end of the driveway.

"Hey, Winnie."

She ducked her head out of the path of the porch light and tried to make out the identity of the man now parked at the end of her driveway in an unfamiliar car. "Hello?"

The man's interior dome light came on and put an end to any further need for guesswork. "Oh. Hey there, Lance." She headed up to the road, her gaze moving from her neighbor's face to the car in which he drove. She couldn't make out much about the car in the night, but she could tell it was sporty. "Looks like you got your new car. Congratulations."

"She's a real beauty, isn't she?" he asked, grinning.

"Why is it that men always refer to their cars as females? Is there some rule about that?"

"I don't know, but I'll research it and get back to you . . ."

She laughed. "That's okay. I imagine you have enough to do with your classes. How's that going? You liking the college? The students? The faculty?"

The faculty . . .

And just like that, she was seated across the table at Beans with Jay all over again, his eyes sparkling as he looked at her . . .

"I like it. The students in my entry-level history class could care less about what I'm teaching. They just want to mark off the required class and move on. But some of my more advanced classes have the kind of students that bring out my not-so-inner geek and solidify my decision to keep teaching."

She saw Lance's mouth moving, even caught some of what he was saying (and yes, he was a history geek), but she just couldn't stop thinking about her date with Jay and the fact that he wanted another one.

With me . . .

"As for the faculty, I know my peers in the history department but not really anyone beyond that. I'm sure that will come in time, as they hear more about me and I get more acclimated to the campus and its offerings."

"Are you anywhere near the Cully Business Building?" she made herself ask.

"Two buildings over. Why?"

"I know you're only a few months into the semester, but if you get a chance to stop by there, introduce yourself to Jay Morgan.

238

He's about our age and he's one of the business teachers. Nice guy."

Really nice guy . . .

Cute, too . . .

Lance lifted his hand from its spot along the base of the car window and pointed at Winnie. "He must be if he's got you smiling like that."

Uh-oh.

"Anyway, I probably better let you get inside. I'm sure you've got things to bake for your new business, and I've got a mile-high stack of papers I need to tackle if I want to sleep in tomorrow morning." He moved his left hand from the door to the steering wheel and his right hand to the gear shift. "Have a great rest of your evening, Winnie."

"You, too, Lance. Good night." She lingered at the curb for a moment as the narrow red squares of his taillights disappeared down the last driveway on the street. When Lance and his car were completely gone from sight, she turned and headed back toward the house, her too-full purse growing cumbersome on her shoulder.

She knew Lance was right. She needed to bake. Then again, how long did it really take to make a dump cake? Even one she needed to invent on the spot? Thirty minutes bak-

ing time, an hour if she factored in experi-
mentation and prep?

Pulling her phone from her purse, she il-
luminated the screen and the clock. Nine
thir—

A faint creek off to her left rooted her feet
to the bottom porch step and sent her heart
racing. "Hello?" she called, sliding her focus
left. "Is — is anybody there?"

"It's just me, Winnie Girl."

She resisted the urge to sag against the
stair rail and, instead, concentrated on holding her voice steady. "Mr. Nelson? Where
are you?"

"Corner of the porch."

Stepping up the trio of steps that separated
the porch of their home from the front
walkway, she craned her head left, the
wraparound corner difficult to see thanks to
the moonless night and the location of the
porch light. "I don't see you."

"I'm here."

She made her way around the wicker settee, the card table with the man's chessboard, and one of a pair of wooden rocking
chairs normally positioned in such a way as
to provide the best view of Serenity Lane.
When she reached the far edge of the porch,
she turned right and felt an odd chill skitter
down her spine at the sight of Mr. Nelson

sitting alone, staring off into space.

Sure, the man spent time alone on the front porch every day, but that alone time usually included the chessboard, the day's comics, or a ringside seat for the truest of all weather reports. "What are you doing out here in the dark?"

"Sitting."

"I see that, silly, but —"

"When I got back from Bridget's and saw you weren't home, I looked in on Lovey. She seems to be settling in nicely."

"In terms of my windowsill, my chair, and my bed . . . if I'm not in it, Lovey's world is A-OK. She still hates me, though." She paused for Mr. Nelson's usual it-will-work-out response, but it didn't come. "Um, so . . . how was dinner? I heard Bridget made you pot roast?"

"It was dry and overcooked as usual, but at least I'm still alive to notice."

"Of course you're still . . ." Her sentence drifted off into the night as the meaning behind the man's words hit home. Pivoting on her heels, she slipped her purse off her shoulder and onto the ground, crossed to Mr. Nelson's matching rocker, and carried it back to the darkened corner. Once she was settled and facing her friend, she took his hands in hers and held them gently. "I know you're hurting over Bart's death, Mr. Nelson. We all are. He was a good man."

"A good man who should still be here." Mr. Nelson looked down at Winnie's hands, squeezed them, and then wiggled his out and onto the flat wooden armrests. "Instead, he's in the ground, and that stepson of his is ready to hand Bart's house key to any old Tom, Dick, or Harry off the street."

She opened her mouth to respond but closed it as the elderly man continued. "Within a couple of weeks, someone else will be living in that house — someone who ain't Bart and Ethel. Maybe they'll have little ones; maybe they won't. Maybe it'll be a married couple; maybe it won't. Maybe it'll be that ambulance fella who looked at the house today, or maybe it'll be someone who ain't never stepped foot in Silver Lake until now. But not a one of 'em will know that Bart laid the stonework for that patio out back all by himself . . . to surprise Ethel while she was down South visiting with her sister. Not a one of 'em will know that the bedroom at the top of the stairs was the purplest purple you could imagine for all of about a week when Mark was six or so."

"Purple?" she asked, settling back for a story she already knew she wanted to hear. "Why?"

"Ethel got it in her head that purple was pretty. Bart told her that was true for flowers and shirts and even grapes . . . but not bedroom walls. Still, he went to the paint store, ordered up some purple paint, stuck a paint brush in my hand, and put me to work. We put a nice thick coat of it on those walls, too."

She closed her eyes and tried to imagine the room as Mr. Nelson described, a smile tugging at her lips almost immediately. "And?"

"When it was all done, he called Ethel into the room to show her what we'd done. She took one look at the walls, scrunched her nose the way she did when she didn't like something, and said, 'Maybe we should leave purple to the flowers, after all.' "

She smiled through the tears as she pictured her dear friend standing in the middle of a newly painted room, nose scrunched. Not a day went by that she didn't think of Ethel. Sometimes the thought came in a glance out the window. Sometimes it came while searching through the cookbook Ethel had given Winnie for Christmas — the recipes it held handed down from generation to generation of Ethel's own family. When Winnie had balked and suggested she save it for family, Ethel had corrected her and told her she *was* family.

"Oh, Mr. Nelson, I miss them . . . I really do. But when I get to talk about them with you, it's almost like they're still here."

For the first time since she approached him, she saw him smile. It was slight, but it was there. "I feel it, too, Winnie."

Pitching forward on the rocker, she placed her hands on his knees and held his gaze. "So it's up to us — you, me, and Bridget — to make sure that whoever moves in *does* know about the stone patio . . . and the purple room . . . and the significance of each and every flower Bart and Ethel planted around that house."

"And what happens if they don't care?" Mr. Nelson asked, his eyes wide.

"Then Bridget will write about them in her column, you won't share any chess tips, and I'll . . ." She cast about for just the right form of retaliation and then shot her index finger into the air as she settled on the perfect one. "I'll sic Lovey on them!"

Mr. Nelson laughed and covered her hands with his own. "Lovey isn't the toughie you make her out to be."

"You mean the one she makes herself out to be. To me, anyway."

"She'll come around, Winnie. You just wait and see."

Her Mr. Nelson was back . . .

"I think it's probably time we both call it a night, don't you think?" she asked, smiling. "It's been a busy day."

"Was it a good day?"

She thought back over her first day with the Dessert Squad — the ups (two customers — one of which was Jay), the downs (hello, Lovey), an unexpected date, and time with her beloved Mr. Nelson. It didn't get any better than that . . .

Inhaling the cool, crisp night air, she let her feelings show on her face and in her answer. "It was a *great* day, Mr. Nelson."

"I'm glad, Winnie." She pulled her hands away as he slid forward on his chair and reached for his cane. "I've been thinking. I don't think Mark hurt Bart."

Scooting back her rocker, she widened the gap Mr. Nelson needed to stand and then followed him across the porch and toward the door, doubling back momentarily to retrieve her purse. "You really think Sissy did it?"

He stopped at the door and fixed his gaze on the house across the street — the house that was no longer lit by Bart's hand-carved lamp. "Since she's the only other person that makes any sense, I guess so."

"Why is Mark off your radar?"

"Because even though I think he's rushing the sale of that house for all the wrong reasons, I can't ignore the fact that he cared about Bart enough to bury him with that damn coin he loved so much. Most people wouldn't have given something like that a second thought. But Mark did. That's gotta count for something, don't you think?"

CHAPTER 20

Looking back, she probably shouldn't have lain down on her bed after finishing her talk with Mr. Nelson. If she hadn't, she wouldn't have had to hit the ground running the moment her alarm clock proclaimed it morning. And if she hadn't, she would have bypassed the moment of terror that came with the realization she was low on flour at a critical point in the baking process.

Still, she'd managed to develop a recipe that was sure to be a hit (last-minute flour run and all) and deliver her first Dump (Him) Cake to the Bryant Hall Dormitory at Silver Lake College by the requested noon arrival time. The fact that it was now one o'clock and she was taking her first bite of food since the subpar cinnamon crumb cake with Jay the previous night was beside the point.

Halfway through the sub sandwich Renee had mercifully made for Winnie upon her return from the campus, she looked up to find her friend staring at her with obvious amusement. "Is . . . some . . . thing . . . wrong?" Winnie asked between bites.

"I've never seen you eat so fast before."

Winnie took another bite. "I've never . . . been this . . . hungry before."

"I can see that." Renee looked down at her own sandwich and placed half of it on Winnie's plate. "When was the last time you ate something?"

She considered the question, revisited her food intake over the past twenty-four hours, and then proceeded to answer. "You mean aside from two or three bites of a not-so-great cinnamon crumb cake at Beans last night? Breakfast. Yesterday."

Drumming the fingers of her left hand on the table, Renee conceded the rest of her sandwich to Winnie with her right. "First, you're a nut. Second, you didn't tell me you were going to Beans . . ."

"It was a school night for Ty." She took a moment to come up for air and then moved on to the first of Renee's sandwich halves. "Besides, I was there on someone else's invitation."

The second the words were out she knew she'd made a mistake wording her response the way she did. And, sure enough, Renee's eyes widened, her brow arched, and a knowing smile pushed any lingering concern over Winnie's eating habits right out the door.

"So how was he?"

"He, who?" It was a rhetorical question, of course, but it bought her some time . . .

"He, who? Yeah, okay, go ahead and play coy. It's not like I'm your best friend or anything." Renee pushed her empty plate to the side of the table to accommodate her elbows. "Details. Puh-lease . . ."

"Details? You mean, like the fact it *wasn't* Greg I met at Beans?"

Renee's brow arched still further. "The redhead that works with him? The one who's looking at the house across the street?"

She made a mental note to talk to Bridget and Mr. Nelson about that latest development and then shook her head. "Nope, not Chuck Rogers, either."

Dropping her forearms all the way down, Renee drew back. "Wait. Did you enroll in one of those online dating sites?"

"Nope."

"Then —"

"I delivered a Smart Cookie to him at his office yesterday."

Renee's inhale was so loud even Lovey — in her noon-hour slumber — lifted her head

249

and glared. "The business guy?"

"Business *teacher*," she corrected as her thoughts traveled back to the previous morning and the most engaging man she'd ever met.

"The one with the teenage daughter?"

She set down her sandwich long enough to take a sip of her ice water and pull a potato chip from the open bag between them. "Caroline. She's sixteen."

"And the woman he had this child with?" Renee prodded. "I take it he's no longer married to her?"

"Of course he's not. She took off when Caroline was five and hasn't been back since."

This time, Renee's gasp was laced with more disgust than surprise. "You're kidding."

"No. Seems this woman wanted to be a star in Hollywood."

"Is she?"

She alternated between the chips and the second half of Renee's sandwich and recalled the part of her conversation with Jay that featured his ex-wife. "I think she might be."

"Who? Who is it?"

"I didn't ask." And she hadn't. It hadn't mattered. It still didn't. "He's a really nice guy, Renee. Smart. Funny. Real."

Renee's expression turned dreamy. "Tell me more. Tell me everything."

"Well, last night, after you left, he called and asked if I'd like to get some coffee with him sometime. He threw out a few possibilities, and it just made sense to do it then. So he dropped his daughter off at the dance studio next to the shop and waited there until I arrived."

"Okay . . ."

"He asked about *me*, Renee . . . about where I live and what I like to do in my free time."

"You bake and hang out with old people."

She swallowed the last bite of sandwich and declared herself full. Then, rising to her feet, she wandered over to Lovey. "I told him that. Almost verbatim."

"Yikes."

"That's just it, Renee. There was no 'yikes,' no fidgeting of his fingers, no looking at the clock wondering when he could escape." She reached out to pet Lovey but pulled her hand back at the animal's responding hiss.

"Let her sniff your finger," Renee instructed.

She waved aside the suggestion and moved to the next window. "It was like my choice of friends didn't matter. In fact, he wanted to hear about them all. So I told him and he actually *listened.* I even pinched myself under the table to make sure it was really happening."

Renee left the table to come stand beside Winnie, the smile on her face impossible to miss. "I'm happy for you, Winnie. You deserve a great — wait . . . what's this guy look like?"

"He's got these gorgeous blue green eyes that sparkle and dance every time he smiles. And he smiles *a lot.*"

"Keep going . . ."

"His hair is light brown, but he has a hint of gray near his temples that is really quite flattering."

"How old is this guy?" Renee asked.

"Late thirties, I think. Maybe forty, but definitely no older than that."

Renee widened her lips and nodded, obviously trying to imagine Jay based on Winnie's description. "Nice body?"

She paused at the question and tried to remember, but all she was able to relay was his height (maybe six feet to her own five-five) and weight (proportionate, with no sign of a beer gut) and follow it up with an emphatic, "He's perfect."

"Do you think you'll see him again?"

"He said he wants to." She turned from the window, did a little dance, and then threw her arms around Renee. "I like him. A lot. And I think he might like me, too."

"How could he not?"

"I love you, Renee." She planted a kiss on the side of Renee's cheek and then stepped back, her mind ready to function again now that her stomach had been fed. "Now, we need to get to work."

"What work? We haven't gotten any new calls today."

"Which is exactly why we need to get to work." She headed back to the table, carried their lunch plates to the sink, and then handed the idea notebook to Renee. "We got two calls yesterday because of the article Bridget finagled for the weekend paper. And we got the call for this morning's delivery based on the customer having seen the ambulance in the campus parking lot yesterday. Word of mouth sells. So we need to get more of that out there."

Renee reclaimed her seat, uncapped her pen, and waited for Winnie to continue.

"But we can't just sit back and wait for word of mouth to do everything. We'll be dead by the end of the week."

"But three calls in the first two days is pretty good," Renee argued. "We literally started yesterday."

"True. But our profit from those three calls is probably less than thirty bucks total. I can't live on that and neither can you."

Renee nibbled on the end of her pen and then pointed it at Winnie. "Can Bridget write another article?"

"She just did."

"Maybe the girl who called us about the dump cake can write an article for the campus paper."

Winnie snapped her fingers and then pointed at Renee's notebook. "Good! Write that down."

"You could drive through downtown Silver Lake every night for a few weeks in the ambulance. Surely that would get people's curiosity up."

"Good! Add that one, too." She reached back, grabbed hold of her ponytail, and brought the tip around to the front. Brushing it slowly across her hand, she let her mind drift in a different direction. "Maybe we should put together a proposal that we can get out to a few of the local companies with a list of desserts we could deliver with motivational names. I mean, you hear about these companies who do team building and stuff like that. Seems to me they might also be inclined to send in some treats to boost morale, too. We just need to come up with some more cleverly named desserts and get them in front of the powers that be."

"I like that." Renee tapped the pen against her chin, only to pull it back and point it at Winnie. "What about getting some menus to the people who teach the prenatal classes at the hospital? Surely a mom who is weeks away from going into labor could use a little rescuing. Again, we need to come up with the names, but I could so see a new dad-to-be wanting to do something like that for his wife."

"Excellent!" She gestured toward the notebook and then wandered around the table to Renee's side. "Hey, do you have Ty this weekend or is he with Bob?"

"Technically I have him, but he's going to some sort of game with Bob on Saturday, why?"

"I was thinking, maybe I could go on a baking frenzy. We'll invite Mr. Nelson and Bridget to join us, too, and have everyone throw out dessert names that we could use for pregnant women, or to boost employee morale, or whatever. Who knows, maybe we'll come up with some really good stuff."

"You'll be there, right?" Renee asked.

"Of course."

"Then I'm sure we'll get some good stuff.

You're a dessert-naming genius."

"You're the one who came up with Dump (Him) Cake," Winnie reminded. "That was perfect for the girl today."

Renee drew up her shoulders and pursed her lips proudly. "I did, didn't I?" Then, without waiting for confirmation, she picked up her pen and held it to the notebook. "I just thought of another way to spread the word. We could put up flyers about the Dessert Squad in some of the shopwindows downtown."

"Like Batkas would let us do that . . ." She heard the sarcasm in her voice and knew it was born of experience. "C'mon, Renee, you know that guy would see the Dessert Squad as competition for his precious revitalization efforts."

"The Emergency Dessert Squad is a new business," Renee protested.

"Not one paying lease in any of his buildings . . ."

Renee's shoulders slumped, and she dropped her pen back to the table. "You're right. But" — again she picked up her pen, and again she prepared to write — "Batkas can't keep a lease-paying tenant from advertising us in their window, right?"

"Meaning?"

"Maybe Jack at the hardware store will

put a flyer up in his window. And maybe Sherry at the gift shop will, too."

It was certainly worth a shot. Even if the landlord took issue with it and made them take the flyers down, at least they would have been there for a little while . . .

"I would think that guy, Mark, who is moving into our old spot would put up a flyer for us, too. I mean, you were friends with his mom and stepdad."

She reined in her mental side trip and stared at Renee. "What was that?"

"Mark — Bart and Ethel's son." At Winnie's nod, Renee continued. "He's leasing Delectable Delights. Well, not *Delectable Delights,* per se, but the space Delectable Delights was in until last week."

"For what?" she snapped.

If Renee noticed Winnie's curtness, it had no impact. "A pool hall, believe it or not. Crazy, huh?"

"A pool hall?" She slid into the empty chair closest to Renee's. "How do you know this?"

"After Ty's baseball practice, I took him downtown to get some ice cream." Renee held her free hand up in true crossing guard style. "I know, I know, I should have taken him home for dinner first. But I didn't."

"Go on."

"Ty wanted to see the old store and so we walked down the block with our ice cream to see it. I was expecting to see our counter and display case through the window, but it was gone. In fact, the only thing inside was a ladder and a couple of paint cans. And Mark, of course." Renee ran her hand through her pixie haircut and scrunched her nose like she was trying to determine if she liked a particular smell. If Winnie didn't know better, she'd think Lovey had done something wrong. But since she did know better, she knew it just meant Renee was thinking. "Anyway, I guess he recognized me from being over here for all those late-night gab fests we used to have during the separation. At least that's all I can figure. Anyway, when he saw us looking in the window, he came out to say hi. I told him I was sorry about Bart, and he thanked me. Ty, of course, asked him why he was painting our old bakery, and that's when he told us about the pool hall. Said it was something he's always wanted to do."

"But Batkas was charging a crazy amount for that space," Winnie protested.

Renee's robust shoulders lifted and fell with a sigh-accompanied shrug. "I guess Mark can handle it."

"But how?"

"I don't know. Maybe he's gotten an offer on the house. Maybe he's banking on the fact he will. I don't know. I just know about the pool hall and that he's really excited to get the place up and running." Renee pulled her hand up off the table and inspected her nails. "Me? I think it's amusing that everyone seems to think Silver Lake is going to become some sort of hangout destination. I mean, this is *Silver Lake* we're talking about. The whole reason we get the influx of city folks during the summer and on spring and fall weekends is *because* it's quiet, yes?"

Renee had a point — one that had been argued by many a shopkeeper up and down Main Street over the months leading up to the rent hike. But it was a point that had been discarded by a man hell-bent on proving everyone wrong.

She supposed she nodded, maybe even mumbled some form of agreement, but in reality she was still mentally digesting the news about Mark and drafting the best way to break it to Mr. Nelson.

CHAPTER 21

On one hand she felt silly driving three houses down when she could just as easily push the stretcher that same distance. On the other hand, though, Renee was right. The ambulance was as much a part of the Emergency Dessert Squad experience as the dessert itself.

The only thing she'd yet to rationalize (with or without Renee's help) was Lovey's presence in the passenger seat. She supposed she should have been forewarned of this outcome when the brown and white tabby first followed her down the stairs and out to the driveway. But, honestly, she'd chalked it up to Cat Lesson Number One.

Or was it Cat Lesson Number Two?

Either way, she'd all but ignored the ungrateful little beast as she loaded the brightly colored cupcakes into the back of the vehicle, secured the door, and walked around to the cab via the driver's side.

If she'd been thinking with her head instead of her heart, she'd have returned to the driveway the second she realized Lovey was riding shotgun. And she almost did. But something about the notion of moral support in light of her latest rescue recipient had won out in the end.

Still, she couldn't help but issue a stern warning to the cross-looking animal as she pulled alongside the curb at 21 Serenity Lane. "Now hear this, Lovey. I have a job to do. Without this job, I can't feed you. And while I'm sure you think any number of traitors would take you in, Gertie left you to *me*. So you're not going anywhere, got it?"

Hiss . . .

"Great. Just great . . ." She met Lovey's glare and raised it with one of her own. "I think we need to have some Cat Owner Lessons. Cat Owner Lesson Number One — You can't pour cat food on your own."

Lovey yawned and looked out the passenger side window.

Shaking her head, she opened her door and pointed at the cat. "You stay right here and don't move!"

In a flash Lovey was across her seat and out the door.

"Cat *Owner* Lesson Number One, Lovey. *Cat Lesson Number One!*" She slammed the door shut and walked around to the back of the rig. With hands that were becoming a bit more adept with everything, Winnie lowered the stretcher onto the road, topped it with the cupcakes (which looked adorable, by the way), and closed the back of the ambulance. Then, squaring her shoulders with the help of a rather large inhale, she pushed the stretcher up the walkway and over to the Donovans' front door with Lovey leading the way.

"Please, Lovey," she whispered when they stopped at their destination. "Go back to the car. Please."

Lovey blinked and looked away.

She was contemplating the sanity in continuing to argue with a cat when the door swung open and a puffy-faced Sissy appeared. At first glance, she thought the young mother had been crying, but a second look yielded the real truth . . .

Sissy was mad — fist-clenching, voice-seething, vein-popping mad.

Winnie swallowed. "I — I'm here with your I-Scream Cone Cupcakes."

Sissy stepped back, waved Winnie and the stretcher inside, and didn't balk in the slightest when Lovey invited herself in, too.

"Lovey, no!" Winnie yelled. "You can't go —"

The vein along Sissy's right temple eased as the woman crouched down to the floor and unfisted her hand long enough to pet Lovey's back. "Aren't you a cutie pie . . ."

Lovey?

After what seemed like an eternity, Sissy rose to her feet, took a deep breath, and led the way into the kitchen. Lovey, of course, looked up (triumphantly, mind you) as Winnie went by, yet remained behind for a quick power lick.

"You take direction well. This delivery time is perfect."

She brought the stretcher to a stop and then looked around the kitchen. "Where would you like me to put your cupcakes?"

"Over there, on the center island." Sissy leaned against the wall closest to the family's table and fisted her hands all over again. "I figured these cupcakes would be a nice pick-me-up for Ava this evening after voice lessons."

"Ava is mad about something?" Winnie carried the tray to the counter and then returned to the stretcher and her bag for the bottle of sprinkles she packed specifically for the purpose of freshening up the dessert's appearance.

"Ava is sad," Sissy corrected. "*I'm* mad."

"Oh?" She shook a few extra sprinkles on

four of the twelve cupcakes and then, when she was sure Sissy wasn't paying attention, she quickly swapped the sprinkle jar with the Donovans' saltshaker and held it up for Lovey to see.

Lovey opened her mouth in a silent hiss and then wound her way around Sissy's legs.

Like a balloon voided of its air by the prick of a needle, the anger all but drained from Sissy's body as she slid to the ground and reached for Lovey. "I kept hoping the judges would unanimously decide to delay the pageant until Ava was able to participate, but they didn't. Brianna Rawlins is, in fact, the new Little Miss Northwest Ohio!"

"Little Miss Northwest Ohio?" she echoed only to have her brain fill in the answer all on its own. "Wait. That was the pageant Ava was in over the weekend, isn't it?"

"The pageant Ava was *supposed* to be in — and would have won — if it weren't for that horrible old man."

Bart . . .

"Because of him and that damn flowerbed of his," Sissy continued, "Ava missed out on the crown and the Tasty Toothpaste commercial!"

Mindful of her presence in a customer's home, Winnie capped the sprinkle jar, put it back in her bag, and readied the stretcher for its return to the ambulance. After all, staying in Sissy's house any longer than absolutely necessary wasn't advisable, especially if the woman was going to continue trashing Bart.

Unfortunately, Sissy kept talking (and holding Lovey). "I've never understood why Brianna has scored so well in previous pageants. Her hair is poker straight and rodent brown! And her eyes are blue — *sapphire* blue! I swear her insufferable mother has that child wearing colored contacts. How else could you explain that color with that hair?"

Lovey looked up at Winnie, and Winnie, in turn, studied her reflection in the black lacquer framed mirror just outside the entrance to the kitchen.

Hair — brown (though mousey sounds so much better than rodent).

Eyes — blue (sapphire might be a bit strong, but definitely ocean-y).

"And her face! It's — it's heart shaped!" Sissy argued. "Anyone who knows anything about true beauty knows that the best shape is oval. It tapers much more gracefully toward the chin and has prominent cheekbones. *Runway models* have prominent cheekbones! Brianna has a heart-shaped face. It's all wrong!"

She leaned forward ever so slightly and examined her facial shape — something she'd never really given much thought to until that moment.

Her chin — it didn't really taper . . .

And her cheekbones weren't necessarily prominent . . .

"Your shape is easy, Winnie. It's round — like a bowling ball." Sissy jerked her hand back as Lovey turned and hissed at her. "Well, aren't you just a nasty little thing?"

Lurching forward, Winnie tried to grab hold of Lovey, but she was too late; the cat was off Sissy's lap and out of the kitchen like a shot. "I'm sorry, Sissy. I — I don't know what came over her. She's not normally a hisser."

Liar, liar, pants on fire . . .

"Not to anyone other than me, of course," she finished under her breath.

Wait. Had Lovey just defended her?

No.

No way.

Shaking the ludicrous scenario from her thoughts, she began the walk back to the front door, the stretcher gliding across the floor effortlessly. "Lovey? Where are you? It's time to go."

She came around the back of the stretcher to open the door and then jumped back as

Lovey dashed past her and across the front walkway to the ambulance. "Okay, cool . . ." Then, returning her focus to the stretcher and the woman standing on the other side of it, Winnie called her best professional smile into action. "I hope the I-Scream Cone Cupcakes are a hit with Ava when she gets home."

"I can hope. But really, once she hears who won the title and *her commercial,* I'm not sure anything will work." Sissy pressed her fingertips to her lips so hard, they lost their color. After a moment, she pulled them back and let loose an angry moan. "When I think of the stepping-stone Tasty Toothpaste was supposed to be, I just want to kill that man all over again!"

"Again?" Winnie grabbed hold of the closest porch column to steady herself. "What do you mean, a —"

"Only instead of a pillow this go-round, I'd use something different. Like maybe the shovel he used to plant those damn daisies he's now pushing up from six feet under."

Again and again she replayed Sissy's words as she drove past the house she shared with Mr. Nelson and turned left at the end of Serenity Lane. Where she was going, she wasn't entirely sure, but she just knew she needed to drive.

And think.

On the way back to the ambulance with the stretcher in tow, she'd been convinced Sissy had murdered Bart, the woman's own words akin to a confession in Winnie's book. Yet by the time she slid into position behind the steering wheel, she wasn't so sure anymore.

Maybe the words had been spoken in more of a generic nature — a here's-how-I'd-have-done-it kind of thing . . .

Movement out of the corner of her eye reminded her she wasn't alone, and she pulled her eyes off the road long enough to acknowledge her feline companion. "I don't know if that reaction to Sissy back there was simply you being ornery or you sticking up for me, but either way, thanks."

Lovey stared back at her but said nothing. Not a meow, not a hiss, nothing.

She brought her focus back to the stretch of road in front of her and concentrated on her breathing.

Inhale . . .

Exhale . . .

Inhale . . .

Ex—

"I swear, Lovey, if that hateful woman had something to do with Bart's death, I will find out and I will make sure she spends the rest of her life behind bars where she belongs."

She stopped at the four-way intersection and then continued straight, her mind vaguely registering the parts of Silver Lake that remained before she left the city limits entirely.

There was Buckeye Convenience Store (a twenty-four-hour drive-thru) . . .

The turnoff to the public lake access . . .

Silver Lake Convenience Store (a twenty-four-hour drive-thru) . . .

The connector road leading to the weekend homes inhabited by Cincinnati's most wealthy . . .

Lakeside Convenience Store (you guessed it, another twenty-four-hour drive-thru) . . .

Silver Lake Park . . .

With a quick check of her rearview and driver's side mirror, Winnie made a wide U-turn and doubled back toward the park. Turning into the gravel parking lot, she slid into a quiet spot near a large tree, rolled down the window, and cut the engine.

"Only instead of a pillow this go-round, I'd use something different," she whispered. "I don't know, Lovey, what do you think? Do you think Sissy was confessing or do you think —"

269

A blur of brown and white fur leapt across her thighs and out the window before she could finish her sentence or shift her body fast enough to block the escape.

"Lovey!" she shouted, poking her head out the window. "Get back here right now!"

Lovey turned, made eye contact, and then sauntered off toward the one lone person on the playground — a female, sitting on a swing, her feet still planted on the ground, the side of her head resting against the chain tethered to the metal upright above.

Clamping her lips closed around the string of not-so-nice descriptive terms for an animal that had once meant so much to one of Winnie's most beloved friends, Winnie shoved open the door, stepped out onto the gravel lot, and slammed the door shut. "Lovey, this is the last time I take you anywhere!"

If Lovey heard (which she did), she didn't care (surprise!) and, instead, kept walking, the object of the animal's focus now regarding them (okay, just Winnie) with tangible wariness.

The female (a teenager, Winnie could now tell) bent over at the waist, held her index finger out for Lovey to smell, and then looked up at Winnie. "Is this your cat?"

"Legally, yes," Winnie mumbled before

transitioning her thoughts and her attitude to the smile the innocent party deserved. "I guess I wasn't thinking when I rolled down my window just now. Fish don't do that."

They just die when you put salt in their tank . . .

"You're right. They don't." The girl took a moment to scratch the area behind Lovey's left ear . . . and then her right . . . and then back to her left as the cat flopped onto her side. "Ohhh, yeah, you like that, don't you, sweetie?"

"Her name is Lovey," Winnie said, awe-struck.

"Lovey," the girl repeated as her hand left the cat's ears and continued down Lovey's full length. "Hello, Lovey, I'm Caroline."

Caroline?

As in Morgan?

Before she could ask, the girl continued, her voice taking on a wispy, faraway quality that was at times difficult to hear. "I used to think it would have been fun to have a pet — a dog, a bunny, a fish, a cat like this . . . Someone who could lick away all the tears I didn't want my dad to see."

"Fish don't have tongues," Winnie pointed out only to berate herself (silently, of course) for having done so.

"I was five. I didn't think that hard."

"Sorry. I'm not exactly a fish expert, myself." Winnie crossed to the vacant swing next to the young girl and lowered herself onto the flimsy piece of curved rubber. "I take it you didn't get one?"

"A fish?"

"A pet of any kind."

Lovey stood up, flopped onto her opposite side, and looked up at Caroline expectantly. Like a trained sea lion, the girl responded, gliding her hand along Lovey's soft fur. "No. No pets. My dad actually offered once or twice when I was like ten, but I said no."

"Why?"

"He'd already gotten stuck taking care of me all on his own. I didn't think he should have to take care of a pet, too." Caroline pulled her hand back as Lovey stood, stretched, and wandered over to check out a piece of grass. "When I was five, my mom decided she didn't want me or my dad anymore."

Winnie opened her mouth to speak, to introduce herself and say that she knew Jay, but something about the way the girl worded her sentence elbowed its way to the front. "I — I don't know what to say. I —"

"It's okay. She's famous now. Just like she wanted to be." Caroline wrapped her hand around the chains on either side of her body

272

and used her feet to start the swing. "I saw her in a magazine the other day when I was at the store with some of my friends. One of them — Courtney — actually said I kind of looked like her. I thought about telling them right then and there that she was my mom, but I didn't. No one would believe me anyway seeing as how she's never told the press she was married to my dad or that I even exist."

"Her loss."

Caroline slammed her feet into the ground, stopping the motion she'd managed to gain. "Excuse me?"

Uh-oh.

"I — I said it's her loss. Because" — she stopped, swallowed, and started again — "it *is.*"

"How do you know? You don't know anything about me."

"I know you're good with my cat." It sounded lame the second it left her mouth, but it was something . . . "And I don't think there's a career on the face of the earth that's more important than being a mom."

"Are you a mom?" Caroline asked.

"No."

"Married?"

"No."

"Then you really don't know what you're

273

talking about, do you?" Caroline wiggled off the swing and turned to face Winnie, anger lighting the blue green eyes she shared with her father.

"I know *me,* Caroline. I know what I want for *my* life."

"And what is that?"

"Right now? It's to get my business off the ground and make it a success. After that, if I'm fortunate enough to meet someone I want to spend the rest of my life with, I'd like to have a family."

"But your business comes first?" Caroline prodded.

"Right now, yes. Because it's all I have. But once I have a family, that won't be the case."

"You say that *now . . .* "

"And I'll say that then, too." She watched Lovey make two laps around an oak tree and then squat in a pile of dirt. It was on the tip of her tongue to tell the cat to wait, but she stopped herself, opting, instead, to stay in the conversation with Jay's daughter. "Being a parent is the greatest gift of all, Caroline. Just ask your dad. I'm quite sure he'll tell you the same thing."

Caroline shrugged and kicked at the first in a series of railroad ties outlining the play area. "He does. All the time. We're a team

— the two of us. Us against the world. Forever and ever. He won't let anyone hurt me, and I won't let anyone hurt him."

An odd sensation skittered up Winnie's spine and propelled her up and off the swing just as Caroline looked down at her phone and made a face. "Oh. Wow. It's getting late. My dad will be home from his class in twenty minutes, and he'll be worried if I'm not there."

"I could give you a lift," she suggested. "After I round up Lovey."

"Nah, that's okay. I live on the other side of those trees right over there." Caroline pointed toward a line of pine trees on the eastern side of the park. "But I can help you get your cat. She seems to like me."

Sure enough, with little more than a snap of her fingers, Caroline managed to coax Lovey over to the playground and into her arms. Rising up on her feet, the girl jerked her chin toward the parking lot. "Okay, so where's your car?"

Winnie started to answer with the help of her index finger but stopped mid-point. "Don't you have to go home?"

"I do. And I will. But I can carry Lovey to your car first."

"Okay, great. I'm parked over there," she said, leading the way. "Under the oak tree."

Two steps later, Caroline stopped. "But that's an ambulance."

"It is. But not for people. It's my brand-new —"

"Emergency Dessert Squad," Caroline said, reading the side of Winnie's ambulance. "That's *yours* — I mean, *you*? The lady who rescues people with desserts?"

"That's me." She couldn't help but smile at the teenager's description.

The lady who rescues people with —

In a harried whirl of loose fur and incessant hissing, Caroline shoved Lovey into Winnie's arms and took off.

"Wait! Caroline! Are you okay?"

Mere steps from the tree line, the teenager turned around to glare at Winnie, her face contorted with the same rage now spewing from her mouth. "Stay away from my dad!"

CHAPTER 22

"See, this is yet another reason why I never got married."

Winnie pulled her feet from their spot atop the porch railing and let them drop onto the floor in front of her rocking chair. "Why's that, Mr. Nelson?"

"Because all that silent brooding you ladies do is detrimental to my chess game." With a sweep of his hand, the pieces on his side of the board went to the right, and the pieces on the opposing side went left.

"Why'd you do that?" she asked. "I thought you were winning."

"Not hard to do when I'm the only one playing." Mr. Nelson retrieved his cane from the floor at his feet, righted it, and used it to stand and make his way over to the vacant rocking chair beside Winnie. He pointed up at the ceiling. "So what's so fascinating up there besides the fact we need to paint in a few weeks?"

She looked at him in the last of the day's light and tried to make sense of what he was saying, but she had nothing. Nada. "I'm not sure what you're talking about."

Again, he guided her eyes upward with his finger. "You've been staring at that same spot for close to an hour now. I even tried out a few of the jokes I heard at the bingo hall this afternoon and you didn't so much as crack a smile at any of 'em."

"You told me jokes?"

"Four of 'em." Mr. Nelson let his hand drift down to the armrest of his rocker as he settled into the chair. "Granted the first three weren't the best, but that last one? I was so tickled by that one, I didn't hear Margaret Mary call B-5. If I had, I'd have gotten myself a five-dollar gift card to Burger Barn!"

"Sorry to hear that, Mr. Nelson. I know how much you adore that place . . . and the waitresses."

He stopped rocking and leaned across the gap between their chairs. "I adore *you* more, Winnie Girl. Always have, always will."

Swallowing hard at the sudden tightness in her throat, Winnie dropped her head against the back of the chair and pinned her gaze to the ceiling once again.

Mr. Nelson is right. We do need to paint . . .

278

"Care to tell me what's bothering you?"

"Nothing is bothering me, Mr. Nelson. I'm fine."

"And I'm twenty-five and full of muscles," he groused. "Feel better now? We're both lying."

He was right.

She felt as lousy at that moment as she had when she first wandered down to the porch after dinner (icing and leftover cake batter). Sitting there, in silence, wasn't helping her, and it certainly wasn't helping Mr. Nelson's chess game.

"I don't know how to put this, exactly."

"You don't know if you don't try."

"I clicked with someone the other day."

Mr. Nelson studied her for a moment. After what seemed like a minute, maybe two, he resituated himself in his chair but kept his focus squarely on her face. "Did he hurt you?"

"No. No! It's nothing like that." She breathed in the potpourri of scents that was Serenity Lane — Bridget's dinner wafting across the yard, Harold Jenkins's pipe as he rode down the road on his motorized scooter in the hopes of catching Cornelia taking her sheltie, Con-Man, on his last walk of the day — and tried to assemble her thoughts in some sort of easy-to-follow order.

"Then what's got you so down in the mouth?"

She didn't need a mirror to know what her friend saw on her face. And she didn't need a therapist to know what was wrong.

"This guy got me, Mr. Nelson. He got my demeanor, my humor, my drive, my choice in friends — all of it. And something about being in his presence made me . . . *happy.* Really, really happy. Like I am when I'm out here with you and Bridget."

"You're not happy *now.*"

"It's not the company — I assure you that," she said over a rumble in her stomach.

"So then what's the problem?"

She pressed a hand to her stomach as a second, louder rumble rivaled the sound of Harold's scooter en route back to his home. "Sorry."

Reaching into his shirt pocket, Mr. Nelson extracted a pretzel and held it out to Winnie. "Eat."

"No, I'm . . ." A third and still louder rumble drowned out her protest, and she accepted the offering. After a quick inspection for shirt lint, she popped it into her mouth. "This guy has a daughter. A sixteen-year-old, to be exact. Seems the ex-wife split

280

town eleven years ago and hasn't looked back. The kid has a whole lot of lingering anger — stoked to the surface, no doubt, by normal teenage angst. The last thing he needs and she wants is someone else in the mix."

"Did he say that?"

He held a second pretzel across the gap. She ate it, sans lint inspection. "No. But the message from the daughter was crystal clear. In fact, her exact words were, *'Stay away from my dad.'* "

"That doesn't mean he agrees, Winnie Girl . . ."

"She's sixteen. She's still at home. He kind of has to." She looked down at her shirt and began plucking off previously unnoticed clumps of Lovey hair. "Besides, I'm despised enough in my own home thanks to Lovey. Why put myself in a position to be despised in someone else's?"

It was a smart decision. She knew this. But still, it didn't negate the disappointment.

"Then look elsewhere. There are plenty more fish in the sea — or, should I say, lake." Mr. Nelson leaned forward and directed Winnie's attention to the car rolling to a stop in front of their house. "And lookee here, there's a fish a floppin' at your

281

doorstep right now."

She lifted her hand in a perfect mirror image of Mr. Nelson's and waved at the face peering out from the open window, but other than registering Lance's basic features (long face, strong jawline, curly auburn hair), her gaze was already on to the car — the car she'd obviously underestimated in the dark the previous night.

Whoa.

Actually, no . . . Make that a double whoa.

Mr. Nelson's elbow found its way into her upper arm. "You should have seen the ladies when I got out of that beauty at the bingo hall this afternoon, Winnie . . . You'd have thought I was James Bond or something."

Pushing off the rocking chair, she crossed to the railing and used it to support her lower body as she leaned forward. "Wow. I could tell it was sporty in the dark last night, but I had no idea your new car was that gorgeous," she called out to Lance.

"Been wanting one of these my whole life." Lance ran his hand along the top of his door as if he, too, was seeing his new car for the first time.

"Funny, I would have pictured you in a Model T with the way you are about American history," Mr. Nelson said as he joined Winnie at the rail.

Lance grinned so wide Winnie couldn't help but smile, too. "Yeah, but this works better on those days I might otherwise be late for class." Then, just as quick as his grin had ventured across his face, it disappeared. "Now don't you worry, Mr. Nelson, I won't be racing down Serenity Lane."

"Pacing?" Mr. Nelson echoed in confusion. "Why would you be pacing? That's what us old folks do!"

She turned, pointed at the elderly man's ear, waited for him to adjust the volume on his hearing aids, and then repeated Lance's word. *"Racing, Mr. Nelson. He said, racing."*

"Ahhh. Yes. If you're doing any of that, young fella, I better be in the car with you."

She shook her head at the both of them and then helped herself to the last of the pretzels Mr. Nelson had stashed in his shirt pocket. "Men! You never grow up, do you?"

"Nope," Lance and Mr. Nelson said in unison.

"Hey, looks like your Dessert Squad is really getting around, Winnie. I saw you over by Silver Lake Park on my way home from my afternoon classes."

Silver Lake Park . . .

And, just like that, she was back in her funk.

Or would have been if Mr. Nelson's bony

elbow hadn't nudged her right back into the conversation . . .

"I have high hopes for it, but now, standing here, looking at you in that car, I'm wondering if I should go back and get a degree in history, instead," she joked. "I'll tell them Lance Reed sent me."

"What? Are you kidding me? I'd be the most despised man in this town if you stopped baking, Winnie Johnson."

"He's a floppin'," Mr. Nelson whispered. "Flop, flop, flop."

She rolled her eyes, checked his pocket one last time, and then smiled out at their neighbor. "Thanks, Lance."

"No problem. Well, hey, I better head out. I've got an eight A.M. class every day except Tuesday, and I didn't get to all my grading last night."

"Good night, Lance."

"G'night, Winnie. G'night, Mr. Nelson."

They watched him pull away from the curb and head down the street, the red glow of his taillights brightening and then disappearing as he turned into his driveway.

"He's a nice fish, Winnie."

"I'm not looking for fish, Mr. Nelson. This other one just kind of jumped on the plate in front of me. And I liked him."

I still do.

"It'll work out, Winnie Girl. You mark my words."

It wouldn't, but she still appreciated his concern. "So how are you? Feeling any better about the possibility of getting a new neighbor?"

His smile faltered, but he managed to regroup before she could call him on it. "Better? No. But I can accept it. I have to. We all do." With one hand on the rail and the other on his cane, Mr. Nelson turned and made his way back to the general vicinity of his chair. "What I can't accept is why someone isn't behind bars for killing Bart yet."

"Maybe something is happening behind the scenes that we're not privy to," she suggested. "You know, maybe the police are closing in on a suspect as we speak."

"There's no closing in, Winnie. Not in this town. We'd all know it if they were." He ran his free hand along the top of the chair and then raked it across his unshaven face. "No, the chief is too busy running traffic studies to decide whether that four-way stop on the eastern edge of town should actually be a light."

She wished she could argue, but she couldn't. The powers that be in Silver Lake were focused on revitalization, not on finding the killer of a man who wasn't too far from death's door to begin with.

"I'm still paying attention, Mr. Nelson. In fact, I want to find out where Sissy Donovan was the morning Bart was killed." She looked from Mr. Nelson to Bart's darkened house and back again. "You didn't see her that morning, did you?"

"I saw her the day before. When Ava knocked out her tooth running from Bart . . ."

"I know. But it was the next morning he was killed. Sometime between eight and nine, remember?" She considered the usual activity on Serenity Lane at that time and threw out some possibilities. "Ava's bus comes at what? Eight — eight ten?"

"Seven fifty-five. Though sometimes it's been as early as seven fifty-two. You should hear that one yelling at the driver when he shaves off them three minutes."

"*Ava* yells at the driver?"

"No. Sissy does. In front of Ava."

"So Sissy is always at the bus stop with Ava in the mornings, right?"

"She is."

"Does she ever leave Ava to wait alone?"

"Never."

She tried another avenue. "Have you ever seen them approaching the bus stop from a different direction? Like, say, Bart's drive-way?" She knew it was a long shot, especially considering that would have meant Ava being present when her mother suffocated an old man, but it was worth a chance.

Mr. Nelson's brow furrowed in thought as he undoubtedly forced his mind back to the previous week. When his head started shaking, she knew he'd come up empty.

"What about Cornelia?" she asked on the heels of a frustrated exhale that was far louder than she'd intended. "Is she walking Con-Man that early? And if she is, maybe she . . . or Harold . . . saw an unfamiliar car or an unfamiliar face that morning?"

"If there was someone who didn't belong on our street that morning, I'd have seen him myself," Mr. Nelson insisted around a series of yawns. "I — I was . . . right there . . . like I always am. Playing chess."

Playing chess . . .

Translation: in his own little world . . .

She made a mental note to talk to Cornelia and Harold the first chance she got. Maybe they saw or heard something.

Stepping forward, she whispered a kiss across the man's forehead and then gently guided him toward the front door. "Well, keep thinking. If something comes up, let me know. Until then, Sissy Donovan remains a person of interest."

CHAPTER 23

Winnie glanced at the timer tasked with monitoring the third and final batch of thumbprint cookies and groaned. Loudly.

"What? We're coming up with some good stuff here." Renee thrust her hand into the near-empty chip bowl and pulled out one of the only remaining intact pieces. "Of course, I've probably gained five more pounds in the process, but Bob's no longer counting, so who cares?"

There was no mistaking the catch in Renee's voice at the mention of her ex-husband. There was also no mistaking the anger that catch stoked inside Winnie.

Bob was a fool. Plain and simple. Changing him would be like trying to change the fact that Bart was dead. All she could do was work with the aftermath.

In Renee's case, that aftermath was finding a way to build up the woman's self-esteem. In Bart's case, that aftermath was making sure justice was served.

"Renee, you're gorgeous just the way you are. If you doubt me, go knock on Mr. Nelson's door downstairs. Or walk down Main Street in those heels of yours."

Renee helped herself to another chip. "I stand by my original question. What's with the groan just now?"

She looked down at the idea notebook and all the new dessert names and shrugged. "I don't know. It was kind of a two-folded — maybe even tri-folded — groan."

"You decipher; I'll get the cookies." Grabbing the oven mitt from the table, Renee stood and crossed to the oven. Then, flipping on the interior light, she checked the cookies and declared them done. "I have to say, Uh-Oh You Jammed Your Finger-Print Cookies has to be one of the most creative rescue desserts so far. I can only imagine the coach's face when you bring these by his office."

"I wish ones to rescue a person's motivation would come as easily as that one did. Then we could take the menu into some of the companies in and around Silver Lake."

One by one, Renee transferred the cookies from the baking sheet to the cooling rack. "So is that one of the reasons for the groan? The lack of motivation-themed dessert names?"

"Yup."

"I came up with one last night, but it doesn't have anything to do with motivation." Renee gave a quick check on the first two batches and then turned around to face Winnie. "Ty thinks it's silly, but I think it's kind of cute. Wanna hear it?"

"Sure." She exited off the left side of her chair and reached for the disposable platter on which she'd deliver the cookies to the Silver Lake Hornets coach.

"It's for a guy who's head over heels in love with someone."

Winnie arranged the first dozen cookies around the center of the plate and then reached for the second, pausing to take in her friend as she did. "Oh, this should be good . . ."

"Ready?"

"Yup."

"Nut 'n But-er cookies or cake." Renee's eyes narrowed and then widened with pride. "Get it? It's like saying, 'nothing but her' . . . and it'll be a butter cake or a butter cookie with nuts in it!"

She stopped mid cookie placement and laughed. "Cute. Very, very cute." And it was. It just didn't help attract companies . . .

"Can I add it to the book?" Renee asked.

"Add away. It's great."

"Cool." Renee crossed to the table, added the dessert to the menu list, and then returned to the counter to help Winnie. "Didn't you say you were going to make these *white chocolate* raspberry thumbprints?"

"That's right."

"Then shouldn't we drizzle on the white chocolate before you put them on the plate?" Then, waving off her own question, Renee added a few cookies herself. "Don't answer that. The white chocolate is already in the warming bag."

"Thanks." Winnie finished plating the first two dozen cookies and then wandered over to check the next batch. Another few minutes and they could be added as well. "I couldn't do this without you, Renee. I hope you know that."

"Yes, you could. But it's fun to pretend otherwise." Renee retrieved the bowl of chip dust from the table and carried it over to the sink to be cleaned along with the cookie pans. "So, back to the groan and its second reason . . ."

"Bart's killer needs to be found. It's been a week and a day. Surely someone saw something."

"What about Mr. Nelson? He's always sitting on the porch in the morning."

"But he was playing chess."

Renee filled the left side of the sink with soapy water and dunked the chip bowl inside. "Oh. So he saw nothing."

"Exactly."

Once it was good and soapy, Renee dipped the bowl into the right side of the sink and then sprayed off the rest of the soap. "You know, we *do* have a police department in this town, Winnie. They're the ones who should be stressing over who killed your neighbor."

"We don't have a suspect yet," Winnie pointed out. "At least the cops don't."

"Meaning?"

"Meaning I'm leaning heavily toward Sissy Donovan." Pulling her rescue bag with its warming compartment onto the counter, she began to pack the essentials for her next rescue — plates, napkins, forks, and a jar of red sugar crystals. As she worked, she shared details of her conversation with Sissy the previous afternoon. When she was done, she added the last of the cookies, grabbed her purse, and headed for the door. "I gotta get these over to the college now."

Renee turned off the water and quickly dried her hands. "You need any help?"

"No, I've got it."

293

"You sure?"

"I'm sure." She stopped at the top of the steps just long enough to glance back at her friend before beginning her descent down to the ambulance. "Call me on the cell if any new deliveries come in."

Winnie was on her way back to the ambulance when she heard her name from across the faculty parking lot at Silver Lake College. She contemplated the many positives associated with pretending not to hear, but, in the end, she just couldn't do it. After all, the whole reason she was back on campus for the third time in three days was because of the person now slaloming his way around cars to say hello.

She brought the stretcher to a stop and raised her hand in greeting, but Jay kept coming. And while one part of her wished he wouldn't, another part (the part that wanted to squeal with excitement) was glad he did.

"I was hoping I'd catch you," he said as he glided to a stop on the opposite side of the stretcher. "So how'd it go?"

"How'd it . . . *go*?" She knew she sounded like a moron, but it was the best she could do at the moment.

"With Coach Simpson." He raked his long

fingers through his hair and dropped his focus onto the empty stretcher between them. "I'd wanted to be there when you made the rescue, but a student showed up at my door as I was getting ready to head over to the athletic building, and he needed my help."

More than anything, she wanted to dull her senses when it came to Jay Morgan and the megawatt smile now making its way across his face, but he didn't make it easy, that was for sure. Especially when said smile was topped off with eyes trained on no one but her . . .

"Winnie?"

When it became apparent he was actually expecting a reply, she willed herself to say something, anything.

Keep it short. Keep it sweet.

"He loved it. So did his entire staff, based on how many of them were taking pictures and videos when I came through the door and started administering IV to his dessert."

"Awesome. That'll surely get you some more customers in the days and weeks to come."

"Thank you. I — I know you were a huge factor in today's delivery." She hated that her voice broke a little, hated the reason for it even more. But the last thing she wanted to do was reach for something that couldn't happen. "Well, I imagine you've got a class to teach, so I better let you go."

He consulted his watch and then helped guide the stretcher over to the ambulance. "My next class isn't for another forty-five minutes, so I've got time."

"Oh." She unlocked the rear latch, took control of the stretcher, and loaded it into the rig. Once everything was secure and ready for transport back to the house, she closed the door. "Well, I probably should be returning to my, um, house . . . in case another rescue request comes in."

There was no denying the way his smile faltered and his eyes dulled, but still, he pressed on. "Okay, then how about this weekend? There's a great local guitarist playing in one of the cafés downtown on Saturday night. Maybe we could go to dinner together and then check that out afterward?"

Music?

Dinner?

She tried to ignore the image now playing in her head — an image that had her sitting at a corner table laughing and talking for hours with the handsome man now waiting for her answer. But it refused to go away. Instead, it expanded to include the very real, very wonderful feeling of his hand on hers . . .

"Winnie?"

Call it silly, call it childish, but all her life she'd believed in Mr. Right — believed she'd know him as such the second they met.

She still believed that.

In fact now, thanks to the man holding her hand at that exact moment, she *knew* Mr. Right existed.

The only part she hadn't seen coming was the part about him having a daughter who wanted nothing whatsoever to do with Winnie.

Impossible circumstances . . .

Blinking against the sudden wetness in her eyes, she tugged her hand from his grasp and stepped back. "I have to go, Jay. Thanks. For everything."

CHAPTER 24

Short of fast-forwarding to the weekend and its vast opportunities to be antisocial, the next best scenario for avoiding the pain knocking at her heart was baking. Especially when that baking came with a fast-approaching deadline that was little more than an hour away.

"I considered telling the school we couldn't turn around an order for four dozen cookies this quickly, but I also didn't think we should be turning away business so soon in the game."

Winnie looked down at the dough in her bowl, added a drop of vanilla, and then pressed the power button on the electric mixer one more time. "You did the right thing, Renee," she said over the whir of the beaters. "The more we do, the more word of mouth we'll drum up. The more word of mouth we drum up, the more customers we'll get. The more customers we get, the

298

more likely it is Ty and Lovey won't starve."

"Phew!" Renee ripped off the last of four pieces of parchment paper and lined the final pan called into service to help recognize Silver Lake Elementary School's Big Thinkers Club. "I just wish you could have had more time at the college."

"Why? I did everything I needed to do. The coach and his staff were thrilled."

"I was thinking more along the lines of you getting to have some time with this new guy — *Jay*, right?" Renee placed the first pan and a cookie scoop in front of Winnie and then leaned against the refrigerator. "So when are you guys going out again?"

Winnie's mumbled response must have sounded enough like a real answer, because Renee continued on, her enthusiasm for the subject building to a hand-clapping crescendo. "Oh! I can help you with your hair and makeup if you want!"

Her hand shook as she dug the scoop into the dough and hoped Renee was too wrapped up in her own thoughts to notice.

"You could even borrow some of my shoes." Renee parted company with the fridge long enough to reach inside and grab a soda. "So where are you going? That'll help determine how we should style your hair. If you're going to dinner, we'll leave it down. If you're going to do something outdoors, like a hike, we can put it into a high ponytail with some flirty waves."

"So, um, what do you think of my adding a chocolate drizzle to these cookies? Do you think the kids would like that?"

Renee paused the soda can in front of her mouth and shrugged. "Sure. Why not? Aside from the fun of watching the drizzling process, it's more chocolate."

"Drizzle it is."

"Anyway, back to your hair —"

"Can you check the oven?" Winnie finished filling the first tray and moved on to the second. "Make sure I set it to preheat?"

Renee took a sip, peeked at the digital display, and then narrowed her eyes on Winnie. "Why are you being such a killjoy right now?"

"I'm not being a killjoy."

"Yes, you are."

She added two more scoops of dough to the second pan and then stepped to the right to start on the third. "I'm getting everything ready for the next job. How's that being a killjoy?"

"I'm trying to talk about your hair and clothes for your next date with Jay, and you're trying to sidetrack me with . . ." Renee smacked her can down on the counter and crossed to Winnie and the baking sheets. "Wait. This is deliberate, isn't it?"

"I always space my cookies apart like this. You know that." She knew she was being evasive, but it was preferable to answering questions she simply didn't want to answer. Maybe another time . . . When her emotions weren't so close to the surface . . .

"C'mon, Winnie. Talk to me."

"I am." She filled up the third and fourth trays with rapid-fire speed and then popped them all into the oven. With her distractions now baking, she seized on another. "Imagine you're stressed beyond belief and something comes along to make it even worse. How's The Last Straw-Berry Shortcake grab you?"

"What did he do?"

Crossing to the table, Winnie reached for a pen and their idea pad and added the dessert to the running list. "It doesn't have to be a guy. Women can have days that push them to the limit, too."

"I'm having one right now, thanks to you." Renee marched over to the table, stole the idea pad from Winnie's hand, and stuffed it into the living room chair next to a clearly perturbed Lovey.

"Me?" Winnie parroted.

"Yes, you. Tell me what happened with Jay right now!" Renee sat on the couch and patted the vacant cushion to her left. "Come. Sit. Talk to me."

"But I've got cookies to watch."

"Cookies that have another six minutes before we even have to check them." Renee patted the couch again. "Come. Sit. Now."

Winnie did as she was ordered but not without a fair amount of feet dragging and mumbling.

"I don't get this, Winnie." Renee tossed one throw pillow in Winnie's lap and used the other to support her own back. "You were over the moon about this guy yesterday."

I still am.

Careful not to share that thought aloud, Winnie did her best to sum up the issue as succinctly as possible. "We're not suited to each other."

"Excuse me?"

"I bake. He . . . teaches."

"And?"

"And, um, his schedule . . . as it is . . . and, um . . . the fact that he has a kid . . . means he has to lead a pretty buttoned-up life."

At first, Renee's laugh was merely startling, but as it continued (and continued) it crossed into annoying territory. "*You,* Winnie Johnson, are the most buttoned-up

302

person I know."

Winnie blinked, and then blinked again.

"Don't you dare pretend you don't know what I'm talking about," Renee protested.

"I — I don't . . ." Pulling her hand from its near death grip on the pillow, Winnie reached up and checked her nose.

Same size . . .

"How many times over the past few weeks have I asked you to go to a club with me on weekends that Ty is with Bob?"

"Um. A few?"

"That's right. And your reasons for turning me down?"

She lowered her hand back down to the pillow and pulled it to her chest. "I think one of the times I was having dinner with Bridget. And . . . another time I was helping Mr. Nelson with something."

Renee's head bobbed along with each reason Winnie shared. When the reasons stopped, so, too, did Renee's head. "Don't forget the time you had two more chapters to read in your book . . ."

"It was a really good book," she said in her defense.

"You're thirty-four. You're single. And you're beautiful. Yet you aren't dating, or even trying to date, because you prefer to be home reading and hobnobbing with the

303

blue hairs."

Winnie rested her chin on the pillow and stared at Lovey (happily licking her private parts). "You know, I've never understood why people say that. *Blue hairs* . . . I mean, what's with that? I'd get saying silver hairs or white hairs or even *no* hairs. But *blue* hairs? It's false advertising."

The ding of the timer saved her from further discussion (and Lovey from completely finishing her preening). "Cookies are done!"

She was halfway to the kitchen when she noticed Renee hadn't moved. In fact, a glance over her shoulder revealed a gape-mouthed woman who looked as if she'd gotten run over by a truck.

Or a Dessert Squad . . .

Laughing at her own funny, she slid an oven mitt onto her hand, opened the oven, and pulled out four sheets of perfectly baked Smart Cookie cookies. "Mmmm. These came out perfect!"

"You're too much, you know that?"

"No, I'm extraordinary —" She thumped the last pan down on top of the cooling rack and jogged back into the living room. Stopping beside Lovey, she reached a hand between the cat (hissing, of course) and the cushion and extracted her idea book. "I just came up with another rescue dessert! You're Egg-straordinary Custard for someone who needs a little stroking!"

It wasn't until she was a solid mile from the house before Winnie finally let herself breathe.

Somehow, someway, she'd managed to dodge Renee's questions (and frustrated glares) about Jay right up until the moment it was time to head out to Silver Lake Elementary School. She'd finished the cookies, filled the IV bag with melted chocolate, packed her rescue bag, and carried everything to the car. Every time her friend tried to insert another question, Winnie had found a way to work it into another dessert name.

With any luck, the members of the Big Thinkers Club would have lots of questions about her Dessert Squad and she could delay returning to the house until after Renee had left for the day . . .

At the traffic light she reached for the power button on the radio, only to pull her hand back at the weight of Lovey's stare. "Don't you start on me, Little Miss, or I'll take you back to the house right now."

No. Renee's still there . . .

Releasing a sigh born of equal parts

305

frustration, irritation, and downright disappointment, Winnie dropped her head onto the headrest and waited for the light to turn green. "I really liked him, Lovey. Liked him a lot. But his daughter needs to come first."

Lovey stood up, stretched, and then lowered herself back down to the passenger seat. If she had an opinion on the subject of Jay Morgan, the feline kept it to herself.

When the light changed, they lurched forward with the rest of the early afternoon traffic headed toward the outskirts of town. Some were probably heading to the mall in nearby Jennings, some to the park to play or work out, and some back home after an early shift at work or a much-needed stop at the grocery store.

Along the way, people stopped and looked at Winnie as she went by. The first few times, she found herself peeking in the rearview mirror to see if she'd forgotten to comb her hair (she hadn't) or to see if she looked as strung out as she felt (she did). But eventually, she began to realize passing drivers and the occasional pedestrian were checking out her ambulance and the Emergency Dessert Squad logo that claimed both sides of the vehicle.

"You know something, Lovey? I think we might really have a shot with this idea." At

Lovey's yawn, she pulled her right hand from the steering wheel and pointed at the cat. "Which means *you* might actually get a cat toy the next time I stop at the store."

She slowed as they approached the school crossing sign and then turned into the upper level parking lot for her pick of at least a half dozen unoccupied visitor spots. Shutting off the car, Winnie couldn't help but smile at the way Lovey jumped up and surveyed their surroundings. "I hate to break it to you, Lovey, but I can't take you with me on this call. It's a school. No pets allowed. Right now, in this weather, it's okay for you to wait for me. But once it starts getting hot, you'll have to stay at home for stuff like this."

Reaching across Lovey's seat, she rolled down the window just enough to provide air flow through the cab and then made her way around to the back of the rig. Two (okay, it was really closer to three) minutes later, she rolled the stretcher and its four dozen You Are One Smart Cookie cookies up to the main entrance and pressed the button for admittance.

She didn't need to look over her shoulder toward the car to know Lovey was watching. She could feel the animal's eyes burning a hole in the back of her head. Still, she managed to smile when the school's secretary buzzed her in.

"You must be with the Dessert Squad." The woman pulled out a phone and snapped a picture of first the cookie-topped stretcher, and then Winnie. "I saw the article in the paper over the weekend and then read something about it on one of those social media sites last night."

"That's great to hear." Winnie reached into her pocket and pulled out a thin stack of business cards she'd printed off the computer. "If you know of anyone who might be interested in a dessert rescue, feel free to pass on my card."

"Oh, I will. I most definitely will." The woman set the cards on the desk just inside the door and then returned her attention to the stretcher and the pole Winnie had affixed to the top edge of the stretcher before coming inside. "Is that an IV pole?"

"Yes, it is." She set her rescue bag on the bottom edge of the stretcher and unzipped it to show the woman the melted icing inside. "Once I get to the room where the kids are, I'll attach the icing bag to the pole and drizzle the top of each cookie as I hand them out."

"Oh, they're going to love that." The woman pointed Winnie's gaze down the hallway. "The children are in the room at the end of the hall."

"Thanks." She zipped up the bag, hoisted it back onto her shoulder, and guided the stretcher in the correct direction. Halfway down the hallway, though, she stopped.

There, in the middle of a bulletin board highlighting the first half of the year, was a picture of Ethel and Bart, smiling at the camera from amid a circle of students Winnie estimated to be about eight years old.

"What's this?" she asked, looking back at the woman now seated behind her desk.

The woman rose and ventured down the hallway to stand beside Winnie. "These are pictures of people in the community who came and spent their time with the children this year. Some talked about their time in the military, some talked about growing up in other countries, and some talked about favorite books. The children learn so much from these types of visits."

She felt bad not being able to maintain eye contact with the woman, but she couldn't stop looking at the picture of her friends.

Ethel looked so happy sitting there, surrounded by children, with the love of her life by her side . . .

"I take it, by your expression, that you knew the Wagners?" The woman shook her head sadly then stepped close enough to the board to run her hand along the picture. "I was shocked that he actually let the children hold his coin, but he did. He said it was a piece of history that belonged as much to them as it did to him.

"Miss Laughner, the fourth grade teacher, kept close watch on the students as they passed it around, though. And I swear you could hear her sigh of relief once it made its way back to Mr. Wagner."

Winnie felt the lump of sadness rising up her throat as she studied the man smiling back at her from the wall. "Bart loved to tell everyone he met about that coin. Every time he told his story, you'd think it was the first time. His excitement never waned."

"He certainly had our fourth graders hanging on his every word that day."

"I'm not surprised." And she wasn't. Bart had a way of making people hang on his every word regardless of their age.

"Do you know what will become of that coin now? Will it go into a museum?"

She gave herself a moment to drink in the couple's happiness and then turned her attention back on the woman at her side.

"Bart has it. And he's probably telling all the angels in Heaven about it as we speak."

"You're probably right."

"Well, I better get these cookies to the kids." Setting her hands on the side of the stretcher once again, she continued down the hallway to the very last room and the dozen or so faces now pressed against the glass-paneled wooden door, watching her approach. The sound of their squeals escaping through the miniscule gap between the floor and the door helped ease the lingering sadness brought on by the picture of her friends.

"Enjoy the moment, Winnie," she whispered under her breath. It was a sentiment Ethel had shared with her often — a sentiment Winnie was determined to heed, one way or the other.

CHAPTER 25

For the first time in thirty-four years, Winnie knew what it felt like to be a rock star. The fact that the dozen or so adoring eyes cast in her direction were merely waiting for her to hand them a cookie was beside the point.

"Boys and girls, Miss Winnie will be happy to drizzle white or milk chocolate onto your cookie provided you form a nice line and use your best manners." Mrs. Hopkins, the Big Thinkers Club advisor, held her right hand in the air and waited as twelve children scrambled into a line amid a background of giggles, quiet protests over position, and then, finally, silence. Nodding in approval, the fifty-something who doubled as Silver Lake Elementary School's second grade teacher brought her hand to her chin and scrunched her face in thought. "For my older Thinkers . . . Miss Winnie has brought forty-eight cookies, and we have twelve members. How should we divide that?"

A larger boy (probably a fifth grader) at the end of the line grinned and poked the slightly shorter boy in front of him. "We each get four!"

Mrs. Hopkins nodded, her face still scrunched. "We could, or . . ."

A girl with two brown braids who wasn't quite as tall as the first boy yet seemed to be about the same age shot her hand into the air.

"Yes, Tina?" Mrs. Hopkins prodded.

"We could invite the Big Helpers Club to have some, too."

Mrs. Hopkins beamed with pride. "I think that would be a marvelous idea —"

"But if we do that, we can't get four," the larger boy said in protest.

"I believe they have ten in their club today," Mrs. Hopkins said, scrunching her face once again.

Tina closed her eyes briefly as she worked through the latest math problem in her head. When she was done, she smiled at the teacher. "We could have two each and four left over!"

The larger boy's groan was helped to a rapid death by a stern look from Mrs. Hopkins. When the advisor was confident her nonverbal message had been received

313

and understood, she returned her focus to Tina. "Since you thought of the idea, why don't you go across the hall to Miss Laughner's room and invite the Big Helpers and their guests over for a cookie."

Then, turning back to Winnie, Mrs. Hopkins nodded toward the first child in line. "Why don't you start handing out the first of the two cookies now so the line won't be too long when the other children join us? If someone is full after one, they can either take their second cookie home at the end of our meeting or set it aside for someone else."

"Sounds good to me." Winnie winked at the little red-haired boy hopping from foot to foot in the front of the line and then waved him over to the stretcher. "So, what would you like? Brown drizzle or white drizzle?"

Cookie by cookie, and drizzle choice by drizzle choice, Winnie was slowly but surely paring the line down, when the door just over her left shoulder opened and a second line of brand-new squealers merged in with a returning Tina and the last of the three Thinkers. "Welcome boys and —"

"Winnie?"

She swung her focus to the left and the two uniform-clad males smiling at her in amusement.

"Greg? Chuck? What are you guys doing here?"

Before either could answer, a tiny little girl about midway down the line pointed at the men. "They let us go inside their ambulance!"

An even smaller little boy peeked his head around his classmate and pointed at the IV pole next to Winnie. "They have that same thing, too!"

Greg approached from the left, studying Winnie's drip bag and stretcher as he did. "Looking good . . ."

She forced her eyes to remain on the little boy rather than on Master Sergeant Hottie and his equally intrigued sidekick, Chuck. "The one Mr. Greg and Mr. Chuck showed you is a *real* one . . . one that helps people who are sick or hurt. Mine is just a pretend one."

"Yeah, but yours has chocolate in it." The larger boy from the Thinkers Club crammed the rest of his inaugural cookie into his mouth and then rejoined the line. "My mom says chocolate helps people, too."

Winnie laughed along with the teachers as she returned to drizzling duties for the rest of the first-round kids. When she was done, she set the decorating tube down, wiped her hands on a white cloth, and focused on the paramedic and his EMT. "Did you just get here?" she asked.

Chuck's finger shot halfway into the air over the plate of remaining cookies and began a silent but obvious count while Greg answered Winnie's question. "We've been here for about an hour. The kids toured the ambulance and then we went back into their room and answered questions about what they saw."

"But I didn't see the ambulance when I pulled in . . ."

"We're parked in the lower lot."

"Ahhh."

Chuck's finger stopped moving. "Think there will be any left for me?"

"C'mon, Chuck, they're for the kids." Greg met Winnie's eyes and then rolled his own. "Chuck has a one-track mind when it comes to food. If he's not thinking about food, he's eating it. And if he's not eating it, he's thinking about it."

"Hey. I don't like waste," Chuck quipped. "None of us should."

Mrs. Hopkins stepped over to the stretcher and swept her hand toward the cookies. "You are each welcome to try one." Then, turning to the head of the Big Helpers Club, she said, "Jeannie, there is one for you as well."

"Miss Laughner, they're really, really good," came a little voice from the other side of the room.

Miss Laughner smiled at the student and then held a hand out to Winnie. "I'm Jeannie Laughner, fourth grade teacher during school hours and advisor for our school's Big Helpers Club two Wednesday afternoons a month."

"Miss Laughner . . ." It took a moment, but the name finally registered in her head, momentarily claiming her smile in the process. "I was admiring one of your photographs on the bulletin board in the front hallway as I was coming in."

The woman's thinning but still dark eyebrows furrowed ever so slightly. "Oh? Which one?"

"The one of Bart and Ethel Wagner. I understand Bart came in and showed his special coin to your students."

Chuck plucked a cookie from the pile and placed it next to Winnie's IV tube. "Can I do a mix of white *and* milk chocolate on the top?"

Without a word, she retrieved the first tube, drizzled white chocolate across the cookie in a pattern of interesting swirls, and then swapped it for the second tube and its more traditional, darker contents.

When she was done, she handed the cookie to Chuck and pointed to the remaining cookies. "Miss Laughner? Mrs Hopkins? Greg?"

"Oh yeah."

Mrs. Hopkins laughed and pointed at Greg. "What he said."

Miss Laughner nodded but brought the conversation back to Winnie. "Mr. Wagner was wonderful with my students. His stories about life and his coin had the children on the edge of their seats . . . even the ones who react to very little."

"No surprise there." Chuck plucked a cookie crumb off his uniform shirt and popped it in his mouth. "I couldn't have been a whole lot older when I heard his story the first time, either. In fact, on the way home in the car with my dad that day, I seriously considered abandoning my baseball card collection in favor of coins."

Winnie's answering smile came equipped with a sudden moistening of her eyes. Oh, how she missed Bart and Ethel . . .

"That's why I can't figure out why anyone — especially a mother of one of our students — would rip his picture in half."

Dropping the icing tube back onto the

stretcher, Winnie stared at the fourth grade teacher. "But I saw the picture just now. It was perfectly fine."

"Because I ran off another copy and tacked it back up."

"The *why* is simple, Jeannie," said Mrs. Hopkins. "She did it out of anger. Much like her daughter or any other second grader reacts when someone won't share on the playground."

Winnie bobbed her head to the right to gain a better view of Mrs. Hopkins, but just as she did, Miss Laugher spoke, reclaiming her focus in short order. "But she's not a child."

Mrs. Hopkins narrowed the space between them, briefly glanced over her shoulder in search of any potential eavesdroppers, and then lowered her voice to a raspy whisper. "Wait until you give the pageant princess a less than perfect grade on something. You'll rethink that statement."

Pageant princess . . .

The women exchanged knowing glances while Greg and Chuck looked from the plate of cookies to Winnie and back again.

Pageant princess . . .

"Boys and girls," Mrs. Hopkins said, spinning around to face the children, "if you're ready for your second cookie, you may line

319

up when the big hand reaches the five. But you must do so quietly and orderly."

Pageant —

Winnie yanked her gaze up to Miss Laughner's. "Wait. You're talking about Sissy Donovan, aren't you?"

The fourth grade teacher's face reddened. "I — I'm sorry. We shouldn't be talking like this."

"No, it's not that. It's just . . ." Winnie's voice trailed off as she mentally revisited the conversation from the beginning. "Wait! Are you telling me that Sissy Donovan is the one who ripped Bart's picture in half?"

A moment's hesitation was followed by a slow nod. "One of my students saw her do it."

Out of the corner of her eye, Winnie could see the students lining up once again, their anticipation for another cookie as tangible as it had been for the first. "Do you remember when this happened?" she asked while readying the tubes and the cookies for round two.

"Last Tuesday." Mrs. Hopkins stepped to the side and shook her finger at some overeager students at the back of the line. Once they responded accordingly, she turned back to Winnie. "Shortly after our post-lunch recess, Mrs. Donovan brought

320

Ava into school late. I'd assumed they were just stopping by to pick up missed work, but Ava wanted to stay."

"Why did she come in late?"

"Ava knocked out a tooth the previous day and, as a result, spent all of Tuesday morning at some expensive dentist in Larkmont."

"Larkmont? Wow, that's a hike." Greg moved in beside her, his lips stopping just shy of her ear. "Winnie, I think this kid might cry if you don't drizzle his cookie — stat."

"Huh? What?" She stopped, looked straight ahead, and smiled apologetically at the little boy. "I'm sorry, sweetheart . . . white chocolate coming right up." Grabbing the tube between her fingers, she made a smiley face with the melted chocolate and handed the cookie to the boy. Then, taking advantage of every shred of ooh-ahh time the design incurred, she glanced up at Greg. "How long of a drive is that?"

"To where? Larkmont?" At her nod, he looked at Chuck, threw out an initial guess of ninety minutes, and then amended it to an hour and forty-five minutes each way.

An hour and forty-five minutes each way . . .
Three and a half hours of driving in total . . .
Back at the school shortly after lunch . . .
And, just like that, Winnie was back to

square one in her quest to find Bart's murderer.

CHAPTER 26

Somehow, even amid the fog of disappointment and worry hovering around every step she took, Winnie couldn't help but marvel at the way perspective could change. For two years, she'd made this same walk, twice a day, every day — a nearly mile-long trek that had been doubly onerous after standing on her feet for as much as twelve hours at a time. Yet now that she no longer had to rely on her feet for all her transportation needs, she actually welcomed the opportunity to get outside and clear her head.

Her visit to Silver Lake Elementary School had stoked up so much internal angst in its final thirty minutes she simply couldn't handle being hissed at for sitting on the couch . . . or walking across the kitchen . . . or (God forbid) stretching out across her *own* bed. So she'd grabbed her purse, made sure the perpetual hisser had fresh food and water, and took to the pavement, her destination uncertain for the first half of the trip. Eventually, though, as her thoughts skirted between Bart and Jay, she realized she was headed toward her bakery.

Or, rather, the area in which her bakery had been before it was driven from its walls by a delusional landlord who fancied Silver Lake's Main Street as something akin to the kind of popular thoroughfares that drew people to places like Chicago and New York.

She knew she should be pleased with the Dessert Squad's first three days, and she was, but having Delectable Delights virtually snatched from her hands by such idiocy still stung a little. Fortunately (or unfortunately, as the case was turning out to be), suspect lists (or lack thereof) and unexpected date requests had a way of bulldozing over that sting fairly well.

If she hadn't been so thrown by losing Sissy as a suspect, maybe she would have picked up on Greg's cues a little faster, giving herself time to come up with a better reply to his dinner invitation than "Uhhh, um, wow . . . sure."

"Sure," she muttered as she crossed a side street and continued the final two blocks to what was referred to as downtown. What had she been thinking? She didn't want to go out with Greg Stevens. Yes, he was gor-

geous. Hot, even. But Master Sergeant Hottie wasn't who floated her boat.

Jay Morgan did that.

Jay . . .

Suddenly, she was back at Beans, joking and laughing with him in a way she hadn't joked or laughed with a man under sixty-five in years (okay, ever). Seeing him in her head, with his chin propped in his hand, leaning forward against the table as if he couldn't get enough of Winnie, was worth every palpitation she was experiencing at that moment . . .

Or was until a decidedly feminine version of Jay's face claimed center stage and immediately drained the water on which Winnie's boat had dared to float.

No, Jay Morgan simply wasn't an option.

She could almost hear Renee's voice in her head, telling her to keep the date with Master Sergeant Hottie. The problem was whether she should listen.

If she listened, she was being unfair to Greg — a man who seemed to genuinely like her, and whom she saw as nothing more than a potential friend.

If she didn't listen, she would continue living exactly the way she had since moving to Silver Lake. Only now she had a cat . . .

She looked up as she crossed the next side

street and stepped back onto the sidewalk, her old storefront now mere steps away. Pushing thoughts of Jay, Greg, Caroline, and Bart from her mind, she allowed herself to really see the rectangular dark green shingle that hung where her pink and white one had been just eight days earlier.

In the center of the green shingle, in thick black letters trimmed with white, the sign read:

THE CORNER POCKET

"The Corner Pocket," she repeated aloud as her feet automatically stopped in front of the open door. Peeking inside, she saw a painter's ladder, an assortment of paint cans, and the back side of a man clad in paint-spattered jeans and a loose-fitting shirt. The back half of the room that had once held her dessert cases and a few small tables now boasted one solid red wall, a stark white wall with a single thick stripe of yellow running horizontal across the center, and a solid green on the wall currently being painted.

She watched as the man returned his roller to the tray, loaded it up with paint, and applied it to the third wall one careful swath at a time. It wasn't necessarily a decorating scheme she would have thought of, but seeing it come together under Mark's careful hand made it a veritable no-brainer for a billiards hall.

The part she still couldn't rationalize, though, was how Mark — a man well-known in town for a history of gambling (and losing) — suddenly had enough money to open a brand-new business in a space she (a proven business owner) couldn't afford.

"Hey there, Winnie."

She lifted her gaze back to the top of the ladder and waved at the man now alternating between wiping his hands on a cloth and gesturing her inside.

"C'mon in. Tell me what you think . . ."

Nibbling on her lower lip, Winnie fought through the desire to preserve her memory of the storefront's previous incarnation and stepped inside. Slowly.

"Wow, you've really been working hard in here." She heard the slight shake to her voice and hoped it went unnoticed. The last thing she needed was to get all sentimental with her last remaining suspect in Bart's murder.

Mark set the roller inside the tray and then climbed down the ladder. At the bottom, he pointed to the first two walls. "Tell me you get what I'm doing here . . ."

"Sure. The red wall and this green one are the solid balls . . . and the back wall is for the striped balls." Now that she was inside, she found it wasn't so hard. The fact that Mark's version of the space bore absolutely no similarity to hers helped. "And your sign out front is supposed to be the inside of the pool table, yes? With the white trim around the black letters to simulate the eight ball?"

A smile spread across the man's aging face like wildfire. "Awesome! I was hoping I'd pulled it off!"

"And you have." She inched across the series of drop cloths lining the floor around them and pointed toward the back of the room. "Are you going to put the tables in vertically with the back wall?"

Mark reached up, lifted the bill of his painter's hat, swiped the back of his free hand across his forehead, and then adjusted his hat back into place. "That's what I envisioned in my head, but when I got in here with my measuring tape, I realized trying to put in my tables in that way wouldn't give players room to move around the tables. So I'm going horizontally. Gives me room for four tables and maybe even some chairs people can sit in between play or during tournaments."

"Sounds like you've got it all figured out," she mused.

"Been dreaming about it for years but never had the money to give it a go until now."

She felt her eyebrow lift along with her curiosity. "So what's different about now?"

"Dad told me to go for my dream."

She stifled the urge to gasp and was more than grateful for the reprieve Mark's brief glance back at his wall provided. Before she could formulate some sort of response, though, he continued, his voice exhibiting a rare burst of emotion that seemed surprisingly genuine. "When Mom passed, any remaining money from my biological father's estate immediately transferred to me. It wasn't tons, but it was enough to open this place." Mark waved her over to a pair of folding chairs in the center of the room and dropped onto the second one. "Initially, I figured I'd hold on to it. You know, in case Dad went into a rapid decline in the wake of Mom's death. But Dad wanted no part of that. He said he had money of his own to take care of his needs and that I should use my biological father's money to get this place going.

"That's the way Dad was. Always supporting me even when I didn't deserve it. That's why I want to do this place right. I want to finally be the success my parents always believed I'd be, even when I did everything to show them otherwise."

Lowering herself onto the first chair, she found herself swallowing over the same lump that appeared in her throat every time she thought of Ethel and Bart. "So then if you had the money to start this place all on your own, why were you pressuring your dad to sell his house?"

The second the question was out, she found herself wishing for a rewind button. Talk about pushing things . . .

Surprisingly, though, Mark didn't even flinch. Instead, he dropped forward, propped his forearms on his thighs, and hung his head. "I hated the thought of him being alone in that house all day long. I mean, that place was *them,* you know? Mom's absence was suffocating."

"And you thought a nursing home would be better?"

His head shot up, his eyes pinning hers. *"Nursing home?* I didn't want Dad in a nursing home. I wanted him at my place . . . *with me."*

It was a part of the story she hadn't known. One that didn't completely mesh with the version told to her by Bridget . . .

"So you're saying Bart was all for the move?"

His dark eyes disappeared from view for what seemed like an eternity before reappearing beside deep creases. "Dad refused to go. Said his home was Mom's home and he was going to stay there until he took his last breath. He was stubborn that way."

Mark released a weary sigh and then dropped his face into his hands, muffling his words as he did. "But no matter how stubborn he was, there was no denying what being in that house without Mom was doing to him. And he knew it. Looking back, I wish I hadn't pushed the issue so many times. Heck, I even made up flyers on the house two weeks ago and showed them to him." He picked up his head, threw his body back against the chair, and stared up at the ceiling. "Man, he went ballistic when I did that. Yet, when he called me that last night and told me he couldn't do it anymore, he referred to that flyer. Said, 'Get them things out there before I change my mind.' So I did. And then I got the call that they'd found him — that *you* found him."

She closed her eyes against the memory of Bart's lifeless body and forced herself to remain in the present, with the man seated in the next chair — a man whose pain was so raw and so real she could no longer keep the emotion from her own voice. "I'm sorry, Mark. I really am. Your parents were the best."

For a moment she wasn't sure he heard her, but, eventually, he sat up tall and met her gaze head-on. "They loved you, Winnie. I hope you know that."

"I do. And I loved them, too."

Mark's smile was back, only this time, it held a hint of sadness. "I know about the pies you brought him each week for Mom. That was a really awesome thing to do."

Oh, what she wouldn't give to make Bart another pie . . .

Shaking off the thought, she reached across the gap between their chairs and patted the top of Mark's hand. "And I think what you did for your dad with his coin was pretty awesome, too."

He drew back. "What are you talking about?"

"Burying him with it."

His eyes narrowed with confusion. "Buried him with it? I didn't bury him with it." He pulled his hand from hers and palmed his face, grief turning to horror. "My God, I — I didn't even think about that . . . I'm such an idiot."

Slowly he let his hand drop down to his

lap as he, once again, met her eyes. "Do you think it's too late? I mean, should I have him exhumed so I could put it in the casket with him?"

She considered his question and the pain in which it was asked and gave the only answer she could. "No. I think you should hold on to it. As a memento of your dad. Share its history as proudly as he did."

Mark's nod was slow to come, but once it did, it came with a smile. "You're right. Dad got that coin from *his* father, just as I will get it from *my* dad."

"*Will* get?" she echoed.

"I'll stop by the house tonight and pick it up."

She stared at him, waiting for his words to carry some other sort of meaning. But no matter how hard she tried to squeeze something different out, only one response fit. "It's not there, Mark. The case is empty and Bart's coin is gone."

CHAPTER 27

She lifted her fist to the door and knocked
louder, any guilt she should have felt over
the late hour paling in comparison against
the need to vent. Sure, she'd heard of
would-be home buyers taking things when
Realtors weren't looking, but to do that to
Bart? With something that meant so much
to him?

It wasn't right.

It wasn't right at all.

"Mr. Nelson?" she called between knocks.
"It's me. Winnie. Could we talk?"

Pulling her hand back, she pressed her ear
to the door and listened.

Nothing.

Defeated, she stepped back, turned toward
the stairs, and began the slow climb to the
top, trying, with each step, to envision
Lovey as a sounding board. Technically,
with Lovey, Winnie didn't have to worry
about malfunctioning hearing aids and hav-

ing to repeat herself all the —

The door at the top of the steps creaked open, and Mr. Nelson peered out from her entryway. "Well, would you lookee who's here, Lovey. It's your momma."

"Mr. Nelson!" She ran the rest of the way up the steps and into her apartment, the welcoming hiss from the living room barely registering against her excitement. "I was just knocking on your door, hoping you weren't asleep yet."

"Asleep? With you still out and about?" Mr. Nelson pushed the door shut behind her and caned his way into the living room. When he reached Lovey's armchair, he snapped his fingers for the cat to move and then sat.

"How did you do that?" she asked, awe-struck. "She won't give up that chair for *me.*"

"Give it time, Winnie Girl. She'll come around." A quick pat on his lap brought Lovey back to the chair (and Mr. Nelson's lap) with an audible purr. "Been out with that fella you were telling me about, have you?"

"Fella?"

"The one with the daughter."

Jay . . .

She shook the business professor's image

from her thoughts and lowered herself onto the couch. "I was with Mark."

"Hark? That's the fella's name?"

Waving aside his words, she leaned forward and spoke louder. "I was with Mark, Mr. Nelson."

"Mark?"

At his continued confusion, she added more information. "Mark Reilly. Bart's son."

"Mark has a *daughter?"* Mr. Nelson asked. "Does Bridget know this?"

She allowed herself to sink backward against the cushion, grabbing a throw pillow and hugging it to her chest as she did. "If Mark had a daughter, Bridget would know."

Mr. Nelson took a moment to nod in agreement and then turned up the volume in his right ear. "I'm not sure Mark is the right man for you, Winnie."

"We weren't on a date, Mr. Nelson. I just happened to see him when I went for a walk. He was painting the walls in his new pool hall." She thought back to her evening and the rare side of Mark she'd witnessed. "He's doing a nice job. Bart would be proud of him."

"He always was proud of that boy. Sometimes he had to search real hard to find something worth being proud of, but he always managed to find something."

"Bart had decided to sell, Mr. Nelson. Those flyers I saw were *his* idea." At Mr. Nelson's obvious skepticism, she amended her statement to help fill in the gaps. "I mean, the initial idea was Mark's, but the decision to finally put them up was Bart's."

"And you believe that?" Mr. Nelson asked quietly.

"I do."

Any urge he may have had to call her on her sudden conviction remained in check as he turned his attention to Lovey. "Your momma has always been a smart young lady. No reason to think anything different now."

She hiked her legs up onto the couch and ran her finger along the throw pillow's simple design. "Mr. Nelson?" she finally asked, looking up. "What can you tell me about Bart's coin?"

Mr. Nelson's hand stopped as he leaned his head against the back of his seat, a thoughtful smile claiming his lips. "He got it from his daddy. Who got it from a member of President Roosevelt's Secret Service detail."

"I remember something about a floral shop. Is that right?"

"Bart's daddy was a florist. One of President Roosevelt's Secret Service agents had a standing order for a floral delivery to his wife." Mr. Nelson returned to petting Lovey, but his thoughts, his memories, were clearly somewhere else. "See? That's why I never got married. I wouldn't have thought of sending flowers every week."

"You'd have thought of your own things."

"Eh," he said, waving her words away. "I'd have been no good at marriage."

She opened her mouth to offer another protest but let it go. After all, what difference did it make? Mr. Nelson was set in his ways. "Tell me more."

"Bart's daddy filled that order faithfully for more than twenty years. Never forgot a one, from what Bart said."

It was hard not to smile at that. Still, she wanted to hear more. "Okay . . ."

"In thanks for his daddy's dedication, the agent gave him that gold double eagle coin."

"It was made in 1934, right?"

"In 1933," he corrected. "There were more than four hundred thousand of them made."

She pulled the pillow from her chest and slowly turned it around in her hands, her mind working through Mr. Nelson's words — words she'd heard many times from Bart yet wanted to commit to memory now.

"Four hundred thousand sounds like a lot."

"Because it is. Especially back in 1933."

"So the fact that he got it from a member of the president's Secret Service is what made it so special, right?"

Mr. Nelson looked at her across the coffee table, his head starting to shake before she'd even finished her question. "What made it special was the fact that none of those four hundred thousand coins were ever released to the public."

"But why?" she asked, lowering the pillow to her lap.

"During the Depression, President Roosevelt decided to take America off the gold standard. When he did that, it became illegal to have any gold coins."

"But this coin Bart's dad was given was gold . . ."

"Indeed it was."

"So that means it has to be really rare."

Mr. Nelson slid his hands underneath Lovey, scooted the cat into the miniscule gap between his legs and the side of the chair, and then inched forward until he was ready to stand. Wrapping his hand around the top of the cane Bart hand carved for him years earlier, he rose to his feet and began his journey to the door. "Rare just like you, Winnie Girl."

"I wish that were true." She cringed at the woe-is-me tone of her voice, but before she could counteract it with a proper thank-you, he steadied himself with the edge of the now-open door and pointed the end of his cane at Winnie.

"You care about folks, Winnie Girl. Really care about 'em. Especially us old-timers. Most people your age wrote us off a long time ago. But not you. Can't put a price on something that rare. Though, if you could, I'd pay it in a heartbeat."

Winnie pushed the covers off to the side and swung her feet over the edge of the bed. Two hours of forcing her eyes closed, counting sheep (or, rather, raspberry mousse parfaits), and one-sided conversation with a cat who'd long since left the room was indication enough that sleep wasn't going to be forthcoming anytime soon.

She could get a jump on the day's baking. But there weren't any orders yet.

She could track down Lovey and try to become friends, but exercises in futility had never been her forte.

She could turn on Mr. Nelson's old tube television set and flip through the channels. But the last time she did that at three in the morning, she ended up buying a set of measuring cups that melted in the dish-washer.

The only thing left was the computer, which, unfortunately, meant dislodging Lovey from the chair on which she'd suddenly chosen (for the first time, mind you) to sleep away the wee hours of the morning.

Three hisses (and what sounded an awful lot like a growl) later, Winnie clicked the icon for solitaire and began to play. The first game, she won. The second game, she didn't. Halfway through the third game, she switched over to the Internet. She checked Renee's Facebook page (she'd posted a picture of Ty playing baseball) first, and then moved on to Bridget's and the picture depicting the latest blanket the elderly woman had completed.

She contemplated updating her own page but discarded the idea when she realized she had nothing to say. Then, moving the cursor up to the search bar, she typed in Jay's name. A dozen or so people with the same name popped up, but it took Winnie just seconds to locate the correct one thanks to the thumbnail-sized profile picture of the business teacher himself. She clicked on the tiny photo and instantly found herself staring at a larger version of the same picture

— one that showed his smile and his eyes with such startling clarity she actually sucked in her breath.

For far longer than she knew she should, she studied his every feature, memorizing the curve of his face, the arch of his brow, the honest directness of his gaze. More than anything she wanted to know what he was doing at that moment (although sleeping was a good guess), but because they weren't Internet friends, she couldn't see anything beyond his picture.

Finally, she forced herself to log off her account. Next, she checked her Twitter account, scrolling through some of the tweets she'd missed over the last few weeks. A few pages in, she grew bored and abandoned her efforts. Her e-mail account yielded nothing capable of helping pass the time, and she closed out of that, too.

She was just about to shut down the computer and head back into her bedroom to count more parfaits, when she switched gears and typed "1933 gold double eagle coin" into her favorite search engine. Sure enough, more than ten pages of links popped up on her screen, and she clicked on the first one.

Two paragraphs in, she realized she knew everything there was to know, thanks to Mr.

Nelson. Still, she checked the next link and the one after that, the same basic facts repeated again and again.

Halfway down the page of links, she clicked on one that mentioned value and began to read.

Currency can be traced back hundreds and hundreds of years. The older a coin is, the rarer it is. The rarer it is, the more coveted it is by collectors. Today, the most coveted coin — which recently sold for 7.5 million dollars — is the 1933 gold double eagle.

This time, when she sucked in her breath, the sound echoed around the room.

"Noooo . . ." Her gaze returned to the top of the article and quickly skipped ahead to the most important part.

Today, the most coveted coin — which recently sold for 7.5 million dollars — is the 1933 gold double eagle.

"Seven point five million dollars?" Covering her mouth with her hand, Winnie reread the sentence one more time, the third go-round kicking off a chill so powerful she actually began to shiver.

CHAPTER 28

Winnie moved between the stove and the cabinet in a sleep-deprived fog, grabbing cocoa instead of coffee and glasses instead of mugs. Once she finally got her act together, she reached for the kettle only to realize she'd never turned on the burner.

"Ugh! Ugh! Ugh!" She spun the dial to high, lifted her gaze to the ceiling, and released the groan she'd been holding back since the moment Renee arrived.

"Soooo are you just going to stand there and make me guess, or are you going to tell me what's —"

Saved by the telephone . . .

Squaring her shoulders with the help of a calming breath, Winnie turned to see Renee pick up the phone.

"Emergency Dessert Squad, what's your emergency?"

She had to admit, Renee's greeting was cute. Fun, even.

"Sure, Winnie is here." Renee pulled the phone away from her face and held it across the table in Winnie's direction. "It's a hot-sounding guy, and he's asking for you."

"Shhh," she hissed as she crossed to the table and took the phone. "Good morning, this is Winnie. How can I help you?"

"Hi, Winnie. It's Greg."

She could feel the weight of Renee's eyes and quickly removed herself from their path. Rounding the corner between the kitchen and her bedroom, she searched her brain for just the right way to rescind their date. But before she could select the perfect words, he filled in the awkward silence.

"How does six o'clock sound for dinner tonight? And is Italian okay? I figured we could check out that new place that went in on the other side of the street from your old bakery."

Tell him, dummy . . .

"I — I . . . I love Italian." The second she said it she longed for the ability to kick herself. Short of that she simply slapped herself on the side of the head.

"And six? Does that work for you? I checked that flyer you gave all of us at the school yesterday and noticed that your last rescue is at five o'clock."

"Six works."

"Should I pick you up?"

Her head snapped up. "No!" Then, softening her tone, she added, "I'll meet you there."

She could hear his smile through the phone and instantly hated herself for leading him on. Now, instead of getting it over with via phone, she'd have to do it over spaghetti and meatballs.

Nice going, Winnie . . .

"Great. I'll see you then."

She stifled the groan threatening to make its grand encore and closed her eyes instead. "I'll see you then, Greg."

A squeal from the other side of her bed had her opening her eyes and racing for the disconnect button before Renee's overactive imagination morphed into words. "Geez, Renee, you scared me!"

"You're going on a date with Master Sergeant Hottie, aren't you?" Without waiting for an answer, Renee headed straight for Winnie's closet and began tossing dresses and skirts onto the bed. "You're going to knock his socks — and maybe even some other stuff — off by the time I'm done with you."

"Whoa. Slow down." Gathering up as many of the items now heaped on her bed as she could, Winnie carried them back to the closet. "I don't want to knock his socks off. In fact, the only thing I really plan on doing is telling him I'm not interested in dating anyone right now."

Renee looked up from the wraparound dress Winnie had intentionally shoved to the back of the closet (impulse buy) eons earlier and stared at her as if she'd grown three heads. "Make sure you drink some coffee before you meet him so he doesn't meet Miss Cranky Pants too early in the relationship. He needs to be at the can't-live-without-you phase before you show him that side."

"There isn't going to be a can't-live-without-you phase with Master Sergeant — with *Greg*," she hissed. "Ain't going to happen."

Extending her arm outward, Renee held the dress up to Winnie and smiled. "He sees you in this thing and you'll be eating those words. Trust me on this."

"Renee, please. Stop!" She wrestled the dress from Renee's hands and thrust it back into its aforementioned spot in the back of the closet. "I'm not interested in this guy. Not now. Not ever. He's not the one, Renee."

"Not the one," Renee repeated. "What one?"

"*The* one."

Renee stared at her, wide-eyed, and then reached back into the closet. "You can't know that, Winnie, until *after* you go out with him."

"Yes, I can, and I *do.*" She smacked Renee's hand off the hanger toting the wraparound dress and pulled her friend out and away from the closet. "Please, Renee, I mean it. Stop."

She braced herself for yet another round of protest but was pleasantly surprised when Renee refrained. "It's that teacher guy, isn't it? The one with the teenager?"

"Renee, I can't do this right now. I just can't." Hooking her thumb in the direction of the kitchen, she led the way back to the stove and the mug of coffee capable of lifting the fog from her head once and for all.

Or, at least the sleep-deprived part . . .

"Do you want to talk about —"

She made a mental note to send an extra five bucks to the phone company as the ringing of the main phone cut Renee off mid-sentence. Again.

"Don't you go anywhere," Renee ordered before grabbing the phone and switching over to her continually changing dispatcher voice. "Emergency Dessert Squad. What's your emergency?"

348

I'm going on a date with the wrong man?

I'm so tired I could fall over?

I have a horrible feeling my friend was murdered over a coin?

"Hmmm . . ." Renee sat down, quickly located the sheet of dessert options, and slowly ran her finger down the list. "She's a worrier, you say?"

Shaking away her own emergencies, Winnie stepped in behind Renee and clamped a hand on her friend's shoulder. "How about our Worry No s'More Bar?"

Renee looked up at Winnie, shook her head in amazement, and relayed the dessert option to the caller. "Okay, great. We can have that to her at" — again, Renee lifted her gaze to Winnie only to return it back to the order pad — "two o'clock. Will that work?"

Leaving Renee to nail down the particulars, Winnie crossed back to the stove, turned the oven to three hundred fifty degrees, and began pulling ingredients from the cabinet next to the refrigerator. She was just reaching for her mixing bowl and measuring spoons when Renee ended the call. "Worry No s'More Bar?"

"What?" She measured out the correct amount of brown sugar and poured it into the waiting bowl. "No good?"

"No, it's adorable. I just don't know how you can come up with something so perfect so fast."

"It's no different than you coming up with a plan for special time with Ty without even blinking an eye." Winnie moved on to the white sugar and the baking soda. "It's no different than Bridget knowing exactly what angle to take with a story. I mean, if it's your passion, it's a part of you."

"I guess . . ." Renee pushed back her chair and wandered over to the center island. "Anything I can do?"

Winnie scooted a bag of chocolate bars across the counter to Renee. "Sure. Wash your hands, unwrap these, break them into tiny squares, and set them in a small bowl. Once they're all in there, pop them in the freezer, will you?"

"Aye, aye, Captain!"

For the next few minutes, they worked side by side, Renee intent on her wrapper duty, and Winnie focused on the s'more bar coming together in her bowl. Once all the ingredients were mixed, she turned to the bag of graham crackers to her left and crushed them just shy of a dust consistency. In a separate bowl, she mixed the cracker base with melted butter and pressed it into her prepared pan. Once the crust was set, she scooped the cookie mixture on top, spread it around, and popped the pan in the oven while Renee put the bowl of chocolate pieces into the freezer to firm.

"How long?" Renee asked.

"Ten minutes."

"It'll be ready that fast?"

Winnie pointed to the remaining half cup of marshmallows that hadn't made it into the mixture. "No. That's just when I sprinkle these on top. Then it'll be another ten minutes before it comes out and we scatter the chocolate pieces across the top."

"I'm thinking maybe you need to give me some hazard pay," Renee quipped, reaching for (and unwrapping) a single "missed" (yeah, right) chocolate bar. "Having a dessert like that within arm's reach and not being able to eat it surely must qualify as hazard duty, don't you think?"

She cracked a half smile and lifted her coffee mug off the table. "We need a lot more clients before I can cut much of a paycheck at all, let alone consider including hazard pay."

"Is that why you're so blah today? Because you're worried about paying me?" Renee asked quickly. "Because I'm okay right now. Really. I'm here with you because I *want* to be."

"That's a worry, sure." She took a sip of the lukewarm liquid and then wrapped both hands around the mug.

"*A* worry." Renee balled up the chocolate bar wrappers and tossed them in the trash, narrowly missing Winnie in the process. "So then what's *the* worry?"

"I found out something last night that I can't seem to shake from my mind."

Leaning forward, Renee stared at her and waited.

"Bart had a coin he kept in a glass case on the center of his fireplace mantel."

"The one his dad got from one of President Roosevelt's Secret Service agents, right?"

Winnie recovered her gaped mouth and pulled her mug against her chest. "You knew about Bart's coin?"

"Sure. He told me all about it at every block party you dragged me to."

"*Dragged* you to?" She didn't need a mirror to know her left brow had lifted further into her forehead. "Hmmm. I seem to remember you *begging* for an invite."

Renee shrugged. "The food is always really good; the gossip, even better."

She laughed, but it was short-lived. "Okay, so he told you about his coin."

"Uh-huh."

352

"Did he ever happen to mention how much it was worth?" Slowly, she lowered the mug to the counter and trained her focus on the timer above the oven.

Forty-five more seconds . . .

She grabbed the remaining marshmallows, carried them over to the oven, set them down long enough to place a mitt on her hand, and then opened the door and pulled out the pan. Digging her free hand into the measuring cup of marshmallows, she held it over the pan, and sprinkled them across the top of the half-baked cookie bar. When they were in place, she popped the pan back in the oven and reset the timer for another ten minutes.

"That smells amazing," Renee mused before turning her attention back to Winnie's question. "No. He never said. I just know it meant a lot to him."

Winnie spun around to face her friend. "According to Mr. Nelson and every site I found on the Internet last night, the 1933 gold double eagle coin is the rarest coin there is."

"Okay . . ."

"Which means it's worth a whole lot of money, Renee. And by a lot, I mean *a lot*."

"What constitutes *a lot*?"

She walked to the window, looked across

the street at Bart's empty home, and then retraced her steps back to Renee. "Seven point five million dollars."

"Ha-ha. You're funny, Winnie."

"I'm not being funny, Renee. According to a collector's website I went to last night, the last one of these coins that surfaced sold for seven point five million dollars."

Renee's mouth rounded into a near-perfect O. "Wow. I had no idea you had such wealthy neighbors."

"Neither did I. But in all the time I knew Bart and Ethel, he never talked about the monetary worth of that coin. He simply talked about its connection to a former president."

"Maybe he didn't know. Or maybe he didn't care." Renee shifted her weight from stiletto-clad foot to stiletto-clad foot. "Maybe it was really just about the sentimental value for him."

"The coin is *missing,* Renee."

"His kid doesn't have it?"

Winnie shook her head.

"Mr. Nelson?"

Again she shook her head. "Mr. Nelson is actually the one who first noticed it was gone when we were trying to coax Lovey out of the house. He assumed Mark had buried it with Bart."

"And we know that he didn't?"

"Mark told me he didn't."

"Do you think that's why he was murdered?" Renee asked.

It was the only answer that made sense now that Mark and Sissy had been eliminated from her personal list of suspects. "I do."

"Did you tell the cops this?"

"I'm going to. I just want to think on it a little longer. In case I'm wrong. I mean, maybe he moved the coin somewhere else. Maybe he sent it off to be cleaned."

"He polished it himself," Renee offered. "He even showed me *how* he cleaned it two block parties ago."

She felt the sag of her shoulders and glanced back at the oven.

Three minutes . . .

She didn't know what to say.

Renee, of course, wasn't afflicted with that problem. "Sounds like someone knew what Bart was sitting on."

She returned her gaze to Renee. "So you think he was killed for the coin, too?"

"It's missing, right?"

"Yes."

"And it's worth seven point five mil, right?"

"Yes."

"Then I think it's a no-brainer."

"But who could possibly know what that thing was worth if Bart never told anyone?"

"That's simple," Renee said as the timer beeped and she made a beeline for the freezer and the chilled chocolate pieces. "A collector."

CHAPTER 29

She was halfway through her lasagna when she realized Greg had barely touched his Penne alla Bolognese. In fact, not only was he not eating, he'd stopped talking, too.

"You don't like it?" Winnie pointed her fork at the man's plate and then directed it back to her own. "Because mine is *amazing*. Truly, *truly* amazing." (Okay, so maybe the second *truly* was a bit much.)

"It must be considering you haven't said anything since the waiter brought it to the table."

She racked her brain for some sort of fun retort but gave up when she realized he wasn't kidding. "I — I'm sorry. I guess I was just hungrier than I realized."

"Busy day?"

Resting her fork on the side of the plate, Winnie reached for her water glass and took a sip, his gaze narrowing in on her face as she did. When she was done, she set the glass back down and wiped her mouth on her cloth napkin. "We only had two rescues today, but the second one involved a slightly more complicated recipe."

"I see."

"Between *that* and not sleeping terribly well last night, I guess I never really gave much thought to eating until now."

"So it was the lack of sleep that had you saying very little before the food showed up, too?" he asked, not unkindly.

She looked down at her plate and then back up at her dinner companion, her ravenous hunger suddenly not so ravenous anymore. "I'm sorry, Greg. It's just . . ."

The sentence fell away as Jay Morgan walked past the restaurant's front window. Dressed in a simple pair of jeans and a Henley-style shirt, the business teacher seemed distracted as he crossed the span of the window and disappeared from her sight.

"You know that guy?"

She kept her eyes on the window, hoping Jay had forgotten something and would have to double back just so she could see him again . . .

"Winnie?"

When he didn't return in a reasonable amount of time, she reengaged eye contact with Greg. "I'm sorry, did you say something?"

"I did. But it doesn't matter. It's obvious your mind is somewhere else."

His voice was matter-of-fact, but still, she caught the hurt it was unable to mask. Realizing she was the cause, she pushed her plate of lasagna off to the side and leaned forward a smidge. "Greg, I'm sorry. None of this — *of me* — is your fault. I shouldn't have agreed to this date in the first place. I'm just not interested in a relationship right now. I'm too focused on trying to make this new business a go."

"I appreciate you going easy on my ego, Winnie, but I saw the way you looked at that guy just now."

At a loss for what to say, Winnie pulled her plate back in front of her body and took another bite of her dinner. Maybe if she concentrated on eating again, they could get back to the whole silence thing . . .

"What's his name?"

She considered ignoring the question or simply stuffing a piece of bread in her mouth to avoid answering, but since she hadn't had the courage to turn Greg down before he wasted his evening, she went the route of courtesy. "Jay. Jay Morgan."

"What's he do?"

"He's a business professor at Silver Lake College."

"He's a lucky guy."

Slowly, she looked up from her plate. "Lucky guy?"

"To have your interest."

Once again, she gave up on her dinner. Only this time, she did so with a mixture of sadness and disgust. "Greg, I'm so sorry about this. You were so nice showing me your ambulance and answering all my questions last week. I —"

He cut her apology off with raised hands. "Look, I get it. You're not the kind of girl who relishes turning a guy down. So you opt for nice even when it catches you up. It's okay. I get it. Really."

She searched his face for any sign of sarcasm or insincerity, but there was none. Rather, there was simply concern. For . . . *her*?

"I — I don't know what to say."

"Just say we can be friends."

"Friends?" she parroted.

"You forget I've only been here a few months, Winnie." Greg forked a piece of penne pasta and held it just shy of his mouth. "Trust me, I can use a good friend here every bit as much as I can use a romantic relationship."

360

Winnie smiled through the tears she felt pricking the corners of her eyes. "A good friend, I can be. But don't give up on the notion of finding a little romance, either. You are, after all, known far and wide as Master Sergeant Hottie."

The second Greg started coughing around his noodle, she knew she should have waited to share his Silver Lake–wide nickname, but hindsight was called hindsight for a reason. Instead, she retrieved his glass from the table and handed it to him. "If this doesn't work, you'll have to put your arms up in the air so I can come around the table and smack you on the back the way my parents always did when I was choking."

He took a sip of water, coughed, and then took another sip. "No . . . that's . . . okay."

"Sorry about unleashing that nickname on you. I guess I just figured you knew by now."

"No. I had no idea."

"Bridget, the one who wrote that article on you when you first came to town, coined the phrase."

"The old lady?" he asked, still coughing a little.

She started to bristle and willed herself to keep it light. "She's eighty, if that matters."

Returning to his dinner, he took a few

bites and then gestured toward the window with his fork. "So are you dating that guy?"

She felt the lightness drain out of her as her thoughts traveled back to Jay. "No."

"But you like him?"

She smoothed the napkin across her lap and then fidgeted her hands along its narrow hem.

"Does he know?"

"It doesn't matter." She played with the cloth square for a few more seconds and then crumpled it up and laid it on the table beside her plate. "He has a daughter. That needs to be his primary focus."

"He said that?"

"No."

"So you're assuming this?"

"He's a single dad. The ex-wife took off years ago and has nothing to do with the daughter. He's all she has." She traced her finger along a slight crease in the tablecloth and then pulled it back as she became aware of Greg's concern. "Them against the world, that sort of thing."

"He said *that*?"

"No. Caroline, his daughter, did."

Dropping his fork onto the side of his plate, he pushed back from the table just far enough to rest his ankle across his opposite knee. "I was that way once, too."

"I don't understand."

"My parents got divorced when I was twelve. The second my dad moved out, I appointed myself the man of the family. It was my job to look after my mom and keep her safe." A wry smile crossed his lips as his focus drifted to a place far from Silver Lake, Ohio. "When I think back on those first few guys who tried to date my mom, I realize what a little creep I was. I was worse than any father I met during my own dating years. Only instead of talking about guns to scare them off, I caused so many problems they went running for the hills."

She wasn't sure what to say, so she simply nodded.

"Then Doug came along."

"Doug?"

"My best friend."

"Your best friend?" she repeated.

"Well, technically he's my stepfather, but he's become my best friend, too." Greg took another sip of water and then focused his attention completely on Winnie. "He made my mom happy in a different way than I did. It took me a while to see it . . . to *want* to see it, I should say. But it got to a point where I realized my denying her that happiness was just me being selfish. So I stopped."

"You're a good son." It was a simple statement, but certainly one that appeared to be accurate.

"Doug was a good guy. Once I got over myself and let it happen, I realized my mom wasn't the only one he made happy."

"Hence, you calling him your best friend," she mused.

"Exactly."

More than anything, she wanted to believe she could have a chance with her Mr. Right. But she just couldn't block out the things that Caroline had said in the park or the way the teenager's face had twisted in horror at the sight of the Dessert Squad ambulance parked in the lot. Jay must have said something that put Winnie on the girl's radar . . .

"I don't know, Greg. I'm not sure my skin is thick enough, you know? And that's even assuming Jay has any genuine interest in me in the first place."

"He'd be a fool if he didn't."

Again the sting of tears was back, only this time the smile that had accompanied them before was a bit harder to come by. Still, she found one along with a thank-you just as the waitress reappeared with two dessert menus in her hand.

364

"Do you eat other people's desserts?" he asked.

"To twist your words just a bit, I'd be a fool if I didn't." She ran her finger down the dessert options and settled on tiramisu. "Everything I eat is a potential springboard to something better."

"I like that." He, too, consulted the menu, and then called the waitress back to request their desserts. When the woman left, he rested his elbows on the edge of the table. "So this guy and his kid, and you not wanting to hurt my feelings because of them, is why you seemed so distracted when you walked in here at six o'clock?"

"No. I mean, partially, I guess. But only the part about you. I really wasn't thinking about Jay until he walked by the window just now."

"Then? What's up? What's the other part?"

The other part . . .

Meaning, the part she hadn't been able to shake since two o'clock in the morning . . .

"What do you know about a rare coin from the 1930s?" she finally posed.

"Nothing. I'm not a collector. I have a thing for old ambulances, sure, but I'm not a collector." He finished off his last sip of water and then leaned back and smiled at Winnie. "But Chuck would probably know."

365

"Chuck?"

"Yeah. You remember, he tried to eat all the kids' cookies at the school the other day . . . Average build. Red hair. He's why I was at that reception for your deceased neighbor."

"Yeah, I know who you're talking about," she said. "I just don't understand what he has to do with an old coin."

"I told you at the restaurant on Saturday. Chuck collects baseball cards. Has since he was a little kid, from what I gather. He's real active in the Silver Lake Collectors Club. That's how he knew your neighbor."

"And how he knew my neighbor's coin was worth millions?" she whispered.

CHAPTER 30

Chuck . . .

For not the first time since the EMT's name was mentioned across a white linen-draped table, Winnie felt a cold shiver take root in her chest and spread its way across her body. Only now, instead of having to cover her reaction with a sip of coffee or a bite of (highly average and way too chewy) tiramisu, she could verbalize her thoughts aloud and know that they were safe within the confines of Gertie's ambulance.

Peeking into the rearview mirror, she saw Greg still standing on the sidewalk beside her now-empty parking space looking as if he wasn't sure what to do with the rest of his night. Part of her still felt bad for crushing his hopes for a real date, but another part of her — the part that valued honesty and despised games — knew she'd done the right thing.

She truly wasn't interested in a relationship with Greg, Lance, or anyone else Renee or Mr. Nelson had subtly (or not so subtly) tried to foist on her. But adding them to her friend base? That she could do.

Especially when they hand me a brand-new name for my suspect list . . .

Yet even as the redhead took center stage in her thoughts once again, Winnie found her brain at war with itself.

Chuck Rogers was an emergency medical technician. He'd picked a career that was focused on saving people, not killing them. So the notion that he'd suffocate an elderly man to get his hands on a coin didn't really mesh.

Then again, she'd be willing to bet that money — especially to the tune of seven and a half million dollars — had converted its fair share of previously upstanding citizens throughout history.

At the far end of Main Street, she turned right and then left, the not-so-quiet whir of the fifty-plus-year-old engine providing just the right amount of background noise with which to think. There was no denying the fact that Chuck had knowledge of the coin prior to Bart's death. Greg, himself, had filled in that little detail at the repast.

Add in the fact that the baseball card collector had been seen looking at Bart's house within days of his passing and —

"A criminal always returns to the scene of the crime!" She pulled into the driveway, cut the engine, and sighed with relief at the sight of Mr. Nelson and Bridget waving at her from the front porch. Pushing the driver's side door open, she stepped onto the pavement and returned the wave.

"How'd it go with Master Sergeant Hottie?" Bridget called from her spot on Winnie's favorite rocking chair.

"Pastor Lotty?" Mr. Nelson shook his head with obvious disgust. "I thought that fella was married."

Even in the gathering dusk, Winnie could make out Bridget's exasperated eye roll and her downstairs neighbor's confusion as she stepped onto the porch and made her way over to the rattan chair positioned within arm's reach of the chessboard. She pointed at the pile of black pieces to the left of the board and eyed Mr. Nelson. "So you lost? I mean . . . won?"

"He put himself in checkmate about thirty minutes ago. I'm surprised you didn't hear the crowing from wherever you were eating on Main Street."

"We were at that new place, Luigi's — dinner was good, dessert was average. Mario's is still better." She swung her gaze from Bridget to the man sitting in the opposing rocking chair, happily stroking Winnie's brown and white tabby cat. "Well, you certainly gave yourself quite a run, Mr. Nelson. What did that game last? Two, three days?"

"Three days." Mr. Nelson smiled proudly at Winnie and then reached into his front pocket and extracted a five-dollar bill. "I won five dollars."

"It's not winning when you give it to yourself, Parker."

Mr. Nelson hooked his thumb in the direction of Winnie's rocking chair and scrunched his face tight. "Anytime I find myself wonderin' why I didn't get married, Winnie Girl, all I have to do is look at our next-door neighbor here. Bingo — mystery solved."

She readied herself for a war of barbs between the pair, but it was for naught. Any offense Bridget might have taken from the man's words was pushed aside for what really mattered.

"Parker said you left at six for your dinner with" — Bridget turned a disapproving eye on Mr. Nelson and enunciated loudly and clearly — "*Master* Sergeant *Hottie* and yet, here it is, seven thirty, and you're already home. No movie? No after-dinner walk?"

"No. Just dinner."

"People in his line of work *do* have crazy hours," Bridget mused. "Maybe next time he'll have a bigger window."

"It was *my* choice to wrap it up when we did, Bridget."

"Oh? Did it not go well, dear?"

"It went as well as can be expected considering our very different mind-sets."

Bridget stopped rocking. "Meaning?"

"Meaning he went wanting it to be a date, and I went knowing I didn't."

"I was wondering why you didn't dress up more . . ."

She looked down at her soft black jeans and white short-sleeved sweater and tried not to take offense. It was a nice outfit, but certainly not anything that screamed "date," much to Renee's (and now, obviously, Bridget's) chagrin. Even her hair was in its normal workday ponytail.

"I happen to think my Winnie Girl looks pretty as a picture."

"Thanks, Mr. Nelson."

Bridget scowled at the man and then turned her attention back on Winnie. "Did you fight, dear?"

"Pastor Lotty is a man of the cloth. He shouldn't be fighting," Mr. Nelson said, as he, too, brought his chair to a standstill.

"And he shouldn't be dating if he's married."

Bridget reached across the space between their chairs and turned the dial in Mr. Nelson's ear. Then, shouting loud enough to be heard by just about anyone with an open window in a one-block radius, she said, "*Hot*-tie. Not *Lot*-ty. Good heavens, Parker, you could drive a teetotaler to drink."

Mr. Nelson looked across the porch at Winnie. "Hottie? You went out with a fella named Hottie?"

"His name is Greg. Greg Stevens. You've met him. He's the one who came over last Sunday to see the Dessert Squad."

"He seemed like a nice fella. A little stiff, maybe, but nice."

"He's former army," Bridget interjected. "And so handsome."

"So what went wrong?"

"Nothing went wrong, Mr. Nelson. I'm just not interested in him as anything more than a friend."

And potential case solver . . .

Abandoning Mr. Nelson's chess chair, Winnie moved around the porch, stopping every few steps to collect her thoughts. When she was ready, she crossed to the portion of railing directly in front of the rocking chairs and faced her friends. "I want to run something by the two of you."

"Is this about the Dessert Squad?" Bridget asked, resuming a slow rock. "Because a buzz is growing, dear. Growing fast."

She couldn't help but smile at the news. "I hope you're right. We've had a decent first week so far, all things considered, but there's going to need to be a lot more business to keep us running. Especially if I'm going to be able to keep Renee on the books." Leaning her back against the railing, she settled in for what she knew could be a lengthy talk. "But no, that's not what I want to run by you."

Ever the competitor, Mr. Nelson quickly matched and surpassed Bridget's rocking pace. "Is it a plan to win over that little girl?"

"Little girl?"

"The one that goes with that fella you *are* interested in."

Bridget brought her rocker to a brief stop, her focus flitting between Mr. Nelson and Winnie. "There's a fella with a little girl?"

She breathed in the lingering scent of bacon (Mr. Nelson's favorite food regardless of the time or meal) still wafting from the man's open front windows and imagined herself eating a piece instead of having to tiptoe through a verbal minefield. Say the wrong thing, and it would be midnight before she got to bed . . .

"There is a man that I like, Bridget. But he has a daughter — a teenage daughter, as a matter of fact." She captured the ends of her ponytail with her right hand and brushed them across the palm of her left hand. "But I'd rather talk about that another time. Right now, I just want to toss around a theory pertaining to Bart and the person I think may have killed him."

Both rockers stopped in unison as their respective occupants leaned forward. "You know who killed Bart?" Mr. Nelson and Bridget asked together in matching tones.

"Possibly."

Who?" Mr. Nelson and Bridget echoed together.

"Now hear me out." She released her ponytail and flicked it back over her shoulder. "I could be way off base here, but it fits. Or, at least, I *think* it fits."

"Tell us," Bridget prodded.

She inhaled sharply and then let her theory serve as its countering exhale. "I think it's Chuck. The EMT."

Again, Mr. Nelson tried to adjust his hearing aids but found that they were already on full volume. "That red-haired fella in the uniform?"

"Yes." She kneaded her temple with her fingertips in an attempt to ward off a headache she felt brewing just under her skin. Tension, no doubt. "He came to the repast with Greg, remember? And when Greg explained why they came, he said it was because Chuck had known Bart from a collectors club he's been in since he was a boy."

"I know that collectors club. Been meeting one Saturday a month for decades," Mr. Nelson said. "Bart started it. In the beginning, they met at the old coffee shop. But after a few months, they moved to a meeting room at the Presbyterian church on the corner of Oak and Timber."

Those were details she hadn't known, but they certainly helped set the stage. "Apparently, Chuck started going with his dad when he was a kid. The dad, if I remember from what Greg said on Saturday, collected Lionel trains. Chuck was into baseball cards."

"He still has that collection," Bridget chimed in, "or did when I ran a who's who profile on him when he started with the ambulance district."

"So what's this got to do with Bart?" Mr. Nelson asked. "Other than they were in the same club together?"

375

It was a variation of the same self-argument she'd had off and on throughout dessert with Greg. If Chuck had known about Bart's coin all these years, why kill the elderly man now?

Because, with Ethel gone, he only had to kill one of them . . .

It was, of course, her leading theory and one she was eager to finally bounce off her neighbors.

"Do you realize that Bart's coin was worth seven and a half million dollars?" It was a rhetorical question, really, because it didn't particularly matter if they did or didn't. What mattered was the fact that Bart's coin was missing and there was every reason to connect that fact with the man's murder.

Still, Mr. Nelson's gaped mouth and Bridget's near-deafening intake of air told her they hadn't known.

Their reaction wasn't a surprise. Most people wouldn't know what a 1933 gold double eagle coin was worth. Unless, as Renee had surmised, they were a collector, too.

Like Chuck.

"You think that fella killed Bart for his coin?" Mr. Nelson asked, the shock in his voice still evident on his face.

Winnie nodded.

"But Mark buried Bart with that coin!"

"No. He didn't."

"He didn't?" Mr. Nelson echoed.

"No."

"But —"

"Mark told me he didn't, Mr. Nelson."

"Then what'd he do with it?"

"Nothing. He didn't even know it was missing until I told him."

Mr. Nelson's eyes widened, but it was Bridget who held up her index finger like a teacher silencing her students. "But if this young man came into the kind of money you're talking about, Winnie, why would he be looking at *Bart's* house? I mean, we have a beautiful street, but the houses by the lake are far more la-di-da. And he wouldn't have to remember suffocating an old man to death every time he walked into his kitchen to toast a bagel."

It was a good point, and one she'd not really considered until that moment.

"Unless his looking at the house was a ruse."

Bridget turned a sharp look in Mr. Nelson's direction. "How would looking at Bart and Ethel's house be a ruse?"

"To see if he left behind any evidence that could implicate him in the crime."

"Exactly!" Winnie hadn't meant to shout,

377

but it was validating to hear someone else give voice to the thoughts that had been nibbling at her brain since Greg unknowingly forged a connection between Chuck and Bart. At least now, if she was way off base, she wasn't alone.

"Well, there's only one way to know if he's a viable suspect, isn't there?" Bridget leaned forward, retrieved her purse from the floor beside her rocker, and shoved her wrinkled hand inside. Seconds later, she pulled out her phone, scrolled through her extensive contact list, pressed a button, and held the phone to her ear.

"What are you doing?" Winnie whispered.

Her inquiry was met with a glare and a hush from Bridget, and a laugh from Mr. Nelson.

"Yes, good evening, Sam. This is Bridget O'Keefe with the *Silver Lake Herald*. I understand one of your EMTs — a Chuck Rogers, I believe — was one of two called to the scene when Mr. Bart Wagner's body was found."

"What is she doing?" Winnie tried again, this time directing her question at Mr. Nelson rather than Bridget.

Mr. Nelson waved her off and leaned across the armrest of his rocking chair to increase his chance of hearing everything the second it happened.

"Yes, Chuck Rogers . . . and Tom Colgan. Can you tell me when their shift started that day?"

Suddenly Bridget's call made all the sense in the world. If they could verify that Chuck's whereabouts were unaccounted for on the morning of Bart's murder, maybe they could convince the police to question —

"They started their double at ten o'clock the previous evening?" Bridget looked up, met first Winnie's and then Mr. Nelson's eyes, and gently shook her head.

It was official. They were back to square one.

CHAPTER 31

Winnie pulled the lemon meringue pie from the refrigerator and braced herself for yet another probing question.

The first few, she'd expected, of course. And, for the most part, she'd been right on the money (and darn close to verbatim, thankyouverymuch) . . .

How'd it go with Greg?

Did you change your attitude and give the poor guy a shot?

You do realize you're nuts, don't you?

Granted she would have given the same answers (*fine, no, if you say so*) whether she'd had prep time or not, but still, it was always good to be prepared. If nothing else, it helped save her energy for the conversations that had invariably followed — most notably the ones detailing the various single men Renee knew in and around Silver Lake, the benefits of sleep in the war against the raccoon eyes Winnie was apparently sporting, and the erasure of her latest potential suspect in Bart's murder.

"Are you absolutely sure you're thinking clearly —"

"Yes," she groaned. Then, sliding the pie in front of her friend's face, she added, "So, how does it look?"

"Delicious." Renee consulted the order sheet on the table in front of her and tapped her pen across the top. "When Life Gives You Lemons, Make Lemon Meringue Pie — another great name for what will surely be yet another popular rescue."

"Let's hope you're right." Winnie loaded plates, napkins, and plastic utensils into her rescue bag and then zipped it closed. "Now tell me again which building and room number I'm going to?"

"The Cully Business Building at Silver Lake College. Room 404."

She hated the surge of excitement that coursed through her body at the mention of anything connected to Jay, but not as much as she hated the overwhelming sadness that immediately squashed it like a bug.

Ughhhh . . .

"You want me to make this run?" Renee asked, lifting the order sheet from the table and rising to her feet. "This one doesn't require any drizzling, right?"

"No, no drizzling, but I'll run this out, anyway. I can't shy away from jobs just because I've got a giant-sized crush on a guy who has way too much going on in his life to reciprocate." Winnie hiked the bag over her shoulder, slid her key ring around her index finger, balanced the plated pie atop her hand, and strode toward the door. "If we get another order that can be delivered before closing, go ahead and call my cell."

Lovey jumped down from the windowsill and met Winnie at the top of the stairs.

"Looks like Lovey will be accompanying you," Renee quipped.

Winnie peered down at the cat. "Are you going to be nice?"

Hiss . . .

"I guess that would be a no, then, wouldn't it?" She found a smile for Renee and then headed downstairs with Lovey and a healthy dose of dread in tow.

She was just about to hit the button to close the elevator doors when a member of campus security poked his head around the corner. "Ma'am, this is the fifth time in a row these doors have opened and I've seen you standing inside. Is there something I can help you with?"

"I . . . um . . . I'm looking for . . . um" — she glanced down at the address Renee had written out for her and then back up at the balding man — "Room 404. I — I have a delivery."

His gaze left hers and landed on the stretcher at her back. "Hey, I know you!"

She swallowed. "You do?"

"Sure. You're with that Dessert Squad everyone keeps talking about!"

She tried to think of something clever to say, but considering the fact she'd just opted to spend a good five minutes or so in an elevator to avoid the possibility of running into Jay, she settled for simple. "I am."

"Whatcha got today?" He leaned around her body to afford a better view of the pie resting smack dab in the middle of the stretcher. "Oh. Wow. That's a lemon meringue pie, isn't it?" Without waiting for her answer, he went on, licking his lips every few words as he did. "My mama used to make me one of those on my birthday every year."

"This particular pie is our When Life Gives You Lemons, Make Lemon Meringue Pie." She returned his ensuing smile with one of her own and slowly turned the stretcher for disembarkation from the elevator. "Apparently, whoever is in office 404 needs a morale boost."

"Room 404 is a supply closet."

"Oh." She looked down at the card in her hand and then back up at the guard. "My dispatcher wrote down 404. Maybe it was 304?"

"Nope. That's a closet, too." He planted his hands on the end of the stretcher closest to the elevator door and helped pull it into the hallway as the silver doors swished to a close behind Winnie. "C'mon, I'll help you find the person waiting on this order."

She wanted to protest, to turn around and head back home, but that was hard to do when a man at least twice her size was taking point. Besides, her reputation couldn't afford a failed delivery.

They stopped at room 401. No one placed an order for a dessert rescue.

They stopped at room 402. No one placed an order for a dessert rescue.

They stopped at room 403. No one placed an order for a dessert rescue.

They bypassed room 404 and its perfect place to hide and moved on to room 405.

The guard knocked on the open door. "Jay? Did you place an order with the Emergency Dessert Squad by any chance?"

She heard a chair scrape across the floor mere seconds before the answer that drained any and all remaining moisture from her mouth. "I did, Paul. Thanks."

The guard stepped back and waved Winnie toward the door. "It looks like we found your patient."

"Looks like it," she managed to eke out.

"My mom used to make a pie just like that for me when I was little," Paul said, directing Jay's focus off Winnie's bright red face and onto the stretcher. "You'll have to tell me how it is when you're done."

"I've got a better idea." Jay walked over to the stretcher, picked up the plated pie, and held it out to the guard. "Take it with you back to the security office for you and the rest of the guards."

Paul's eyes widened. "Are you serious?"

"Sure."

"But you ordered this, didn't you?" he asked.

"I wanted the Dessert Squad here . . . and" — he gestured toward Winnie — "she is. So I'm good."

Paul looked from Jay to Winnie and back again, and then took the pie. "Wow, man, thanks." And then he was gone, the pie and the man disappearing behind the elevator doors at the end of the hall.

"Why did you order a pie if you didn't want one?" she asked.

"Oh, I'd have eaten it. But did you see the guy's face when he talked about the pie just now? He looked like a kid on Christmas morning."

"I suppose."

"Well, now that you're here, why don't you come in and sit for a few minutes."

She brought her hands down to the edge of the stretcher and pushed it ever so slightly in the direction of the elevator. "I — I can't. I've got to get back and see if there are any new orders."

"Wouldn't your dispatcher call if any jobs came up?"

"I guess. But still, I should get back. Lovey is waiting in the car."

"No, she's not."

She stared at Jay as his heart-stopping smile ignited across his mouth. "Yes, she is."

"Actually, she's right there." He pointed at two large golden eyes staring back at them from the same shelf-like space below the stretcher where Winnie kept her rescue bag during transport.

"Oh, Jay. I'm sorry. I didn't know she was there. I'll get her out of here right now."

"No. Please. Come inside. We'll shut the door while we talk, and no one will be the wiser."

Lovey, being the traitor that she was, jumped down and scurried into Jay's office.

Great . . .

"I don't suppose you want a cat?" she mumbled.

"Nope."

She considered a slew of arguments she could wage in favor of simply leaving, but in the end she did as he requested. After all, he had ordered a rescue. What he did with the pie was his business.

Once inside, she chose to stand rather than sit, although, technically speaking, Lovey didn't really give her any other option, considering the cat had claimed the one chair that wasn't Jay's.

"You can take my chair," he offered, stepping into the office and closing the door.

"No. I won't be staying long."

"Winnie, I know why you're suddenly backing off."

"I'm not backing off. I just need to focus on my business like I told you."

"Winnie." He met her in front of his bookshelf, hooked a gentle finger beneath her chin, and gently guided her gaze back to his. "I know you met Caroline the other day."

She felt a familiar sting in the corners of her eyes and blinked it away. "So?"

"I know my daughter. I know how *protective* she is of me . . . and of *us*. I also know she has an issue with jealousy."

"I don't know what that has to do with me." She stepped back and watched his hand fall back to his side.

"One of the mothers connected to her dance class picked up her daughter a little early the other night."

"Okay . . ."

"Apparently this woman must have seen the two of us at Beans and commented about it to Caroline. She asked me about it on the ride home from class, and I told her about you. She's pretty good about reading my body language, and I guess she figured it out."

"Figured what out?" she asked.

"That I like you. A lot."

It was everything her heart wanted to hear, yet nothing her head was prepared to deal with at that moment. Trying to steady her breath against the thumping in her chest was hard enough.

Fortunately, Jay kept talking, buying her time to try and figure out her feelings. "Unfortunately, Caroline hasn't seen me get excited about anyone other than her until now. So she's not exactly happy about this."

"Which is why we need to leave it alone." She hated to say the words as much as she hated to hear them, but that didn't make them any less true.

"I'm allowed to have a life, Winnie. I'm allowed to see where this could go with us. I just need you to give it a chance. Give me and my daughter a chance. I think she'll come around."

"And if she doesn't?"

"I think she will."

"And if she doesn't?" Winnie repeated, her voice cracking.

He reached out, encased her hand with his, and squeezed so gently she actually swore she could feel her heart melt. "I think she will."

She opened her mouth to ask her question one more time, but closed it when she saw the hope reflected in his blue green eyes.

Hope for them . . .

"I — I don't know what to say."

"Say you'll let me walk you to your car now, and that we can spend a little time together this weekend — dinner, a movie, a walk in the park, whatever you want."

She knew she should protest if for no other reason than a need to protect her own heart from being hurt, but she couldn't make herself say no. Instead, she simply nodded and followed Jay (and Lovey) back out into the hall.

Slowly, they (with Lovey stowed away beneath the stretcher) made their way down the hall, into the elevator, and, eventually, out to the parking lot. When they reached the ambulance, Jay helped her load the stretcher into the back and Lovey into the passenger seat. "So," he said, closing Lovey's door, "can I call you tonight?"

"If you want to —"

"Hey Winnie! See you on Serenity Lane . . ."

She glanced toward the back of the ambulance just in time to see Lance wave and continue on his path toward the parking lot's exit. Turning back to Jay, she used Lance's drive-by to slow her heart rate and collect her thoughts. "Have you met Lance Reed yet?"

Jay drew back. "As in the new addition to the history department?"

"Yes. He's my neighbor."

"Driving *that*?"

"He just got it a few days ago." She led the way around the back end of the ambulance and over to her door. "Makes me wish I paid better attention in my history classes," she joked.

"What do you mean?"

"People who bake desserts for a living can't afford a car like that."

"People who teach can't, either." She opened her door but remained standing next to Jay. "Unless they teach history."

His laugh encircled her like a pair of warm arms. "Trust me, Winnie. Working here didn't pay for a car like that."

Her cell phone vibrated inside the front pocket of her jeans, and she pulled it out. The caller ID screen listed an unfamiliar name. "Excuse me one second, Jay." Then, holding the device to her ear, she took the call. "Hello, this is Winnie."

"Winnie? This is Chuck. Chuck Rogers. I work with Greg, and I met you the other day when you came to look at one of our ambulances, and then again at the school."

And for a while, I thought you murdered my friend . . .

"Yes. Hi," she said, instead. "What can I do for you?"

"Greg called me today and told me you had some questions about a rare coin?"

Aware of Jay's nearness, she did her best to keep her voice as light as possible. "Yes."

"I'm assuming it's about Bart Wagner's gold double eagle?"

Caught off guard, she simply repeated the same "yes."

"That thing was worth a fortune. But Bart had no intention of ever selling it. The memory and its tie to his late father meant more than any amount of money. I understood that. I feel the same way about my dad's old trains."

She mulled over his comments only to find a question pushing to the forefront of her thoughts. "Do you know if anyone in your club took a special interest in Bart's coin?"

"We've all known him for years. And while the history behind it was unbelievably cool, it wasn't anything new, you know? I mean, we knew the story already. Had for ages. That's probably why we were all so excited when we got a new member last month. First new member in something like five years, I think."

"New member?" she echoed.

"New member, new set of ears . . ."

"I don't understand."

"Everyone in that club has seen my baseball card collection a million times. Everyone in that club has heard one another's stories a million times. A new member means a new set of ears."

"Ahhh." She held the phone closer to her ear in an effort to try and drown out the chatter of a half dozen or so students walking through the parking lot. "Chuck? Do you happen to know this new member's name?"

"Sure I do. It's Lance — Lance Reed. Guy is a total history buff and super smart. Moved to town a month or so ago to teach at the community college."

CHAPTER 32

Looking back, she wasn't entirely sure how she got out of the parking lot without running anyone over. Or how, exactly, she left things with Jay. But there were no dents in her car, and she vaguely remembered saying something about Bart, his coin, and justice being served. For now, that would have to do.

Especially considering the way everything about Lance as Bart's killer rang true.

Collector or not, a man who taught history would know — probably better than anyone else — just how rare Bart's coin had been. And, according to Jay, community college history professors didn't pull in the salary needed to buy the kind of sports car Lance was driving around town.

Then again, less than twenty-four hours earlier, she'd been convinced Chuck was the killer . . .

Pulling over onto the road's gravel shoulder, Winnie retrieved her phone from Lovey's seat and dialed Bridget's number.

"Hello?"

"Bridget, it's me. Winnie." She saw Lovey stir but kept her focus on the woman in her ear. "I need to ask you something."

"My feet are feeling much better today, thank you. I soaked them in Epsom salt last night and that seemed to do the trick."

"I didn't know your feet were hurting."

"Oh? I was sure I'd told you. Then again, maybe that was Cornelia I mentioned it to . . ."

Stifling the groan she felt building in her throat, she did her best to proceed with caution. "Bridget, I really have to ask you something. Something unrelated to your feet."

"Go ahead, dear."

"It's about Lance."

She closed her eyes against her next-door neighbor's answering squeal — a sound not much different than one Renee would make under the same circumstances. "Has he asked you out?"

"No!"

Bridget sniffed at Winnie's rebuke and then grew silent.

Removing the phone from its holding spot against her cheek, Winnie checked the connection. Still there . . . "I'm sorry if I sound a bit short, but —"

"Parker and I — we just worry about you, dear. We want you to find someone as special as you are. If that's Lance, then that's wonderful."

If she weren't trying to put a face on Bart's killer, she'd probably find their conversation amusing, but she was and so she didn't. "Bridget, please! I just need to double-check my memory from that day."

"What day?"

"The day Bart was murdered." She wrapped her free hand around the steering wheel and braced herself. "Do you remember when I got home from work? It was my last day at the bakery, and I was feeling a little blue."

"I remember. But things have really turned around, haven't they? Your Dessert Squad is the talk of the town — no small thanks to me and my article, of course."

"Yes, of course. And thank you again for that." She stopped, took a breath, and glanced over at Lovey happily licking her hindquarters. "While we were on the porch, before I found Bart's body, you and Mr. Nelson were telling me about the incident with Ava, remember?"

She heard a frustrated sigh in her ear.

"Yes. And Parker kept cutting me off, telling you all the best parts of the story."

"I'm calling *you,* aren't I?" she reminded.

"That's just because Parker doesn't hear the phone when it rings."

She considered protesting if for no other reason than to stroke the elderly woman's ego, but it was pointless. Besides, it didn't matter. Not now, anyway. Instead, she cut to the chase. "Bridget, what did you say about Bart before Ava ran through Ethel's flower bed that day — or, rather, the previous day?"

"I don't remember telling you anything."

"You did," she insisted. "It was about Bart and his frame of mind just before Ava set him off . . ."

"I don't know. I — wait. Yes. Bart had looked so happy. He was even smiling for the first time since Ethel passed."

She needed more to make her case. But she wanted to hear it from Bridget's mouth rather than in her own head where it could be mixed with an entirely different memory. "Do you remember why he was so happy?"

"I wasn't privy to what actually went on, of course, but I suspect that young man had just told a joke that struck Bart's funny bone."

"Young man?"

"Lance. I saw them step out onto Bart's porch together, and Bart was *smiling.*" Winnie heard a few odd noises and surmised that Bridget was shifting the phone from one hand to the other. Sure enough, the woman's voice resumed its normal strength. "Or was until that little girl decided to run through that flowerbed."

"So Lance had been inside Bart's house?"

"He had indeed. Why do you ask?"

Ignoring the woman's question, she tossed out one last one of her own. "Do you happen to know whether Lance was around that next morning? The morning that Bart was murdered?"

"That was a Tuesday, yes?"

"Yes. Tues—" The day disappeared from her lips as a memory from another conversation took center stage in her thoughts. A conversation and a voice that was suddenly as clear as the soft purr coming from the passenger seat . . .

I've got an eight A.M. class every day except Tuesday . . .

She sucked in her breath, the reality of what was sitting in her lap simply too hard to ignore. The only question that remained was what to do with the information.

Did she go to the police or did she go straight to —

"Thanks, Bridget. I've got to go." She disconnected the line, tossed the phone onto the seat next to Lovey, and pulled back onto the road, her destination clear. "You better believe you'll see me on Serenity Lane, Lance . . ."

Ten minutes later, she piloted the ambulance into Lance's driveway and cut the engine. "Well, we got him, Lovey."

Lovey popped her head up and blinked.

"You stay right here, okay? I won't be long." Then, realizing the cat wasn't going to answer, she stepped out of the vehicle and headed up to the house. She wasn't entirely sure what she was going to say when he answered the door, but she'd figure it out. Bart had deserved better. If nothing else, she'd be sure to tell Lance that . . .

She half walked, half jogged her way up to the door and knocked, her anger rising with each answering step she heard. When the footsteps stopped, the door swung open.

"Oh. Hey. Winnie. This is a nice surprise. Come on in. I was just about to fix a snack of some sort. Do you like nachos?"

She supposed she nodded, but she wasn't sure. She did know that she accepted his invitation and stepped into his hallway — a decision she couldn't help but second-guess as she heard the click of the door over her shoulder.

Still, she owed this moment to Bart.

And Ethel.

"C'mon, we can talk in the kitchen while I pull everything together." He led the way toward the kitchen at the end of the hallway, stopping every few feet to wave at a different aspect of his new place. "I've put an offer in on this house. To buy it outright. The second it goes through, I'm gonna gut this place and start all over. New walls, new floors, new furniture, new windows, new everything."

"Sounds expensive." She didn't bother to look at the rooms they passed. They didn't matter. There would be no gutting, no buying, no changing of anything. Except maybe the color Lance was wearing . . .

"It will be. But I've got it covered." When they reached the kitchen, he gestured her toward a chair and then ripped open a bag of nacho chips he'd already placed on the counter. "Do you like your cheese with or without a zip?"

"Either is fine." She sifted through a pile of travel brochures on the table and held up one pertaining to Greece. "You like to travel?"

He shook the chips onto a plate and then popped a bowl of cheese into the microwave for forty seconds. As the cheese heated, he leaned against the nearest counter and smiled at Winnie. "I'm about to find out as soon as the current semester is over."

"So you're going to keep teaching?" she asked, returning the brochure to the pile. "Even though you don't have to?"

"I'd teach history if I was the richest person in the world."

She considered his answer, swiveling her body to face him as she did. "*In the world* might be a stretch, but I'd say that seven and a half million probably solidifies you as the richest person in Silver Lake. Maybe even the whole county."

If she'd been thinking beyond her own need to call Lance out, she'd have taken advantage of his momentary shock to run for the front door, but, since she wasn't, she was ill prepared when he lunged forward, his face contorted with rage.

She did manage to struggle to her feet, but not without knocking over her chair.

"You little witch!" He reared his arm back to strike her, but somehow she managed to step out of his reach and alter his balance enough so she had time to think.

Glancing around wildly, she tried to assess her best route to freedom.

Jump over the chair and make a break for

the front door, or find a way to get around him to the back door . . .

She was just about to take the second option when she spied Mr. Nelson peeking around the door's drab curtain panel, the index finger of his non-cane-holding hand poised in front of his lips. If she went that way, she'd put her friend in danger.

No.

Lance recovered his balance and lunged at her again, his sudden and menacing movements so frightening she shrieked in terror.

"Scream all you want, Winnie. No one in this neighborhood of hearing aids and walkers will be coming to your rescue anytime —"

The sound of glass shattering in the front hall made them both jump. Before either of them could process what was happening, an arm reached through the glass, unlocked the door, and shoved it open.

"Jay!" She tried to run toward him but was stopped mid-step by Lance — his left arm wrapped around her neck, his right arm wielding a kitchen knife angled toward her throat.

"Take one more step and I swear I'll —"

The threat changed into a groan as Lance took a blow to the side of the face and stumbled backward, confused. Before Winnie could think, before she could even scream, Jay was past her and on top of Lance. Beside them stood Mr. Nelson and his hand-carved wooden cane.

"Walkers, canes — either way they get the job done." Mr. Nelson poked his cane in the middle of Lance's back and then pulled Winnie in for a tight hug. "You're safe now, Winnie Girl."

CHAPTER 33

She sat on the top step of the porch and smiled out at her friends standing or sitting around the yard in groups of two and three. News of Lance's arrest in the murder of Bart Wagner had spread up and down Serenity Lane like wildfire. In fact, the disgraced teacher's ride up the street in the back of a patrol car had been quite an event.

Today, though, was about something different.

Today was about coming together to celebrate Bart Wagner's life.

It was, as Bridget had said the previous night, a chance to heal and to put the Serenity back in Serenity Lane.

Now, as she sat mere inches away from a semi-purring Lovey (okay, maybe not *purring,* exactly), Winnie had to admit she needed this kind of peace and calm every bit as much as her friends did.

To her left, Chuck and a scooter-riding

Harold Jenkins were deep in conversation. She wasn't close enough to hear what they were saying, but considering Chuck was holding a sleeve of baseball cards and Harold was actually paying attention (rather than winking and blinking at Cornelia Wright), she figured baseball was a safe guess.

Off to her right, Renee (dressed in a pair of formfitting jeans and matching stilettos) was laughing at something Mark had just said. Winnie had called Bart and Ethel's son once she'd gotten back to the house after the debacle with Lance — the man's heartfelt gratitude in response to news of an arrest in his father's death still making an occasional loop through her thoughts.

Mark was a little rough around the edges, but he seemed determined to make a go of his dream — a dream his father had wanted for him every bit as much as he wanted it for himself.

She followed Renee's occasional shy glances around to the side of the house where she spotted Greg playing catch with Ty, the ten-year-old's excitement over having found an unexpected playmate bubbling over into silly jokes. Greg, being the sweetheart that he was, laughed at all the right places. If he noticed Renee looking over at them, he didn't let on.

Ahead of her, just under the large oak tree, stood Mr. Nelson and Bridget, pointing up at a bird's nest hidden among the branches. Mr. Nelson, along with Jay, had saved her life. From what Jay had told her the day before, he'd been worried about her after she'd left the college so abruptly (leaving her rescue bag behind in the process). When he arrived at the house to check on her, Bridget was on the porch with Mr. Nelson, relaying her odd phone call with Winnie — a phone call that led the men to Lance's house (and Bridget to call 911) just in the nick of time.

Somehow, someway, she'd find a way to pay them back. Not just for saving her life, but for making it so special day in and day out.

"You look awfully pensive sitting there by yourself."

Startled back into the present, Winnie turned to find Jay smiling at her from the walkway, his blue green eyes fairly dancing in the afternoon sun. A few steps behind him, and to the left, stood Caroline, her expression the antithesis of her father's.

To Jay, Winnie seemed to represent hope. Maybe even a second chance.

To Caroline, Winnie seemed to represent —

Lovey woke from her nap beside Winnie
to run down the steps and straight into the
arms Caroline swooped down to offer. Seiz-
ing the opportunity the distraction afforded
them, Winnie gave in to the smile Jay's presence warranted.

"I was kind of hoping you'd show."

"How could I not?"

His daughter's name was on the tip of her
tongue, but she refrained from sharing it
aloud. Instead, she gestured toward the preoccupied pair with her chin. "They have a
lot in common."

"Oh?" Jay closed the gap between them
and lowered himself onto the step beside
Winnie. "What's that?"

"I've been forced onto both of them . . .
and they both hate me."

He slipped his arm around her back and
pulled her in for a much-needed (and oh-
so-wonderful) side-arm hug. "From what I
could tell when we just walked up, it looks
like maybe Lovey is starting to warm up to
you."

"Why? Because she wasn't hissing at me
at that exact moment?"

"Exactly."

"Maybe she thought I was Bridget sitting here."

"Nope. She knew it was you."

Was Jay right? Was Lovey finally warming up to her?

"Mr. Nelson told me to give it time. Said she'd come around."

Jay followed her gaze toward the tree and the elderly man now spying at them from behind the thick trunk. "Mr. Nelson is a smart man."

She waved at Mr. Nelson and his slightly more inconspicuous partner in crime, Bridget. "That he is."

"I think the same will happen with Caroline if we give her time."

"You do?"

"I certainly hope so." Leaning over, he whispered a kiss across her forehead, the warmth of his breath against her skin like nothing she'd ever felt before. "She's not going to make it easy on us, Winnie, but I refuse to give up. You're much too special."

Refuse to give up . . .

Refuse to give up . . .

She grabbed hold of his free hand and held it close. "So, you're telling me not to give up, yes?"

"That's exactly what I'm saying."

Poking her head around the corner, she

called out to Renee. "Hey, I just came up with another dessert. We'll call it Never Give Up-side-Down Cake."

RECIPES

YOU'RE A PEACH PIE

Pastry for double-crust 9-inch pie
1/2 cup sugar
1/4 cup packed brown sugar
4 1/2 cups sliced and peeled peaches
3 tablespoons cornstarch
1/4 teaspoon ground cinnamon
1/4 teaspoon ground nutmeg
1/8 teaspoon salt
2 teaspoons lemon juice
1 tablespoon butter

1. In a large bowl, combine both sugars. Add peaches and gently toss. Cover and let stand for one hour.

2. Line a 9-inch pie plate with the bottom pastry. Trim and set aside.

3. Drain peaches and reserve juice.

411

4. In a small saucepan, mix the cornstarch, cinnamon, nutmeg, and salt. Slowly add in reserved juice and stir. Bring to a boil, then cook and stir for 2 more minutes to thicken. Remove from the heat. Add in lemon juice and butter, and stir. Gently fold in peaches and pour all into crust.

5. With a rolling pin, make a lattice crust from the remaining pastry. Seal edges and flute if desired. Cover edges loosely with foil.

6. Bake at 400 degrees for 50–60 minutes or until crust is golden brown and filling is bubbly. Remove foil. Cool on a wire rack.

WORRY NO S'MORE BARS

1 1/4 cup graham crackers — crushed
4 tablespoons butter, melted
3/4 cup sugar
1/2 cup brown sugar
1/2 cup butter, softened
1 egg
1/2 teaspoon vanilla
1 1/4 cup all-purpose flour
1/2 teaspoon baking soda
1/2 teaspoon salt
1 cup chocolate chips

1 cup mini marshmallows (with an additional handful for the top)

1 full-sized chocolate bar

1. Line a square baking pan with parchment paper and set aside.

2. Combine crushed graham crackers and 4 tablespoons of melted butter. Press into bottom of prepared pan to form a crust.

3. Cream 1/2 cup of softened butter. Mix in both sugars and cream again until fluffy. Add in egg and vanilla. Mix again.

4. In a separate bowl, combine flour, baking soda, and salt. Add to butter mixture and combine.

5. Add in chocolate chips and marshmallows. Stir.

6. Spoon cookie dough on top of graham crust and spread (dough will fill in any gaps as it cooks).

7. Bake at 350 degrees for 10 minutes.

8. While bar is cooking, break chocolate bar

into pieces and place in freezer.

9. Sprinkle reserved marshmallows on top of cooking bar and continue baking for another 8 to 10 minutes.

10. Remove from oven and place chocolate bar pieces on top. Cool completely.

YOU ARE ONE SMART COOKIE

1 cup butter, softened
3/4 cup brown sugar, packed firmly
3/4 cup sugar
1 teaspoon vanilla
2 eggs
2 1/4 cups all-purpose flour
1 teaspoon baking soda
1 teaspoon salt
2 cups semisweet or white chocolate chips
1 cup milk chocolate or white chocolate chips for drizzle

1. In a large bowl, combine butter, both sugars, and vanilla. Beat until light and fluffy.

2. Add eggs, one at a time, beating well after each addition.

3. Slowly add flour, baking soda, and salt.

Beat until well blended.

4. Stir in chips.

5. Spread in greased 16-inch round pizza pan (14-inch if you want a thicker cookie).

6. Bake at 350 degrees for 20 minutes.

7. Cool cookie in pan.

8. Drizzle with melted chips.

ABOUT THE AUTHOR

As a child, **Laura Bradford** fell in love with writing over a stack of blank paper, a box of crayons, and a freshly sharpened number two pencil. From that moment forward, she never wanted to do or be anything else. Today, Laura is the author of *Éclair and Present Danger,* the debut novel in the Emergency Dessert Squad Mysteries, and the national bestselling Amish Mysteries, including *A Churn for the Worse* and *Suspendered Sentence.* She lives in Yorktown Heights, New York, with her husband and their blended brood. Visit her website at laurabradford.com.